the darkest note

REDWOOD KINGS BOOK 1

NELIA ALARCON

Copyright © 2022 by Nelia Alarcon

All rights reserved.

No part of this publication may be reproduced, distributed, or transmitted in any form or by any means, including photocopying, recording, or other electronic or mechanical methods, without the prior written permission of the publisher, except as permitted by U.S. copyright law. For permission requests, contact the author at neliaalarcon.com.

The story, all names, characters, and incidents portrayed in this production are fictitious. No identification with actual persons (living or deceased), places, buildings, and products is intended or should be inferred.

Book Cover by GetCovers

First edition 2022

Prologue

I DON'T CRY when I get the call from the police.

I don't cry when I identify the body, when I see the dark hair and bloated skin.

I don't cry when they hand me the note my mother left behind.

To my sweet Cadey,

When I sat down to write this, my fingers kept trembling and I bawled like a baby all over the page. You don't know how many papers I've used up trying to find the right words.

There's no perfect way to say this, so I'll get to the point.

It's over for me.

But it's not because of you or Vi.

Sweetheart, you are everything a mother could possibly ask for. Smart, strong, perfect.

I remember when I first heard you play piano. You had no idea what you were doing, but you managed to pick out a melody. It was raining that day. And my heart was dragging on the floor, but the minute you started playing, the sun came out.

That's who you are to me, Cadey. You are my sunshine. It's just that I've been battling this dark cloud way before you and your sister were born. I don't have the strength left to fight it anymore.

I'm sorry I'm not good enough.

I'm sorry I have to leave you behind in this cold, cruel world, but I know that you're going to take good care of your sister. And I know you're going to be strong.

Don't worry. I'm not leaving you completely alone. I've contacted your brother to come and take care of you both.

I'm aware that might come as a shock. I never told you about him. Mostly because I was too ashamed to admit that I'd given up a child.

Surprised? There's a lot that you don't know about me, Cadey. And that's for your own good. Please don't resent me too much. It's my dear wish that you never see the full extent of what I've done.

It's almost time for me to go. I'm starting to get teary again. There's still so much I want to say.

You and Vi can stay in the apartment so you don't have to change schools. I've already worked it out with the bank.

I wish I had more to leave for you, but that's all I can manage for now. Your brother will take care of the rest. Try not to aggravate him too much. He isn't all that excited about meeting you two, but it's not personal. Trust me.

I have to go now. Remember that I love you and Vi more than anything in the world. I'll meet you on the other side.

- Mom

I don't shed a single tear as I crumple her note and hand it back to the cops.

I certainly don't cry when I tell the mortician to burn her body to a crisp.

Chapter One

—AUGUST, FOUR MONTHS LATER—

CADENCE

The saddest key in music is Dmajor.

It's the key that rings through my head whenever I think of my mother, fingers trembling, arms dotted with pucker marks, body stretching far beyond the empty cupboard to the stash she keeps in the jar.

Some mothers store cookies in those potted tubs shaped like bears or seashells or flowers.

My mother stored weed.

She'd puff it in my face and laugh, low and haunting. It was always that tone.

D#major.

Like a vampire coughing up blood.

I love you and Vi more than anything in the world.

The line from her suicide letter plays on a loop in my mind.

I thought if I burned the words they'd disappear, but the ashes rose from the dead and started haunting me.

I love you and Vi more than anything.

Mom had nothing but audacity.

Love? Her twisted version of love was a descent straight into the darkest chords, full of brokenness and black keys.

I always saw the chaos in her, but I never let it stain me. I created a space inside my head where the music would die. Because if I couldn't hear music at all, then I wouldn't hear her notes either.

But now that she's gone, music has tiptoed its way back into my life. Or more like it slammed into me at a hundred miles an hour and now I find myself on a ride with no idea how I got there and no clue how to get off.

"Like a wreeeecking ball!" A soulless, upbeat version of Miley Cyrus's hit blasts from the speakers on the stage.

I'd descended into my thoughts to escape the noisy cover, but it seems like the music's gotten even louder.

Three girls wearing dressed-up versions of bras and booty shorts gyrate to the rhythm.

The girl in the center suddenly rises in the air, propelled by a thin harness. Her legs spread wide as she flies over the crowd, flashing everyone in attendance.

Heads tip back in adoration. Roars erupt from the audience like they're all her worshipers and this is some kind of cultish mating ritual.

I wonder if it's too late for me to rip my wig off and run.

"I thought you'd dipped, you skank!"

A hand grabs me before I can make my escape.

I force a smile on my face and ease around.

"Me? Run from this," I gesture to the blonde performer who's soaking in the 'woof, woof, woof' erupting from the guys in attendance, "lavish display of musical prowess?" I blink innocently at my best friend. "Never."

"You're such a music snob, Cadey. Now bend down so I can unbutton your shirt. You're not showing enough cleavage."

I swat her hands away. Breeze tilts her head up and gives me a scolding look.

"Don't you dare undress me," I murmur.

"Do you see the act you're following?" she whisper-shouts. "More of your clothes need to come off. Stat."

I look down at the leather jacket, white shirt and unreasonably short skater skirt that Breeze forced on me. Black heels, giant hoop earrings, green eye contacts and heavy makeup complete the look. It's all a part of my best friend's fool proof plan to rid me of stage fright—a plan we came up with when I scored the role of Mary in our school's Christmas play.

Six years later, I still need the wig to perform in front of crowds, but at least I'm performing. I guess you can call it a rousing success.

"Maybe this is proof that I don't belong at Redwood Prep," I murmur.

"It's too late. You already accepted the scholarship." She fixes the red bob that's covering my long, brunette hair from view. Blue eyes focused, she fusses until the strands meet her approval. "And you know why you can't turn this down."

She's right. My entire future is at stake, but is it worth spending senior year as the 'new girl' at Redwood Prep, home to the elite and stupidly wealthy? Girls from the wrong side of the tracks get eaten up and spit out here.

As if summoned, the trio who just performed glide off the stage in their sparkles and glamor. They look left, catch sight of me and then laugh rudely as they walk away.

Breeze whirls around, nostrils flaring. She's already on the defensive. "What's so funny?"

"Breeze." I grab her arm to keep her at my side. The only thing shorter than my pint-sized best friend is her fuse. "Don't engage. I don't want to get on their radar."

"You can't spend your entire year being invisible," she argues, eyebrows tightening to punctuate her point.

Actually, that's my sole plan. Starting next week, I'll be a ghost floating through the halls of Redwood Prep. On the weekends, I'll trade the sprawling lawns and elegant fountains for chain-link fences, graffiti and garbage. Once I'm on my turf, I'll come alive long enough to get my bearings and do it all again the next week.

The curtains on stage wheel closed and the backstage crew frantically sweep all the glitter and confetti from the floor. There's dedicated staff for the task. I've never seen a high school production this size and it just goes to show how seriously Redwood Prep takes their music program.

"Focus. It's almost time," I tell Breeze when I see she's still evil-eyeing the Mean Girls trio.

Breeze huffs and adjusts the collar of her funky quilted shirt. "At least *you* have actual talent!" she yells loud enough for the entire backstage to hear.

"That's yet to be determined," I murmur.

She flicks me with her French-tipped nails. "Shut up. We are not allowing self-doubt to have a seat at the table."

"Self-doubt is the only one at the table," I grumble.

"What was that?" Breeze frowns and leans in. Then she quickly jumps back. "In fact, I don't want to know. It was probably something self-deprecating and not true." She flaps her hands. "Let me repeat myself, Cadence Cooper. You are going to kill it out there."

Even with my stomach twisted into knots, her words lure a smile from me.

A member of the crew approaches at that moment. "Hey, are you Sonata Jones?"

He squints at the clipboard as if he's not sure he's saying that right.

Breeze snorts and covers her mouth with one hand. I pretend not to notice. Creating new stage names for every performance is a thing I do. It helps me pretend that I'm someone else while I'm playing.

I nod. "Yes, that's me."

He gives me another weird look before saying, "Our final act isn't here yet, so we're going to intermission. You'll be up as soon as they arrive."

"Are you kidding me?"

He gives me a blank look.

"What act is so important that you'd go into intermission rather than cut them from the lineup?" I demand. "Isn't this supposed to be a student showcase?"

It's not that I *want* to perform for the students at Redwood Prep tonight, but I'm halfway through my next-on-stage jitters. The thought of prolonging the torture makes me physically ill.

Clipboard Guy purses his lips. "Look, it's already unprecedented to have an act we've never heard of open for The Kings." His stare turns icy. "Feel free to bow out if you have an issue."

"You'd kick *me* out rather than the ones who couldn't be bothered to show up on—"

The rest of my words die a flailing death as my best friend bumps me out of the way with her hip and shrieks, "The Kings are playing tonight?"

I give Breeze a bewildered look. "You know them?"

"Of course I know them. How do *you* not know them?" she accuses.

Clipboard Guy stalks away as if he can't be bothered.

My phone chirps, drawing both our eyes to the device in my hand.

Breeze leans forward nosily. "Your brother?"

There's a painful scratch against my heart when I shake my head. Trying not to let Breeze see how much it affects me, I shrug it off. "As if he would care enough to call me before I performed."

If he did call, it probably wouldn't be to say anything encouraging.

Her eyes turn wide. "It says 'unknown number'. Maybe it's a scammer." She flicks her wrist. "Hand it over. I'll deal with it for you."

"It's not a scammer." I shut the phone off because I don't want to think about anything other than the performance.

"Who is it then?" Breeze insists.

"I don't know."

"If you don't know, how are you so sure it's not a scammer?" She plants her hands on her hips, causing her bangles to dance.

Yup. *Definitely* not a conversation I want to have right now.

I lift my head and point to the stage. "Look, they're bringing out the piano."

Breeze looks that way and her eyes brighten. "I'm going to check it out. You stay here and try not to hyperventilate."

I eye her suspiciously as she crosses the stage. When I see her chatting it up with one of the guys in the crew, I realize why she was so eager to leave my side.

Typical.

I've known her since we were in diapers. Breeze will never give up an opportunity to flirt.

With her effusive presence gone, I'm back to being stuck in my own head.

I glance towards the exits one last time, wondering if I should back out now rather than step into this new and frightening chapter.

But those thoughts skitter away when the door bursts open. The air backstage shifts and something deep inside, some primal part of me, warns me not to look directly at whatever caused the disturbance.

I force my gaze up anyway because I never listen to that voice.

Three deities stalk backstage, all broad shoulders and brooding eyes. They move as one, like a pride of lions about to close in for the kill, bodies knifing effortlessly through the crowd that parts for them.

Predators. And proud of it. Their presence sets off a chorus of squealing from the people backstage.

They ignore the noise. Unbothered. As if this clamoring, this worship, is only right.

I can't look away even if I want to. A steady thrumming fills my head. The perfect background music to their gait. A diminished chord progression.

A# D# G

Wild and dramatic. The sound of a hurricane at its

peak, winds strong enough to uproot a tree and send it lashing into a building.

They draw closer. The music in my head swells as I notice the finer details of their faces. Hard jaws and cheekbones chiseled by the gods. Straight noses. Full, pursed lips.

The two at the front look exactly alike although one is blonde and the other is raven-haired. The third has thick brown hair and almond-shaped eyes.

They're all wearing faded shirts that stretch across their large, barrel chests and taper down to narrow hips. Blue jeans cling to long legs that go on forever. Their incredible height sets them above everyone else and their gait is better than any model on any catwalk. Ever.

I've never seen people who look as hauntingly beautiful and effortlessly intimidating in real life.

Are these The Kings? The boys who were powerful enough to shut down the entire show?

The two brunettes at the ends break off. One is twirling drumsticks while the other clutches a guitar bag. The blond in the middle gets flocked by two girls who edge up under his armpits for a selfie.

Clipboard Guy huffs toward me.

I rip my eyes away from the three guys, realizing that I'm flushed and a little breathless.

"Okay, Soprana," Clipboard Guy says.

"Uh, it's Sonata."

He waves away the correction. His eyes jump from the three newcomers and back to my pale face. "Curtains go up in three."

I nod my understanding.

He turns and yells in his headset loud enough for everyone to hear. "Surano's opening for The Kings in three! Get the lights ready!"

The three forces of nature—there's no other word to describe the way they suck the air out of the room—notice me at the same time. The two on either end smirk and glance away, but the blond keeps his killer eyes on me.

Dear *Bach,* he's beautiful.

The lights burn an orange glow across his tan skin so it seems like he's bathing in fire. He raises a muscular arm—that looks like it lifts more than the guitar on his back—and squeezes the strap. I swear my soul presses in right along with it.

He smirks and my breath is ripped away by a charisma that doesn't ask but demands my attention. Everyone disappears. All I can see is him. His dark eyes trap me in place. Violent and merciless.

I feel every step he takes in my direction. The rhythm of his stride ricochets down to my toes.

It's frightening, the chokehold he has on me. I don't know where it's coming from. I only know that—if bad news had a face—it would be this guy.

Tattoos climb under his braided leather bracelet with the gold beads and disappear into the worn sleeve of his shirt. From the shaggy blond hair to the easy way the tight T-shirt wraps around his pecs, it all screams danger. Damage. Destruction restrained to the body of a Greek sculpture.

My heart starts racing at an unhealthy speed. The music in my head screeches to a halt. I don't have a chord progression for him. I don't even have a melody. He's too much. He pushes out every sound, every thought until he's all that's left.

I want to look away, but I can't take my eyes off him.

"What are you doing?" Clipboard Guy is back. And he sounds annoyed.

Breeze is beside him. Her smile is dreamy and I wonder if she hit it off with the guy she targeted on stage.

"You ready for this?" my best friend asks.

I drag my eyes away from The Kings and am eternally grateful that Breeze catches sight of them when I'm already enroute to the piano.

I hear her excited squeals and figure Clipboard Guy is getting attacked by her swatting. My best friend's arm turns into a paddle board when she's overjoyed.

The piano falls into my line of sight and I feel the draw the way I always do. An undercurrent, similar to the one I felt when I spotted that guy backstage, vibrates the air around me. Except this tug isn't violent. It's gentle. Warm water on naked skin. Sunlight kissing my palm. Enveloping. Whispering that I could drown and like it.

I tried my hardest to resist the call, especially when mom found out that I could make money playing music. She turned something beautiful and precious and stained it with her junkie fingers.

Even so, even when music felt dirty, it still sang to me. Dug under my skin and told me that I could never run away.

I feel my skirt flare around my hips as I take my seat behind the piano. It's a Steinman and I'd be confused, dazzled even, if I didn't know that this is Redwood Prep. Of course they have one of the most expensive acoustic pianos lying around for random students to use in their end-of-summer showcase.

I lift the lid and run my fingers over the gleaming keys. The weight of it takes my breath away. I've been practicing on the keyboard I lugged out of a thrift store. Those keys sounded like a dying toy and the key bed was so cheap that it sprang like a jack-in-the-box whenever I touched it.

Just outside the curtain, an announcer yells my name to the crowd. No one claps. Not even out of politeness.

They don't know me.

They don't welcome me.

I take a deep breath and settle my nerves. It doesn't matter. They will never know me. The real me.

And there's safety in that.

I'm not Cadence Cooper.

In this red wig and heavy makeup, I'm braver than her. Cooler. And this audience doesn't have to like me, but they will respect me. They'll listen to what I have to say.

The curtains roll back and a spotlight bursts to life, aiming right at my head. I feel the warmth of the light and hear the shuffle of bodies packed close together in front of the stage.

I keep my eyes on the piano.

The first few notes are a haunting melody. Dark. Oily. They flow through the auditorium like imps set loose from the darkest depths.

I shift octaves, taking the crowd on a journey. Faster. Faster. I pound the keys with all my heart, throwing myself into the moment because that's the only way I know how to play.

And then I pause.

The lights go dim.

A new, heavy beat pours from the speakers. It's the track I gave to the sound guys. The music is heavy on the bass and kick. Hip-hop to the max. I layer my melody on top of it. The threads intertwine like lovers who are opposites in every way yet helplessly drawn to each other.

The crowd starts to come alive. I hear their distant cheers and astonished gasps from somewhere outside of myself.

I knew that would happen. I chose this piece based on data. It's the song that raked in the most cash when I bussed in the park.

My fingers dance above two black keys as I hold out the crescendo, building to a climax along with the backing track. My back is bent over the keyboard. My hair's all in my face.

Adrenaline pounds in my veins. My soul moves right across the keys, dancing in the flames and blowing heat all over my face.

At last, I strike the keys once. Twice. Three times.

The note suspends and then bursts like a bubble, leaving nothing but silence. I push the red strands out of my face and stand.

Someone starts a slow applause.

It catches on like a flame.

Then it sweeps through the auditorium, building to a roar.

The rich folks of Redwood approve.

Whistles follow. The roar strips me of my joy and leaves something nasty in its place. The shame comes swiftly, drenching my skin. It doesn't matter how many layers of clothing I have on. I feel naked and vulnerable.

Breeze is to my right, in the wings. She's gesturing for me to come her way. Clipboard Guy is standing behind her, clapping. An impressed look is on his face.

I struggle to breathe.

Out.

I need to get out of here.

I rush to the opposite side of the wings where the sound booth is set up. Skating past the crew who give me wide-eyed stares, I tear through a long, concrete hallway and crash through the exits.

It's only when I'm outside and far from the crowd's prying eyes that I feel the oxygen hit my lungs. A second later, the door bursts open and spits out Breeze.

She stumbles toward me. "Damn, Cadence. You were… that was… holy crap. You were incredible. Even the Kings stopped and took notice. I saw Dutch staring you down like he wanted to pick you up and," she curls her tongue, "lick your face."

"Dutch?" I don't know why, but the name sends a tingle down my spine.

"The lead singer of The Kings. The blond one. His brother's Zane." She fans her face. "Hotness personified. He's the drummer and the social media king. Finn, he's their adopted brother but he's just as sexy with his eyes and his mouth… *oh*." She chews on her bottom lip. "I've been listening to their music for months." Breeze clutches her hands and does a little hop. "I can't believe I got to stand so close to them tonight."

"They're professionals?" I wonder. It would explain why they got preferential treatment. Although they seem a little young to be famous rockstars.

Her jaw drops. "Do you really not know?"

I shrug. Between taking care of Viola, working, and keeping up with school, I don't have time to keep up with the latest trends.

"They're *amazing*. Their singles have, legit, gone viral. Plus they're Jarod Cross's kids."

"Who—"

"If you don't know who Jarod Cross is I will literally smack you across the face," my best friend threatens.

I frown at her. "Of course I know who Jarod Cross is. What I was *going* to say is who cares? They're a bunch of rich, entitled musicians with a famous dad. Does that give them a right to show up late and hold up the entire show?"

Yeah, I'm still not over that.

"Their dad practically owns this school." She blinks. "Out of everyone at Redwood Prep, they're the only ones who have the right to do whatever they want."

A rolling electric guitar riff screams from the building. Breeze whips around, her eyes bright. "Oh my gosh! They're starting!"

"You go ahead. I'll take off now."

"What?" Her jaw falls in disappointment. "You're not going to stay? I guarantee you're going to love their set. They're amazing."

"Viola's home alone," I tell her. My little sister is thirteen going on thirty-five, but I still don't like it when she's alone with no supervision.

Her bottom lip trembles. "Okay. I'll come with you."

There's not a bone in her body that means that.

I let her off the hook. "It's okay. You stay."

"Really?" She squeals.

I nod.

Breeze jumps on me and hooks her arm around my neck. "Best best friend *ever!*"

I watch her scurry inside and turn to face Redwood Prep's sprawling courtyard. The school is as big as a college campus and twice as distinguished.

I rip my wig off and turn back into the Cinderella with rags.

Unknown Number: Nice wig, New Girl. But friendly advice, you might want to leave that on until you clear the campus. If not, I won't be the only one who knows your secrets.

Unknown Number: Call me Jinx, by the way. Welcome to Redwood Prep. And good luck. You're gonna need it.

Chapter Two

—SEPTEMBER, ONE MONTH LATER—

DUTCH

"You got it wrong. We took your deal to piss off our dad. Not because we're stupid."

Finn catches my eye.

I shake my head and throw the phone, still murmuring dollar amounts and empty flattery, over to my brother.

Picking up my guitar, I tuck myself into the backseat of the limo, glad that I have a level-headed sibling who's willing to deal with the greedy music agents and starry-eyed record producers.

"We know who our dad is," Finn says into the phone, his tone edgy with impatience.

Like anyone will ever let us forget.

Jarod Cross's sons.

That and dollar signs are all anyone can see when they look at us. Which is why we've decided we don't give a damn about chasing fame and making a name for ourselves. All we've got is each other and music.

I pluck at the strings, and the heaviness in my stomach lightens a bit.

I'm the only one who wanted to come back home for reasons other than exhaustion and boredom. Being on the road for hours on end made me sick to my stomach most of the time. I'm sure there's a pill or potion I could take for motion sickness, but if there's one that works, I haven't found it yet.

The discomfort increases when Zane sticks his head out of the back seat with a wolfish smile.

My twin plops like a rock into the space beside me. The limo is boxy and stretchier than the average ride. But it's still not enough for him to sprawl like that.

I glare at him when I see his glassy eyes. "Didn't I tell you we were going straight to Redwood Prep?"

"Why do you think I had to fuel up?" He arches an eyebrow at me. The heavy scent of cologne is his attempt at covering the stench of booze.

The only things Zane does with any consistency is hit the drums like a maniac, post cringy shirtless videos online, and drink his face off whenever he feels backed into a corner.

We each have a reason for not wanting to go back to school, but Zane's got it worse than the rest of us.

"We could have stayed if you wanted," I offer.

"Nah. I was getting tired of it too."

I pick the G scale in rapid succession, my fingers blurring over the strings.

"You didn't get much action this time." Zane slaps me

on the shoulder. "What? You're too high class for the groupies now?"

"Maybe."

He smirks and plucks a bottle of water from the minifridge. "You shouldn't be so picky. An easy lay is an easy lay."

I shrug him off. I'm not the type to sleep with fans. It's too easy to run into the crazies that way and I don't have the taste for drama that Zane seems to thrive on.

But my brother is wrong. I did mess around on tour. The problem is... even when boredom had me indulging in a nameless chick with her legs spread open, it didn't rid me of the redhead from the back-to-school showcase.

I can't remember a melody ever sticking in my head the way hers did. She played like an animal. Not in a bad way. It was raw. Bare. Spirited. Like no one had taught her the rules or maybe she knew but didn't care.

It's rare to see something that flawed and unpretentious at Redwood. The redhead served her heart out on a freaking platter and she didn't care if the blood spattered. If things got messy.

I'd noticed her from the moment I walked in. She was beautiful, standing there like a goddess in a leather jacket and a short skirt that showed off legs for days.

Her lashes were thick and a dark black compared to her red hair. Her nose was pert and tilted up at the ends. Her bottom lip was way too big for the top one. It was the kind of mouth that could keep a man up late at night.

I'd wanted to touch her the moment I saw her standing backstage, but when I heard her play, I knew she was the type of fire I sure as hell should stay away from.

Women like her... they're the reason empires fall and

kings turn into losers. The magic in her fingers has that kind of power. And I want no freaking part of it.

Finn motions to me. "Heads-up."

I have to fumble around to set my guitar away and free my hands, but I manage to catch the phone out of mid-air. "Took care of the problem?"

"And made it seem like taking a break was his idea."

When Finn smirks, his eyes turn into half-moons. That expression right there has charmed the panties off more chicks than our quiet brother would ever admit.

Unlike Zane, who posts his naked butt for likes, Finn is the silent killer. By the time you blink, he'll have your girl and her sister under his arm. No words spoken. No apologies given.

Zane leans back in the couch. "You think dad's gone quiet because he's planning the punishment?"

I lift one shoulder calmly. Our father isn't the type to get involved unless he's truly pissed off. Which he was when he found out we'd agreed to open for his arch nemesis Bex Dane. For a whole month. At the beginning of our senior year.

"Nothing he can do to stop us anyway. It'll ruin his pretty reputation." Zane wiggles his eyebrows. "Jarod Cross will eat his own puke to protect his family man image."

A corner of Finn's lips hitches up. He's a big part of that scrubbed-down image. Nothing more humanitarian than adopting a kid from a foreign country for the virtue points.

At least dad thought so after his fourth DUI charge almost turned into an aggravated assault charge. If he hadn't swerved at the right moment, two kids would be without their parents.

Normally, nothing good comes out of dad's meaningless vies for attention, but gaining Finn as a brother was about the best thing he's ever done on one of his repentance tours.

"Damn." Finn's soft voice brings both our heads whipping around.

Zane caps his bottle of water. "What?"

"I hit up Jinx to find out if there's anything at school we should be aware of," Finn begins.

Zane cuts him off. "Why do you support that blackmailer? Do you know how many times I've had to pay Jinx to stay quiet about me?" He groans. "Don't give that creep any more of our money."

"Not my fault you can't keep your pants on in front of security cameras," Finn snaps back.

I lift a hand before the two can get into it. Setting my eyes on Finn, I ask, "What secret did Jinx give you?"

"It's about Sol."

"Sol?" Zane rolls his eyes. "You got fleeced, Finn. There's nothing Sol could have done that we wouldn't know about."

He's not wrong. Solomon Pierce and his family were the only slice of normal in our crazy, rock-and-roll world. We're tighter than tight. What happened earlier this summer proves that.

"Sol got expelled," Finn says abruptly.

My guitar slides out of my lap.

The glaze in Zane's eyes is temporarily overpowered by shock.

"What the hell do you mean?" I bark.

Finn shows me his phone.

Jinx: Four hotties walked into Mulliez's locker and tampered with evidence. Only three came out. Solomon Pierce's suspension turned into an expulsion the day New Girl got her scholarship to Redwood.

"New Girl?" Zane scrunches his nose.

The limo slows to a stop in front of Redwood Prep. I slap my guitar in Zane's lap and scramble for the door.

"Where are you going?" my twin calls.

Finn looks on with a concerned face.

"Take care of my guitar." I point to the instrument and storm inside the building.

The hallway's empty. School started an hour ago, but I wasn't in a rush to get here.

I blow past the principal's receptionist and slam through the office door. Principal Harris is on his phone when he sees me. His bald head turns red and his cheeks puff out in a sigh.

"I'll call you back," he says before setting the landline back in the cradle.

"Why the hell was Sol expelled?"

"Dutch, I was not aware you'd be back in school today. Let me call the teachers to adjust the schedule—"

I slam my hand on the desk. "Cut the bull, Principal Harris. Why *the hell* did a suspension turn into an expulsion?"

He gapes like a fish. "Mr. Mulliez pushed for it. He said it wasn't Mr. Pierce's first time getting into trouble and we'd given him too much lee-way already."

A thread of guilt tugs at my gut. Sol's been a handful, sure. But he only got in trouble this time because he took the rap for us that night.

"You should have called *me*." I poke a finger in my chest.

"I don't see what this situation has to do with you. It was Mr. Pierce who snuck into the teacher's lounge and tried to steal—"

"He didn't steal. My father's camera was confiscated that day. It belonged to us. We were taking it back."

He nabs a handkerchief and dots at the sweat on his brow. "I'm going to pretend I didn't hear that."

"No, you did hear that," I growl. "You're a smart man, Principal Harris. You know Sol wouldn't have broken into school alone."

"Perhaps. That's why I'm not informing your father about this incident."

"Dad's too busy to handle something like this. He's on tour. Whatever you need, you deal with me." I tilt my chin up. "I'm going to assume this matter is cleared up. I'll tell Sol he can come back to school."

"I'm sorry, Dutch. Someone's already taken his spot."

"Who?"

Principal Harris shakes his head. "I can't tell you that." He purses his lips.

Sensing that I won't get any further with him, I storm out of the office.

In the hallway, I bump into Mr. Mulliez, the trash music teacher who's had it out for us since day one.

He couldn't make it as a professional musician, which is why he had to tuck his tail between his legs and slink back to Redwood. He's got an obsession with my father's success and he takes it out on the three of us.

"Dutch, you're back." He gives me a friendly smile that's not enough to convince me of his intentions. "I guess we'll be seeing you in class more often."

I walk past, ignoring his words.

Finn and Zane are still outside.

Zane gives me a worried look. "What did Harris say? Is this about that night we broke in?"

I nod slowly.

My brother runs a hand through his dark hair and curses under his breath.

Finn gets pale. "I've been trying to call Sol. He's not answering."

"His mom probably took his phone and laptop." I pace nervously. "Principal Harris is a dead end. When we weren't around, Mulliez put his claws in and got him to kick Sol out."

"That bastard," Zane hisses.

Finn leans against the railing and crosses his arms. His eyes are narrowed in thought. "What are we going to do now? Sol's parents are stricter than ours. There's no way they'll let him stay out of school until we figure this out. He's probably enrolled somewhere else."

I think about the night Sol stayed back to get the security guards off our tail.

'Go! I'll hold them off.'

The pressure on top of my chest increases.

"Sol is coming back to Redwood," I growl.

"Dad's not going to lift a finger. Not after we spit in his face by going on tour with Bex," Zane points out.

'We're not gonna leave you, Sol.'

'Go!'

My eyes burst open. "Sol is coming back to Redwood," I say again. As if they didn't understand me the first time. "I'll handle it."

My brothers exchange looks but I pretend not to notice.

Jinx told us 'New Girl' had taken Sol's spot and Principal Harris confirmed it.

I don't know who New Girl is, but she's keeping my best friend from his rightful place. She's in my way. And I'll do what I always do with the things that keep me from getting what I want.

I'll destroy them.

And there won't be a brick standing when I'm done.

* * *

Dutch: I sent the money to your account. Who's the New Girl?

Jinx: Cadence Cooper. Shy. Reserved. She's been invisible to everyone since the start of senior year. But be careful with this one. She might seem fragile on the outside, but this wallflower bites.

Chapter Three

CADENCE

The lights flicker before they go out completely, sending me into a darkness so thick it's almost pulsing. Suds fall into my eye, mid-shampoo. I bite down on my bottom lip to hold back my shriek of frustration.

Rick said he would pay the electricity this month. So much for our good, ole' brother keeping his word.

This scenario feels familiar.

Raising our hopes only to let us down? He may not have grown up with mom, but the apple doesn't fall far from the tree.

The suds are a sticky sensation crawling down the side of my face. I flick the moisture away. Anger surges in me, but it's not aimed at Rick. It's a poison-tipped arrow that I can only stab in my own chest.

I'm the idiot for taking him at his word.

Over the past few months, our surprise brother proved that he can fill in mom's shoes perfectly.

Okay, that's unfair.

At least *Rick* doesn't steal our grocery money so he can have a midnight rendezvous with the local crack dealer.

Small mercies are still mercies.

I flail my arms in search of the faucet. The moment it turns on, I get hit with a spray straight from the North Pole.

The hot water cut out ages ago. If we want a warm bath, we have to warm water in a kettle first and pour it in the tub. Since it takes so many extra steps, Viola and I both cut out baths and do showers only.

I shudder under the cold rain and angrily scratch at the soap and suds. My dearest wish is for my baby sister to have a warm bath in a nice, non-rusted tub. Why does it feel like such a fantasy?

Grabbing my towel from the rack, I wrap it around myself and then feel my way through the dark. The bathroom doesn't have any windows so all I've got to guide me is memory.

"Ow!" I stub my toe on something. Peering down, I feel around the object. "What is the scale doing here?" I grumble. "Viola."

Feeling helpless, irritated and close to tears, I wrench the bathroom door open and come face to face with a blinding light. I throw up my hands to save my eyeballs just as that someone turns the flashlight on herself.

I spy ghostly pale skin, dark hair falling messily, and lips dripping in blood.

I let out a glass-shattering scream.

A familiar yelp rattles my ears in return.

When I realize it's my sister, I snap my mouth shut. "Vi, what happened to your face?"

"I was *mid* makeup routine when the lights cut!" She

huffs, stomping to punctuate her dismay. "Didn't you pay the electric bill?"

"Rick said he'd handle it this month." I take her phone from her and lead the way to the kitchen.

"And you *believed* him?" Her crazy, made-up face has '*are you stupid?*' stomped all over it.

The tears that had been dutifully making their way to my eyeballs are halted by a wave of embarrassment. It's one thing to know I messed up, but to be called out by a thirteen year old is another level of horrifying.

I take the responsibility of being an older sibling very seriously. Everything I've done since Vi was born has been to shield her from the harsh realities of our life.

I don't want her to become as jaded as I am. I want her to be free. To have a normal childhood, one that was nothing like mine.

"Don't worry. I'll take care of it," I say, rummaging around the kitchen drawers for the candles.

Mrs. Dorothy, our elderly next door neighbor, gave me a few. She makes candles as a side-hustle to help feed her three grandchildren. Her daughter got pregnant at sixteen, twenty, and twenty-one and then she dipped, leaving all the kids with her ailing mom.

I bet mom would have done that too if our grandmother hadn't died of heartbreak and disappointment first.

"How are you going to do that?" Viola demands.

"That's not your problem to worry about," I answer back in a firm tone.

Grabbing a match box, I strike the match against it. The flames spark to life. Such a tiny flicker and yet the darkness lessens instantly, as if it can't handle the heat.

"Do you want me to talk to him?" Viola presses. "After mom died, he hasn't been around."

Pain knifes me in the gut, but I hide it quickly. "All you need to do is focus on your homework." I reach out and smear my thumb across the mess on her bottom lip. "Stop wasting time with makeup tutorials."

"It's not wasting time. Once I go viral, I'm going to rake in a ton of money and buy us a mansion." She tips her chin up, eyes sparkling with all the hope of a thirteen year old with a dream.

I'm only five years older than her, but I can't help the weariness I feel when I see her fresh-faced enthusiasm. *The world is going to knock that right out of you, Vi.*

Hell, I could do it myself. But, like the plucky little flame that stands alone in the darkness, I want to protect her light for as long as possible.

I draw closer to my sister and tug at her hair. "Fine. A mansion sounds nice."

"Right?" She smiles prettily.

"You can do all the makeup filming and beauty vlogging you want, but make sure your homework's done first."

"How am I supposed to do my homework in the dark?"

I tap the table where the lone candle is sitting. "Right here. It's just for tonight. The power will be back on soon. Think of it as a..." I drum up a smile, "camping adventure. Huh? How cool is this?"

"Unbelievable." She rolls her eyes, but a tiny smile plays at the corner of her lips.

I tap her phone. "I'll keep this until I can get to my room."

Her eyes widen. She shoots from the table and pounces on it. "No, no, no, no."

The alarm bells start going off in my head. "Why don't you want me to use your phone?"

"I..."

I move the device out of her reach and flick through the tabs. "What's on here?"

"Nothing," she says guiltily.

As if on cue, a video of none other than Zane Cross pops up on my sister's phone screen. He's in a dark background with some kind of mood light reflecting white and giving his tan skin a natural glow.

And there's a lot of his skin glowing.

Because he's naked from the top all the way down to the V-lines disappearing beneath his sagging sweatpants.

Zane flashes the camera a lusty look. His eyes are at half-mast and his lips are glistening. As he moves his hips in a slow, undulating roll, he lip syncs, *"Baby, you know you're the only one I want. You like that?'*

"Oh my gosh!" Viola jumps on me, snatches the phone and huddles it close to her chest.

I'm so shocked, I don't even know how to react. "What the hell is that?"

"It's not what you think okay?"

"I don't even know what to think!"

"I'm not thirsting after Zane Cross." She pauses and thinks about it. "Okay, maybe I kind of am." Her voice rises in pitch. "But look at him? Who wouldn't?"

I take a threatening step forward.

She inches backward. "But that's not why I'm studying his videos." Her words spew out in a rush. "I need to grow my makeup channel quickly so I can get monetized. The best way to do that is to collab with a popular account and since Zane has, like, a bajillion views and you're going to the same school, I thought—"

"Whoa. What makes you think that us going to the same school means anything?"

Her big brown eyes peer into mine. "He's one third of

The Kings, one of the hottest bands in town and you guys are probably, like, a few lockers away from each other. "

"And?"

She arches a brow. "Haven't you seen them around?"

"Not once." I shake my head. Not that I'm looking for them. I stared Dutch Cross right in the eyes at the back-to-school showcase which is something I rarely do. I plan to avoid him especially. I can't take the chance that he recognizes me.

Viola's mouth droops in disappointment. "Can't you introduce me to him? Please. It'll really help me out."

I snatch the phone back from her. "Homework. Now."

She pouts.

I whirl around. "And don't you even *think* of contacting Zane. A thirteen year old girl has no business interacting with his kind of content. Ever."

She stomps her foot, but she doesn't talk back. Since mom wasn't much of a disciplinarian—or cook or chaperone or much of anything really—I've been doing most of the child rearing. I'm not sure whether I'm doing a good job or not. I just know that no one will look out for us if I don't.

When I'm back in my bedroom, I set the phone on the bed. Temptation wells within me. I'm curious to see if Zane has any new content. Maybe with his brother Dutch.

My thumb hovers over the phone, but I come back to my senses quickly. I fling the phone away like it's contaminated and pick up my own device.

Rick's number is one of the few in my contacts list.

A part of me wonders if he'll bother picking up, and I'm slightly surprised when he does.

"What do you want, Cadence?"

I can hear the reluctance in his tone and my pride

stings. But this isn't about begging. This is about him making promises and not keeping them.

"You said you'd help with the electricity this month. You know I'm scrambling to come up with Vi's school fees."

"Something else came up," he says irritably.

I rub the bridge of my nose. "Fine. That's okay. But you could have told me. I thought that was one thing off my shoulders and I didn't plan for it. The least you could have done was given me a heads-up that plans had changed."

"Damn, Cadence. What do you think this is? A charity? I had my own responsibilities before you two came along."

My eyelashes flutter. I dig my fingers into the phone. "You're right." I scrape the bottom of my heart to find the last shred of calm and inject it into my voice. "I'm sorry. We won't bother you or your busy life again."

With that, I hang up the phone.

Then I slam it on the bed. Over and over and over. Until the storm in my chest settles into a simmering volcano.

My breath ragged, I straighten and bat my long brown hair away from my face. Mom's 'help' fell through, as I predicted it would.

But that's okay. We've always had to fend for ourselves. Nothing's changed with mom gone.

I gave Rick the benefit of the doubt because we're half-siblings. But now there's a snowball chance in hell that I ask that man for anything.

* * *

Jinx: You still haven't replied to my welcome message, New Girl. I trade secrets for secrets. Wanna play?

Cadence: I don't know who the hell you are, but I'm not

interested in your twisted games. Don't text me again or I swear I'll find you and I will skin you alive.

Chapter Four

DUTCH

Sol's mom wouldn't let us see him or tell us where he was. It hurt because she's always loved us.

We used to sit at her table slurping tamales like hot pockets and butchering conversations with our pitiful Spanish vocabulary.

We learned to salsa at her hands. We picked up a secret obsession with dramatic telenovelas with Sol's abuela. We attended her daughter's quinceañera. Finn was chosen to escort her in because no one trusted Zane to do it and I wasn't interested in donning a sparkly blue suit to match the kid's dress.

But the light went out of Mrs. Pierce's eyes when she saw us at the door this morning. She couldn't smile. There was no laughter or welcome. I saw in her gaze that she thinks we're a bad influence.

She's right.

But damn. That doesn't make it hurt any less. It doesn't make the guilt any better either.

Sol is family. We got him into Redwood Prep. He sang back-up vocals for some of our sets. He was the only friend allowed around our table at lunch. Sometimes, people thought we were four brothers. Most days, it felt like it.

I slow the car down in our designated spot. There's no clear marker or sign to set it apart, but it's established that the Cross park their ride here.

Zane and Finn have their own set of wheels, but they always leave school with a chick on the cheerleading squad. Of course they don't admit that. They tell everyone we ride in one car because we're 'environmentally conscious'.

I drag my bag out of the backseat, kick the door open and set my boots on the pavement.

Finn joins me, his lips set in a thin line.

Zane runs a hand through his hair, wearing his frustration in a dark scowl.

I walk alongside my brothers in thoughtful silence. The stir we cause as we make our way up the stairs of Redwood Prep barely penetrates my senses.

Normally, I can tune out the chatter, but it's noisy today. We've been gone for a month and the kids had enough time to find a new reason to revere us.

As we walk through the hallway, gazes stick to our backs like magnets to steel. No one approaches us though. They know better than to get in our way. Call us stuck up. Call us jerks and bastards. We've had far too many 'friends' try to get close thinking it's a one-way ticket to *the* Jarod Cross. After a few let-downs, we've learned that it's better to keep to ourselves.

The only person who managed to prove he really had our back was Sol. And we let him down in the worst way.

Finn sticks his hands into his pockets. "You said you had a plan, Dutch. You want to enlighten us now?"

"Not in the freaking hallway," I growl back.

Finn gives me a dark look.

I scrape a hand through my hair. We're all on edge, but I don't want to turn on my brothers. Lowering my tone, I glance at him. "I'll tell you in the practice room."

He nods.

'Hey, Zane.'

"Hey, Finn"

'Hey, Dutch'

A chorus of greetings erupt from cheerleaders in short skirts. They flounce down the hallway, their flowery perfume filling my senses.

I'm pretty sure we've taken a turn with the best of them at least once. Although Zane's been known to double-dip.

Girls at Redwood Prep have no problem throwing themselves at us. Most of the time, they don't even care which one of us they're kneeling in front of. As long as they get to work off one of The Kings, that's all they need.

It's getting old.

Or maybe I'm just getting jaded.

Somehow, I've stopped milking up the attention the way Zane seems to.

"By the way, I got a call from Bex Dane's manager. They want us to play at the November Festival this year. You interested?" Finn asks.

"I'm down." Zane pushes his lips toward me. "But our broody leader might pass for the fun of it."

"They're trying to entice us to sign with them. It's so obvious," I say.

Finn shrugs and nods his agreement.

"Dad'll hate it." Zane seems almost gleeful.

"If we do something stupid just to get back at dad, then we're no better than he is."

"He's got a point," Finn says.

"I know. I hate when he does that." Zane sighs. "No offense, Dutch. But sometimes I get the incredible urge to punch you in the... *face*."

My brother gawks at someone coming out of a classroom. Finn and I don't need to turn around to see who's got Zane's tongue. But we do it anyway because we appreciate a good view and the one Miss Jamieson makes is worth the drool slipping down my twin's chin.

A short skirt wraps around Miss Jamieson's sweet chocolate thighs. A nice rack that would win a ten out of ten in any man's books is nicely contained in a crisp silk blouse under a black jacket. Her hair's a riot of curls that taper down to mid-back. Her brown eyes are sharp and commanding, and the way they look now, surrounded by dark grey eye shadow, makes her seem edgy and untouchable.

Everything about her is alluring. She's the sexiest teacher in Redwood Prep and she walks like she knows it.

She also walks right past Zane, whose face is more flushed than a kid without sunscreen.

It's sad the way my brother can't get over that one night with her—a night Miss Jamieson made sure to call a 'mistake' when she found out that Zane was barely legal *and* a student at her new school.

Since then, she pretends he doesn't exist and Zane pretends that flirting with her is just a ploy to piss her off.

"Miss Jamieson," Zane says, easing into the practiced smile that usually leads to a girl getting on her back.

"Mr. Cross." Our Lit teacher stops in front of him, the only sign of her discomfort is the way she tightens her hands on her books. "I see you and your brothers have returned from tour."

Zane holds her gaze and steps closer. "Did you miss me?"

Her lips curl up, but it's not the smile of a gullible cheerleader or a fanatic groupie who's blinded by Zane's good looks. It's a polite, tight-lipped smile with an undercurrent of annoyance.

"I missed you about as much as you probably missed doing your homework. Which," she lifts a finger, "by the way, your reports are still due at the end of the month."

Zane steps up to her. His eyes are roving her face as if he's trying to inscribe it in his memory. His lips curl up. He doesn't hide how much he likes what he's seeing.

Not only that.

He's not hiding how much he wants to be close to her.

I'm not used to that glimmer of affection in his gaze. Zane never lets anyone near enough to get under his skin.

"I might need a little help," Zane whispers. "You know. After-hours."

"Then I suggest you get a tutor," she says, stepping back. Her teeth sink into her bottom lip.

He tilts his head. "I'd rather learn from the source."

Her eyes narrow on him. "I'm sorry, but I'm very busy, Mr. Cross."

"Call me, Zane." He leans close. "You did that night."

Her eyes widen and her books splatter out of her hands. They fall to the ground in a loud thud.

Everyone around us turns to watch.

Miss Jamison's skin would probably be on fire if she wasn't such a dark complexion. When she feels all the eyes lingering on her, she firms her shoulders. Flames pour from her gaze and she wrenches away the books that Zane picks up.

"Thank you," she says loud enough for everyone to hear. Then she lowers her voice and snarls, "Mention that night again and I'll take it as your confession of love to me." She breathes out. "And before you do so I have to remind you that I date men, not little boys. You're not a candidate."

Finn and I both arch an eyebrow.

Zane blinks in a dazed shock.

Miss Jamison's heels click on the tiles as she turns sharply and saunters away, her curls bouncing against her back.

I'm slightly impressed. Miss Jamieson knows who we are at Redwood Prep and she's not afraid to push back at Zane. It takes guts to throw his feelings back in his face without fear of the consequences.

Zane points in her direction. "Did she just..."

"Yeah." Finn slaps his shoulder.

I shake my head. The entire situation is forbidden and messed up and so full of drama that it's no wonder Zane's embroiled in the scandal. Of course, he would pick a teacher over all the easy women who'd love to be chased by him.

"Even if you graduated tomorrow, you're never tapping that again," I say, closing Zane's jaw and steering him away before he smacks into an open locker.

He snarls at me. "Who said I wanted to?"

Finn just smirks secretly.

Zane lifts his chin. "I don't care about her."

"No?" I ask.

"Not even a little?" Finn taunts.

"Look." He points to his pants. "I'm over it. There's nothing. No action."

I snort and push Zane away. "No one wants to see that, you pervert."

"I'm serious." He swaggers forward. "Who'd want a stick-up-her-butt teacher anyway? Honestly?"

"It seems like somebody does," Finn says.

Zane whirls around, almost slamming into our brother. "What?"

"Word on the street is she's got a boyfriend. Some guy in a Lambo picked her up last week. Apparently, they looked cozy."

"How do you know that?" Zane's nostrils flare.

"Someone paid Jinx for the information." Finn tilts his head. "Seems you're not the only student at Redwood who'd like to bang our Lit teacher."

Zane turns fully, his eyes pinned to Miss Jamieson. She's in the hallway speaking to a student. Her laughter rings out over the chatter and thud of footsteps.

Zane's body tenses and a vein pops out before he takes a deep breath.

"Whatever. Like I said. I don't care."

Finn and I exchange glances.

I laugh softly.

Finn chuckles.

Zane pierces us with his gaze. "I hate the both of you." He sticks an accusing hand in my direction. "Who are you to judge me, huh? At least I wasn't afraid to make my move. We all know that you're a lost cause."

"What are you talking about?" I growl.

"Soprano Jones or whatever her name was." Zane points an accusing finger. "You were eye-banging her hard at the showcase, but you haven't tried to find her."

Something deep inside squeezes at the mention of the redhead.

I start walking. "We're going to be late for class."

"Since when did you care about being on time for class?" Zane accuses, speeding up.

Finn lounges behind us, but he's still got that amused look on his face. They're both annoying.

A musical chime fills the hallways, Redwood Prep's version of a school bell. Kids rush past us, hurrying to their classes.

Zane curses. "I don't even remember what class we're supposed to be in right now." He glances at Finn. "Do you?"

"I didn't get a chance to check the schedules."

"It's Algebra," I say.

Zane slings a hand over my shoulder. "I'm impressed, Dutch. You don't normally care about that stuff."

I grit my teeth. It's not that I'm suddenly crazy about math. There's just someone I have to meet in that class.

We enter and a hush falls on the room. I sweep a bored gaze over the kids in the front row, observing methodically until I get to the back.

That's when I spot her.

New Girl.

I recognize her face from the few, grainy photos I managed to dig up on social media, but the chick in front of me looks way more appealing in real life than she did on a screen.

Pale skin, lean waist, nice rack. She's got that fresh-faced beauty thing going with her big, innocent eyes and round face. The skirt she's wearing is a little too short for her long legs and her chest is straining against her top.

The tight clothes don't seem to be for attention. She hunches over in her chair and doesn't make eye contact with anyone as if she wants to blend into the background.

It's a weird contrast of innocent and sexy. Cold and hot. Alluring and stand-offish.

I hate that I notice.

I hate that my pants are starting to tighten.

It only gets worse when I spot her mouth.

Those pouty lips are luscious. The bottom is way bigger than the top. Plump. Pink. Made for sin.

Exactly like the redhead.

Damn.

Am I so obsessed with the mystery girl that every girl is starting to look like her?

"Alright, boys," our algebra teacher enters the room, "if you'd kindly find your seats. Class is about to begin."

I startle a little and stalk to a desk in the middle of the classroom.

Finn and Zane are right behind me.

"What are you staring at?" Finn asks quietly.

I twist around in my seat and jut my chin at New Girl. "Her."

New Girl glances up and catches the three of us staring. A red flush spreads across her face and she instantly stiffens. Turning away as if we're Medusa, she covers her face with a hand and sinks behind her textbook.

Zane twists around too, his chair creaking with the movement. "A transfer? I've never seen her before."

"What do you think about her?" I ask.

"Beautiful but insecure. Strange combination."

"Must be a virgin," Finn adds thoughtfully.

Zane looks impressed. "You on the hunt for a virgin, Dutch?"

I grind my teeth together. "That's not it."

My eyes drag to New Girl again.

Jinx called her fragile and I think that's a good description. Delicate. Dainty. Dangerous. There's something about her lean body in the Redwood Prep uniform that screams 'easily broken', but Jinx made a point to caution me against underestimating her.

Finn gives me a questioning stare. "Who is she?"

"I'll tell you in the practice room," I say, scowling at New Girl who's still ducking behind her textbook.

After class, she's the first one out the door with a swish of her too-short skirt and scuffed tennis shoes.

I rise lazily and slip a hand into my pocket, watching her take off down the hallway. It doesn't matter how hard or how fast she runs, I'm kicking her out of Redwood Prep. One way or another.

"I can't wait until the practice room," Zane says, folding his arms over his chest.

"Too many people are in here," I say.

"That's a problem that's easily solved." Zane rises to his full height and walks a couple steps away.

Immediately, the kids who are lingering turn to him.

"Everybody. Out!" Zane yells.

The hectic thud of footsteps and squeaking of chairs is followed by an immediate silence.

"There. We've got the room to ourselves," Zane says smugly. He swings his leg over the chair in front of me and mounts it backward.

Finn leans toward me. "Spill it, Dutch. What's going on with you and the New Girl?"

I face them. "Remember Jinx's message about Mulliez putting someone in Sol's place?"

The nod.

"*She's* the reason Sol can't come back to Redwood."

Questions jump to life in their eyes.

Finn folds his arms over his chest. "She's the one who took his spot?"

I dip my chin once.

Zane's jaw clenches. "That b—"

"If we get her out, Sol can come back."

"That's if Sol's parents even *want* him to come back," Finn points out.

Guilt twists inside me again, edging to the front of my mind. Sol took the rap for us. There's no other option than to return him to his rightful place.

"Of course they want him to come back," Zane says confidently.

Finn scrubs his chin. "I don't like this. Sol would have found a way to contact us if he could. There's something we don't know."

"You think Jinx knows where he is?" Zane asks.

I give him a sideways look. "You trust Jinx now?"

"She's got eyes everywhere. Maybe those eyes extend to Sol."

"It's worth a shot," Finn agrees.

"Contacting Sol comes later. We gotta have something to offer him first." I hesitate for a moment before I let my brothers in on my plan. "I want to run New Girl out of Redwood Prep and I need your help."

The statement rings in the air.

The silence echoes.

Both my brothers peer up at me, obviously trying to make sense of what I'm saying.

We get what we want because our dad's influence is heavy on Redwood Prep. People stay out of our way naturally. And we have our own code. We don't ever target punks who haven't done us a personal wrong.

New Girl's in that grey area and I know it might not sit

well with them to go after her, but it's what we have to do. What *I* have to do. For Sol's sake.

"What if she leaves on her own?" Finn asks.

"You want us to warn her first?" Zane purses his lips.

I shrug. "Fine. I'll warn her first," I say to Finn, because he seems the most unsettled. "Give her a chance to walk away for her own good."

"And if she doesn't take that chance?" Zane asks.

I focus on the desk where New Girl had been hunched over. "Then I'm going to turn her life at Redwood Prep into a living hell."

* * *

Dutch: Dig up the biggest piece of dirt on New Girl that you have. I'm prepared to pay.

Jinx: Oh-ho. What has New Girl done to get the kings of Redwood all riled up?

Dutch: None of your business.

Chapter Five

CADENCE

It's been a month since I started Redwood Prep and I still get lost in the hallways.

I'd trade the rich wooden decor, pretentious chandeliers and stained glass windows at Redwood Prep for my old high school's peeling paint, dodgy bathrooms, and easy-to-maneuver corridors any day.

Loud laughter fills my ears. It's coming from the cheerleaders in the hallway.

They're all tan-skinned with perfect makeup, white smiles and lean, athletic bodies. They fit so perfectly into this world it almost takes my breath away.

I can't help staring at them. What would it be like if my only worry was whether my French-tipped nails had dried and if Jacey could stick the landing after the triple touch?

It's a mean thought.

No one knows what those girls are going through at home, even if their lives look wonderful on the outside.

Still, no matter their own personal battles, at least they can sooth the pain with expensive cars, wild parties, and bling.

I keep my head down when I pass them, doing my best not to get noticed by the 'Wrecking Ball' blonde and her minions. They barely flick their gazes over me before dismissing me as unimportant.

I breathe out in relief. So far I've managed to fly under the radar, just as I promised Breeze I would. I don't speak up in class. I haven't joined any extra curriculars. And I sure as hell don't talk to anyone.

At first, people were curious about me being new and all. But, with my carefully laid plan, I've been awarded the 'loser' label and left to my own devices.

I was sure the rest of senior year would be smooth sailing.

Then The Kings appeared.

My hopes for a trouble-free semester crashed and burned when the three gods of Redwood Prep sauntered into Algebra yesterday.

They weren't wearing crowns and robes, but they might as well have been royalty the way everyone responded to them. It felt like the entire class would stop breathing if they gave the order.

I told myself not to freak out. I figured they wouldn't pay any attention to the insignificant new kid at the back.

Then a pair of molten hazel eyes knifed me in the gut.

And my world shattered.

There was a hardness to Dutch's look, a hatred that didn't feel earned. I was sure that intimidating gaze had been meant for someone else.

But later on in class, I noticed Dutch talking to his brothers. Zane and Finn had their heads leaning in toward him. All of a sudden, they turned as one. They were watching me. *Staring* me down.

Whatever they were talking about clearly involved me.

I tried to duck behind my textbook, but I couldn't shake the feeling that they recognized me.

Since yesterday, my stomach has been in knots.

The Kings know who I am.

What does that mean for me now that I'm on their radar? And why did Dutch seem so aggravated by the sight of me? Are they upset because I lied about who I really am at the showcase? But why? Why would they care about someone like me?

I dig my sweaty fingers into my uniform skirt, breathing harshly in an effort to calm down.

'They're coming.'

'It's them.'

I feel a stir in the air and excited whispers erupt from the students around me. When I glance up, I see a trio of boys at the end of the hallway.

Dutch is at the front, strolling with a look of quiet intensity on his face. His blonde hair is disheveled and it only adds to his devil-may-care appeal. I curl my fingers tighter, resisting the strange and sudden desire to run my fingers through the wheat-colored locks.

He's wearing a uniform today, conforming to the status quo in name only because the way the sweater vest and white shirt stretches over his broad muscles is downright sinful and definitely against the dress code.

The sleeves of his shirt are rolled up to reveal his leather bracelet and the beginning of tattoos peeking up from his wrist. His khakis go on forever, covering legs that are ridiculously long.

I bite down on my bottom lip as the riff I heard The Kings playing the night of the showcase swells in my head.

C# G# A

It's high-pitched, shrieking, and complicated.

Zane slings an arm around Finn's shoulders. They say something to Dutch.

He smiles and my heart stops beating.

With his overpoweringly beautiful features and haughty expressions, I thought Dutch had reached the pinnacle of male perfection. But seeing his perfect white teeth flashing in the sunlight, I know that he's not just beautiful. He's outright *dangerous*. A heartbreaker in motion. A destroyer of souls. And I should be nowhere near them.

They're getting closer now and if they look up at any minute, they're going to see me. I stumble backward and duck into the bathroom.

I peer through the window pane to check that my escape went unnoticed. The boys don't break their stride even when the cheerleaders follow them eagerly.

From the safety of the bathroom, I watch their profiles. The Cross brothers. The Kings. Fitting. Like royalty, they could have anyone in the land if they wanted to and it's clear that they don't give a damn about the privilege.

"Thank God, they're gone," I whisper, wilting against the door.

"Smart girl." A voice echoes in the bathroom.

I whirl around.

A girl around my age wearing dark eyeliner and a black jacket over her preppy school uniform flicks a lighter and stares at the flame.

"Excuse me?" My voice trembles.

She tilts her head, still eyeing the fire. "Just because

something's beautiful doesn't mean it can't burn your world down."

I blink unsteadily. "Uh…"

"Oh, by the way. One of your buttons popped." She points to my shirt.

I glance down and realize she's right. With a gasp, I curl inward and clutch the fabric. "Thanks. I-I didn't notice."

A corner of her lips hitches up. Without another word, she strides past me and leaves the bathroom.

I shift my glance away from the strange girl and point it at my reflection in the mirror. My hair is long, almost to my butt. I haven't had a chance to cut it. My eyes are brown and my face is a little too round to be eye-catching.

My ordinary looks is directly responsible for my ability to blend in at Redwood. But that might change if people figure out I'm wearing worn, hand-me-down uniforms.

I fumble with the gap in my shirt. How embarrassing. Unfortunately, there's nothing I can do. The ill-fitting outfit was all the office had in my size.

Since I had to borrow money from Breeze just to get my electricity back on, ordering brand new Redwood prep threads is not possible for me.

Thinking quickly, I take out a safety pin from the dusty corners of my school bag and close up the gap. That'll have to work for now until I can locate a button along with a needle and thread.

My heart thuds when I push the door open. Glancing both ways to make sure The Kings are gone, I hurry to my next class.

Thankfully, I've got music next. I push the door and spot a middle-aged man in a sweater vest, flipping through the pages of a sheet book.

When I clear my throat, Mr. Mulliez looks up and smiles.

"Cadence." He nods, his thick hair flopping forward. "What are you doing here?"

I stare at the empty chairs. "Where is everyone?"

"It's Unconventional Theory day. Your assignment is to go out and make music using things around the school that we don't consider instruments." His glasses slides down his nose and he raises his chin to wiggle it in place again.

I laugh and scratch a fingernail against my bag. "Your idea?"

"My idea." He bobs his head, eyes sparkling.

"Why am I not surprised? Only you would think of something that out of the box."

Mr. Mulliez crosses his arms over his plaid blazer. It's a hundred degrees outside, but he doesn't seem to be breaking a sweat at all. "Being inside the box is boring. You should know," he leans forward, "Miss Sonata Jones."

A flush spreads up the back of my neck.

"Besides," he flails his hands, "it's this brilliant mind that got you into Redwood Prep. Let's not forget."

He's right. I owe him for being my advocate and working out my scholarship here.

Coming to Redwood Prep came with a bunch of strict rules about my conduct and grades, but it also included a generous work stipend. I used it to pay most of Viola's school fees.

"I didn't know we weren't having class," I tell him, taking a step back. "When's the Unconventional Theory assignment due?"

"You should have gotten a notification about it." He nods to my phone. "Don't you have the school's app installed?"

I lift the screen and navigate to the fancy Redwood Prep app. "My phone is really old. I haven't been getting a lot of notifications lately."

He nods and studies me, rubbing his whiskered chin. "There's something I wanted to speak to you about."

This can't be good.

I stiffen. "Is something wrong?"

"No, no. Nothing wrong per se." He waves a hand. "As you requested, I changed your name at the showcase and allowed you to perform as someone else. You said it was the only way to work around your stage fright."

I dip my chin, an uneasy feeling coiling in my stomach.

Mr. Mulliez taps his desk. "We agreed that we'd work on that fear of yours. Yet I haven't seen you volunteer to play in class or engage in any musical activities—whether as yourself or as an alter ego."

"I've been busy," I stammer.

"You've been running." He straightens and walks over to me. "Cadence, ever since the night I heard you play for the first time, I knew your approach to music was... different. You see patterns in places where no one else would look to find them. You weave stories into every note. It's something special. Something extraordinary. That's why I went right up to you and offered you a chance to study at Redwood Prep. It wasn't so you could blend in. It was so you could shake things up."

I remember that night with clarity. When Mr. Mulliez first approached my piano, I thought he was going to proposition me as so many of the sleazy customers at the upscale lounge did.

Instead, he changed my life. It was the first good thing to happen to me since mom left Vi and I alone.

I never thought I'd have a chance to enroll in a school

like Redwood Prep. Much less minor in a music program supported by none other than music legend Jarod Cross.

"I'm sorry to disappoint you, Mr. Mulliez. I really am." I stare at the floor. "But I don't want to shake things up. All I want is to graduate, put Redwood Prep on my resume and get a better-paying job. I want my sister to have a roof over her head and food in her stomach. I want to have a normal life with normal problems."

His eyes widen and he gives me a sympathetic look.

I pretend not to notice. "I don't want to change Redwood. I don't want to be in the spotlight. I don't want any of it."

He sighs heavily. "I understand, Cadence." His lips arch up, but it seems like it's a struggle to smile. "I've kept you long enough." He juts his chin at the door. "Start working on your assignment."

"I will." I take a few steps to the door. Then I stop and swerve back. "Mr. Mulliez, it might not seem like it, but I really appreciate everything you've done for me."

"Don't mention it. I, as the kids say, got your back." He thumps his chest twice and then gives me a peace sign.

I snort. "Don't ever do that again."

He laughs and shoos me out.

I push the door open and my smile wobbles. Guilt twists in my chest like a knife. Mr. Mulliez plucked me out of my hopeless existence and gave me a fresh start. I hate that I can't fulfil his expectations for me, but it would cost too much to get over my stage fright and flaunt myself in front of Redwood.

I can't do that.

What I *can* do is turn in the best Unconventional Music Theory assignment Redwood has ever seen. Just to make it clear why my scholarship was worth it.

I head outside and tilt my face up to the sun for inspiration. Redwood Prep's gardens are something out of a fantasy. The lawn goes on for miles with plenty of trees and cute picnic benches nestled under the shade.

I take a step forward when I feel a presence behind me. A voice like raw silk whispers, "New Girl."

I jump out of my skin when I look over my shoulder and see Dutch, Zane and Finn surrounding me. My tongue turns heavy and I instantly back away.

"Want to work on Mulliez's assignment together?" Finn offers.

My jaw drops to the grass. "What?"

"Most of the kids already chose their groups," Zane says easily. His voice is a lot huskier than his twin's. Up close, I can see even more differences between him and Dutch.

Where Dutch looks like he'd bludgeon someone to death if they made him mad enough, Zane looks like he'd smile even when he shoved the knife in his victim's chest.

Dutch is brooding and dark and sullen, while Zane emits 'life of the party' vibes. He doesn't just *know* how to have a good time. He *is* the good time. Unlike his twin who'd suck the life out of any room he enters.

Finn is harder to get a read on. He's not dragging around a dark cloud of doom the way Dutch is, but he's not as wild and loud as his brother.

There's something cold and calculating about the way Finn watches me. A heady mixture of restraint and ruthlessness runs right under the surface, as if he could be worse than his brothers if he wanted to, but he chooses not to take that path.

Zane lifts a hand and rakes it through his perfect, shampoo-commercial-ready hair. The rings on his fingers glint in the sunlight. "We need a fourth member."

"In your band?" I gawk.

Dutch glowers. "Why the hell would we ask you to join our band?"

I narrow my eyes at him. He didn't have to sound so damn offended.

He glares right back. Trade his fancy uniform for spurs and a gun and Dutch would fit right in as a Western gunslinger. Or maybe even a gladiator.

His presence is intense, almost overwhelming. He's around the same size as his brothers, but his energy makes him seem bigger. Like a bull about to impale an innocent bystander.

Dutch's gaze drops, imperceptibly, to my lips and he stares at it as if he wants to know every inch of it well enough to trace it in his dreams.

It's a thousand degrees outside, but my arms erupt with goosebumps.

We're still staring at each other.

I refuse to break his gaze to prove a point.

He doesn't look away either.

Zane chuckles. "You two done eye-sparring yet? New Girl, we haven't gotten an answer."

I glance away from Dutch to focus on the other two members of The Kings. I don't understand why they would need an extra member for this assignment.

First of all, Mulliez made it sound like it was solo work. Second, there's three of them. And they've made it pretty clear they don't need anyone else.

My thoughts start to whirl. Why are they singling me out? Do they recognize me from the showcase? Is this a trap?

The more rational side of my brain comes out to play. Maybe I'm overthinking this. They *were* missing for the first month of school, so it makes sense that they'd be behind in group work. And I have no idea how things work at Redwood Prep. It's totally plausible that they need an extra for the assignment.

What isn't plausible is them wanting to work with *me*.

"I don't know."

The smile cracks on Zane's face. I'm guessing these boys aren't used to girls who'd deny them anything.

The brothers all exchange a loaded look. There's some kind of sibling mind-communication happening and it's weird as hell.

"Well," I shift in the uncomfortable silence, "thanks for the offer, but I'll—"

Zane pushes Dutch forward and he stumbles into me. He smells like wood shavings and sunshine. The feel of his skin on mine causes a full-body shiver.

"Come on, Cadence." Dutch's deep voice casts a spell on me. The timbre is unique. Smooth yet rough around the edges. Like an uncut gem hidden in a dark cave.

What little resistance I had left dies immediately when Dutch steps closer to me. His body is hard, lean and sculpted beneath his uniform.

My traitorous heart cartwheels into my ribs. I curl my hands into fists before I do something stupid—like run my hands down his chest to feel every nick of his abs.

His chiseled chin has a bit of stubble on it and it only adds to his rugged good looks when he ducks his head and peers at me through hooded eyes. "Just say yes. You know you want to."

There's something darkly magnetic about him, although he's the least friendly-looking out of the bunch.

And suddenly, I do want to say yes.

I really, *really* want to say yes.

It's just an assignment, Cadence.

I'd planned to turn in the best work I could for Mulliez. What better way to do that than to work with an actual band who's been on an actual tour?

My lips curl into a small, hesitant smile. "Okay."

"Let's work in the practice room," Finn says. His voice is quieter and smoother than his brothers, but it's the deepest one. Like there's an ocean, no—an entire universe in his chest.

I take a deep breath and make sure my voice doesn't tremble when I say, "Sure. Let's do that."

Zane smiles at me. His grin is panty-melting and I'm not surprised that, of all three gorgeous rockstars, he has the playboy reputation.

Zane drops an arm around my shoulder. "Tell me, New Girl, do you have an actual name?"

A flash of something dark passes through Dutch's eyes, but it's gone in a blink.

"Cadence." I side-step Zane so I'm out of his grasp. "Cadence Cooper."

"Cadence? Like the cadence of a song?" Finn asks.

"Yeah. My dad was a musician. Mom let him pick our names. He called me Cadence and my sister, Viola." My eyes zip to Dutch. He's not saying anything, but his jaw is clenching and unclenching.

A foreboding feeling descends on me, but I brush it away. I haven't done anything to these guys. Or to anyone. I've been invisible at this school for a whole month, not getting into anyone's way or minding anyone's business but my own. They have no reason to seek me out and hurt me.

"Sounds like music's in the family?" Finn says.

"Uh... yeah. I guess you could say it's in my blood."

THE DARKEST NOTE

"Your mom a musician too?" Finn asks.

"No, not exactly." Dad gave me all the good traits. Mom handed down her vices like a hereditary disease.

We're in the hallway now and though it's crowded with students, it feels like someone pressed 'pause' on a movie. No one is moving or blinking. They're all staring at me and The Kings as if we're wild hallucinations.

Heat blasts through my chest and I fight to appear unaffected. I saw how the classroom reacted to Dutch and his brothers yesterday. And I saw it again in the hallway earlier.

They're not flustered by the attention, so I should pretend that I'm not either. Even if this is the most awkward moment of my life.

"Were you at the showcase?" Zane asks, taking me down another hallway.

I tense immediately. "Me? Showcase? No. No I wasn't."

"Weird that Mulliez wouldn't stick someone like you in the show," Dutch murmurs.

I give him a heated a look. It's not that I'm ashamed of being a scholarship kid, but the way he said 'someone like you', as if I'm less-than because of where I come from, sends the hair on the back of my neck standing up.

"Where exactly are we going?" I murmur. We're moving far away from any of the practice rooms in Redwood Prep.

"We're here." Finn lifts a card and slaps it against a scanner. I jump back when a neon light runs up and down the plastic. It beeps and a door clicks open.

I dig my heels in. "Where's *here?*"

"Our practice room," Zane says, giving me a cocky smile.

Finn steps in first.

Zane follows.

Dutch sticks out a hand. "After you."

Tension fills me, vibrating through my body like a broken chord.

"Scared?" Dutch taunts close to my ear.

I stiffen and throw him a fierce look. "Not even close." Then I push the door further and step into the lion's den.

* * *

Jinx: This one is for free, New Girl. A king will never marry his concubine. Don't walk through any doors believing it's your happily ever after. The only path in front of you is the one that leads to destruction.

Chapter Six

CADENCE

It doesn't take long for the alarm bells to go off in my head, overpowering the music that's been on a loop since The Kings cornered me outside.

The smile on Zane's face disappears the moment the door slams shut. He walks over to the window and looks outside it, hands on his hips as if he doesn't want to watch what'll happen next.

Finn retires to a chair, arms folded over his chest and eyes sharp. The ruthlessness that I'd sensed in him takes the wheel. Lips that had seemed vacantly lax have an almost cruel slant. A gentleman replaced by a savage.

But the sense of doom *really* sinks in when my eyes land on Dutch. His scowl is gone, mouth relaxed, as if he's glad to be in his own turf where he no longer has to act civilized. His amber eyes are both bottomless and depthless as he steps closer to me.

I step back.

The smile that inches across his dangerously handsome face is lopsided. He'll enjoy this. Whatever *this* is.

What started as a faint sense of calamity boils down to a steady, untainted thump of distress, like barely visible cracks in the wall morphing into giant gaps that could down a bridge.

"Now that we won't be overheard, there's something we need to discuss, New Girl," Dutch says quietly.

"It's *Cadence*," I correct him, but my voice trembles and it doesn't sound half as intimidating as it should.

He chuckles, low and deep in his throat. "I don't give a damn what your name is."

I whip my eyes to Finn and then to Zane, who's turned around and is watching us like we're a television show that he's barely paying attention to.

The switch in their demeanor is so quick that it feels like diving into water that's *supposed* to be warm and finding out it's ice-cold when your body's already submerged.

I struggle to jump ahead of what's going on, but I can't quite believe any of this is happening. If not for the danger swirling in the air and the alarm bells raging in my head, I'd think this was all a dream.

"W-what do you want?" I stumble back.

"One little thing." Dutch growls darkly. "Leave Redwood Prep. Immediately."

The words thud against my chest and bounce to the ground. If I weren't so shocked, I'd try to pick them up and turn them over. I'd do my best to piece them together until they made sense.

But since I'm not in any state to do that, all I can do is gape. "Excuse me?"

"Leave. This. School."

"What are you—what do you mean?" I stutter.

"You're smart, New Girl, or you wouldn't have been offered a spot here. No matter how much Mulliez begged." Dutch keeps advancing on me. "I need you out. I need you gone. Today."

I keep moving back.

My heart is clanging in my chest. This isn't right. The only place I need to leave is this room. But Dutch is standing between me and the door. And even if I run, Zane and Finn could catch me. They're all lean and powerful. It wouldn't take a lot for them to drag me back.

I can't escape them.

I can't do anything but fight my way through.

"W-who the hell are you to tell me to leave?" I yell. But the bite is lost from my tone when I inch away.

Dutch's hand lurches out and he grabs my upper arm. His grip is strong. Although he's not digging in hard enough to cause pain, it's enough to prove he could break me if he wanted to.

All the tingly feelings I'd felt for him when we met outside disappear, replaced by a pulsing fury. He set me up. The friendliness, the offer of working together, they wanted to *lure* me here.

It's diabolical. It's cruel. I don't have to guess which brother came up with the idea.

"Let me go!" I fight him, flailing my arms and struggling to escape his grasp.

"Watch it, New Girl." He jerks me around and my skirt flails around my legs. I look back, out of breath and realize that I'd been about to knock into his shiny guitar.

Dutch jerks me forward and I collide in his chest. His eyes rove my face. "We all know you wouldn't have been able to afford your tuition if not for our family's money. You had a chance to live on the other side for a while. You're welcome. In return, all we're asking is for you to bow out nice and quiet. You can do that, can't you?"

My nostrils flare. It's one thing to make ridiculous demands out of nowhere. It's another to look down on me because I'm poor. Who the hell does he think he is?

I tilt my chin up. "What if I don't?"

"If you don't," his lips move over mine, so close I can smell his cinnamon-scented breath, "then I will make it my personal mission to destroy you."

His eyes are stone-cold. He means every word.

His flaming antagonism scrapes against the depths of my soul. The part of me that believes in justice and good and fairness shrivels inside.

All my life, I made it through by believing that good exists and things have to work out in the end. I clung to that truth. I had to. When all you're surrounded by is pain and darkness—there's no choice but to hold on to something intangible.

Beautiful idealisms.

Unreachable dreams.

But Dutch Cross just took a baton to my house of cards and smashed it to the ground. I realize just how powerless I really am in this world. Pluckiness? Hard work? Bull crap.

Everything about my existence is moldable. No matter how much pride I have, I'm nothing but a plaything in the hands of the rich and powerful. The hand grabbing mine is proof.

It's disappointment, more than it is the hurt, that spurs the rage through my veins. How dare he steal my hope? That tiny little flower that managed to survive beneath mounds of dirt and garbage. How dare he take such a precious thing from me—my own distorted ideals—and tear it to shreds?

I slam him with my angry eyes and I see the moment he takes note of my expression. A glimmer of amusement passes through his face. And I hate him for that too.

"I wouldn't suggest you choose the hard road, New Girl." His fingers slide down my torso and hook in the gaping hole of my shirt. Somehow, in all the scuffling, the pin came undone. There's a hint of pale flesh peeking at Dutch and his eyes fix there like a predator.

He hooks his ringed finger in the gap and tugs me forward. "I'd really enjoy the chance to break you."

My body trembles from head to toe, but it's not because of my earlier, pitiful infatuation. In fact, I'm more ashamed than ever that I'd fallen for the Cross brothers' spell. Especially him.

The spawn of evil himself.

Dutch is breathing in my fear like a drug. I feel the darkness vibrating in his bones and it rumbles against my skin.

This feels personal.

But why? What could I have possibly done to deserve this cruelty? I've never met these boys in my life. Even if I did, I would have passed them by, knowing that I'm just a speck of dirt on their perfect, pristine worlds.

"There's only one right answer," Dutch says into my ear. "Let me hear it, New Girl."

"You really think you can break me?" I grind out.

One corner of his lips hitches up.

I curl my fingers into fists and launch them at him. He easily wraps his fingers around my wrists and drives me back. I hit the wall so hard that my breath pops out of my open lips.

His body presses against mine. Until I can feel all of him. Until the weight of him is practically sinking into me.

He leans down. The words he delivers hit my neck like tiny daggers. A vampire's bite. "Don't excite me at the thought of a fight, New Girl. I'm trying so hard to end this now."

"Dutch." Zane's voice sounds behind us.

Finn rises from his chair.

The brothers look somber and formidable.

He releases me and I wilt against the wall, a hand to my chest as my heart bangs against my ribs.

I look up through the fringe of hair that's falling in front of my face. Dutch is prowling in front of the instruments, his stare burning with disdain for me. I'm barely human to him. Barely worth respect.

Tears prick the back of my eyes, but I refuse to let them fall. With what's left of my dignity, I pin the hole in my shirt closed.

Since I was a kid growing up in the shadows of poverty, I was always desperate. Gasping for air, for a chance to be free. With mom strung out and my little sister looking to me for food, I had no choice but to wear my poverty on my sleeve.

There were some in my neighborhood who could hide the stench of neglect and hopelessness, but I wasn't one of them. I wore my pain like a badge around my neck and kept my brokenness right at the surface.

It's why I was so elated when I heard that Redwood Prep still used uniforms. Finally, I could blend in and be something close to normal. Finally, people wouldn't be able to look at me and know. *Know* that mom's arms were riddled with needle marks. Know that our beds were inflatable mattresses for most of my childhood. Know that hot meals were a commodity and hot water was a magical unicorn that existed in storybooks.

Leave Redwood Prep?

I think about Viola and her excitement when she heard I'd gotten into Redwood.

'You've got to be kidding me? That's so cool. They've got, like, all the coolest kids there. I follow all of their make-up channels!'

She'd be heartbroken to see me leave the castle in the clouds, not only empty-handed but a quitter.

Because of Redwood, my sister had hope the way I did. A way out. A different way. One that had nothing to do with selling her body or her dreams to scrape through the bottom of the barrel for opportunities.

It means too much. Redwood. The scholarship. It means everything. And I won't let Dutch Spawn-of-Evil Cross pry it out of my hands.

"I don't care what you do," I cry out hoarsely, "I'm not leaving Redwood unless they're carrying out my cold, dead body."

His sinister laughter is the last thing I expect, but it bursts out of his mouth and it's somehow more frightening than any of the scowls and glares that came before it.

The laughter tells me he's not concerned in the least. It tells me I'm a mouse in front of a lion, one whose demise is inevitable and he'll toy around with his meal until it bores him.

The weight of what I'm up against presses into me when I see Finn and Zane trot to Dutch and flank him on either side. They make a formidable picture with their broad shoulders, long legs and chilly, beautiful faces.

"Let's see how long you hold out." He glances at his brothers. "I gave her a chance. You satisfied?"

Finn dips his chin.

Zane frowns.

Hazel eyes burn into me. "Just know that we asked you nicely first." He steps forward, his sneakers kissing mine. "Welcome to Redwood Prep."

If I wasn't sure that his brothers would block me, I'd grab his guitar and bash it in his face.

Instead, I lift my chin and stalk past them. They let me, not chasing me even when I throw the door open and stalk outside. Students stop in their tracks when they see me leaving their private practice room. Astonished gasps ripple like pops of fire.

'What was she doing in there?'

'Is she dating one of the Kings?'

'Who is that girl? I've never seen her before'.

Their whispers follow me as I charge away from The King's lair and stumble down the hallway like a woman possessed.

Did that just happen? Or was it a nightmare ripped straight out of a horror novel?

No, no, no.

I keep running until my legs give out and all I can do is sink against a locker.

Panic gives way to rationalizing. Now that I'm in the sunlight, now that I feel safe, I'm scrambling for an explanation.

Maybe they were bluffing. Maybe, if I just keep my head down and stay out of their way, they'll forget all about the target they put on my back. They'll find someone else to torment.

My heart swells with hope and I latch onto that thread like a drowning bird.

As if hearing my feeble prayers, a disturbance erupts in the hallway.

Phones start chirping.

The *ping* sound reverberates like a gong, rushing down to me with finality.

Movement stops.

Chatter turns to thoughtful silence.

Heads dip like marionettes pulled on strings, all answering the lure of their devices.

The foreboding feeling I'd had in The King's practice room returns. And this time, it's ten times stronger.

I open my phone and maneuver to the Redwood Prep app. That's the only app that would send a notification to everyone's devices at the same time.

"Come on." I pull the screen down and watch the refresh button. It doesn't load. "Come on. Come on." I rub my thumb against the screen, feeling the heat of everyone's stares.

The stupid phone won't refresh.

'Is it her?'

'It looks like her.'

'How could she do that?'

One by one, the whispers start. Accusing eyes shoot in my direction, flogging me like whips at the stake.

I straighten to my full height and try to walk through the hallway without looking shaken. With each step I take, the stares get heavier and heavier.

"Dude, it *is* her." A pimply-faced freshman points and laughs.

Unable to stand the suspense a second longer, I march right up to him and extend my hand. "Give me your phone."

"What?"

Without waiting for a response, I snatch the phone from him.

What I see sends a ricochet of dread drumming down my spine.

It's a photo of me—without my red wig and makeup—and Mr. Mulliez. We're sitting at a booth at the lounge. It was taken the night he offered me a scholarship to Redwood.

Underneath it is a caption.

'*NEW GIRL BANGS MUSIC TEACHER FOR TICKET INTO REDWOOD*'

Bile rises to the back of my throat and I shove the phone back into the freshman's hands. Stomach roiling, I stumble into the nearest restroom and puke my guts out.

The Kings promised they would break me.

But I didn't expect the breaking to take innocent people down too.

* * *

Jinx: All pawns fall first. Still don't want to play, New Girl?

Cadence: Where the hell did Dutch get those pictures from? Was it from you?

Jinx: Trade a secret for a secret. Then I'll tell.

Chapter Seven

CADENCE

I'm fuming when I wrench my front door open and storm inside the messy apartment. The look on Mr. Mulliez's face when I ran to the music room and saw him getting escorted into the principal's office like a criminal is one I'll never forget.

It's going to be okay, he said to me.

Even in that horrific moment, he was more interested in comforting me. As if all of this isn't my fault.

I throw my backpack on the floor, bend over and scream my head off.

Normally, I'd check to make sure Viola isn't home before I release my frustration, but I can't contain my rage. Today, I stood face-to-face with a cold, heartless vortex wrapped in the face of a god. Three of them, in fact.

And I barely survived.

Right now, I'm in critical condition. My heart is leaking

blood and it's all I can do to sew myself up so I can face another day.

Sweat beads on my neck and gathers under my shirt. I lift my cell phone. There's still no new notification on the school app. Not that the picture would still be there even if I had access. I bet the school scrubbed that photo from the records as soon as possible.

Mr. Mulliez has to be okay, right? He'll explain that the picture was out of context. He'll tell them we were only at the lounge that night to discuss my scholarship. Everything will be fine.

I pace the length of my cramped living room, past the drug store makeup kits scattered on the ground, past my cheap piano and Viola's prized light up mirror.

I'm trying not to hyperventilate but I don't think it's working. Mr. Mulliez's entire reputation could be destroyed and it's all because of me.

I'd really enjoy the chance to break you.

I didn't expect Dutch to hit me so hard. He sure knew where to find a place that would hurt.

How could anyone be that cruel?

There's a knock on the front door at that moment.

It can't be Viola or Breeze. Viola has a key and Breeze would just shriek, *"skank, I'm home"* for the entire neighborhood to hear.

I'm not in the mood to entertain door-to-door salesmen, religious groups, or visitors right now, so I ignore the thudding.

The knock sounds again, more insistent this time.

I stomp to the front door and wrench it open. "WHAT?"

"Whoa." A handsome man blinks at me. Chocolate eyes peer into mine. "Calm down, little rottweiler."

"Whatever you're selling, I don't want any of it," I snap, starting to shut the door.

He sticks his head forward. "Wait, I'm Hunter Scott, a friend of Rick's."

At the mention of my brother, my hand falls limp. I haven't heard from Rick since he told me we weren't his responsibility. I figured I'd never hear from him again.

"Rick sent you?"

"Not exactly." Hunter flashes me a handsome grin. Laugh lines form around his mouth, giving him an approachable, warm look. "Can I come in?"

"No, you may not," I say firmly. Having a drug addict for a mother taught me many things. Like how gullibly inviting a strange man into the house when I'm home alone can lead to his hand edging down my thigh.

One broken bottle over the head stopped what could have been a disaster, but it was a lesson I didn't need to learn twice.

The handsome stranger smiles, revealing twin dimples. "Okay, I can see why you wouldn't roll out the red carpet. Your brother's been kind of a jerk to you."

"Kind of?" I scoff. Rick made all kinds of promises to the social worker and then he spit in our faces in our time of need. I don't think his jerkishness needs a precursor.

"Me being his friend probably doesn't endear me to you either," Hunter adds.

"What do you want?" I ask impatiently.

He holds an envelope out to me.

I frown at it. "What's that?"

"I was there when you called Rick and told him about your electricity shutting off."

Flames of humiliation spring to my cheeks. Great. So

our family laundry's been aired to Rick's entire friend group?

"He was a prick to you, but he's having a hard time too." He shoves the envelope toward me. "I'm not sure how much the bill is, but I think that's enough to cover it."

I keep my hands at my sides. Not only do I have to deal with The Kings of Redwood Prep calling me poor, and accusing me of sleeping with a teacher, but now complete and utter strangers think I'm so pathetic they're randomly handing me cash?

"I don't want it," I say, pushing it back to him.

"Look, I know how this might seem. If I were in your position, I wouldn't want to take this either. But here's the thing." He tilts his head and his curly brown hair falls in front of his eyes. "I *have* been in your position before. Oldest sibling. Looking out for my little brother. Trying to make ends meet with the world breathing down my neck. I get it."

I fold my arms over my chest and look up at him.

His lips hitch up slightly. "Your brother's got complicated feelings about his mom. It's inevitable that he'd take it out on you. This is my attempt at asking you to cut him some slack."

"You said you were Rick's friend?"

"We grew up in the foster home together."

That statement knocks the wind right out of my sails. Rick never told us anything about how he grew up and mom, in all her delusional wisdom, hadn't divulged that information either.

I frown suspiciously at Hunter. He's cute and it seems like he has good intentions, but I'm not falling for that play twice.

"I appreciate you coming down here to say all this and

to throw cash at me," I gesture to the envelope, "but I'm fine. Really. So you can go back to Rick and tell him I don't need him or his friends' guilt money."

After swinging the door shut on Hunter, I scoop my bag off the floor and march to my room.

All I want to do is flop onto my bed and let someone more mature than me solve my problems. But that isn't going to work. I need to make dinner for Viola and then I need to report to my shift at the diner. I work as a waitress on the nights when I don't play music at the lounge.

My phone vibrates.

I stiffen, wondering if it's Jinx again. The creepy know-it-all has been hounding me since my first day at Redwood Prep. I have no idea who he or she is but, after what happened today, I definitely don't want any part in her twisted game.

Thankfully, it's not Jinx.

It's Breeze.

Breeze: I heard there was a teacher-student scandal at Redwood. *gasp* Can you believe it? Seems like even the rich have their secrets.

I moan and throw an arm over my face. This is bad. If the news has spread outside of Redwood Prep, there's no way things will end quietly. Mr. Mulliez is in more trouble than I thought.

With a deep sigh, I sit up and roll out of bed. Viola will be home soon and I try to have at least a pb&j prepared for her. She'll whine and refuse to study if she's hungry.

I'm slathering jelly on one side of toast when the front door opens. I expect my little sister to walk in, but I see a walking sandbag instead. The sandbag is hefted to the floor and Viola's dark eyes twinkle at me.

I stick the butterknife in the punching bag's direction. "What's that?"

"I found it leaning against our door. I thought you ordered it."

Heart racing, I throw the knife on the counter and hurry to the bag. "Does it look like we have money to order anything right now?"

I inspect the mysterious item further and notice a note flapping on the side. Snatching it off, I read a man's crab-like handwriting.

This might be a better stress-reliever than screaming. It worked for me.

- Hunter

My eyebrows jump.

Viola grabs the note and reads it, a slow smile climbing on her face. "Who's Hunter?"

"Rick's friend," I mumble, lifting the punching bag and inspecting it. There are a few discolored areas, but it otherwise looks intact.

"Rick?" Viola's expression shifts instantly. "He's talking to us now?"

"Not exactly."

"Oh." Her shoulders slump and she stares at the ground.

"What do you say we try it out?" I offer, hoping to cheer her up.

"Really?" Her voice squeaks. "I thought for sure you'd throw it in the trash."

"It doesn't exactly fit the decor in here but…" I glance around for somewhere to put the punching bag and decide to hang it up on the hook in the living room that's never held a picture frame.

"Can I try first?" My sister asks.

I nod and gesture for her to go ahead.

She bounces in place like a seasoned wrestler and rolls her neck back and side-to-side. Her ponytails bounce on top of her shoulders.

Since Viola's school—my old high school—doesn't require wearing uniforms, she gets to choose whatever she wants. Today, she paired a T-shirt with a daisy in the center with a pair of high-waisted jeans and pure white sneakers.

It's amazing the way she makes thrift-store clothes look so expensive. I know that if she keeps posting with consistency, she might start to get views. I just don't trust that those views can actually turn into money.

Surging forward, Vi slams her fist into the punching bag and makes a guttural roar. "That's for calling my makeup cheap, Tiffany!"

The punching bag whirls around like a runaway piñata.

I stare at my sister with concern. "Who's Tiffany?"

"This poser at my school who thinks she's better than everyone just because she has a thousand followers. Whatever." Viola rolls her brown eyes in that expert way young teenagers do.

Then she gestures to me. "Go on. Your turn."

"My turn?" I shake my head. "I have to get to work."

"You have time." She juts her chin at the punching bag.

"I don't..."

"You know you want to, Cadey."

I step forward hesitantly.

"You can't approach it like that." Viola stands behind me and massages my shoulders. Her fingers are long and slender, perfect for playing piano. Sadly, she has no interest in music.

"How am I supposed to approach it?"

"Like you own it." She puffs out her chest and sticks her

chin up. "Like it's your worst enemy and today's the day you stomp them into the ground." Finally, she drops her stance and returns to the cute, bubbly thirteen-year-old that I practically raised. "Like that."

"Okay." I breathe in and stare at the sand bag, imagining Dutch's beautiful, cocky face. Hauling my fist all the way back, I let a punch fly into the bag. "Jerk!" I think of Dutch's laughter as he told me he'd enjoy destroying my life. "Bastard!" I punch the bag again and again. "Prick! Trash faucet!"

"Whoa, whoa, sis." A hand lands on my shoulder. "You're going to crack the plaster." She nods to the punching bag that's slamming into the wall.

I straighten awkwardly and brush my long brown hair out of my face. I'm flushed and my fist is hurting a little, but I'm lighter already.

"You were right." I smile at Vi. "That does help."

My sister looks at me as if I'm crazy. "Remind me not to get on your bad side."

I laugh and throw my arms around her.

For once, she doesn't squirm. She hugs me back. "Is something going on at Redwood Prep?"

"Of course not," I lie, snuggling her closer. There's no way I'm telling my baby sister that I've gotten on The Kings' bad side. It would only stress her out and there's nothing she can do about it anyway.

"Everything is great," I add.

"In that case," she wiggles away, "would you link me up with Zane Cross? Or even Dutch or Finn." She bats thick eyelashes. "They're super hot and super popular and they're into music. Just like you."

My arms go limp and I step away from her. Voice tightening, I say, "Get to your homework."

"Homework?" She makes a face. "I just got home. Let me relax a bit."

"Viola."

My sister hops into the sofa and scrolls through her phone. "You're going to be late for work," she says smugly.

I glare at her, but she's got a point. I point to the sandwich. "I made you a snack. Do your homework and don't—"

"Open the door for anyone except Breeze. I know. You've only said it a million times."

I walk up to her, bend over the back of the couch and kiss her forehead. "I'll be back after my shift."

"Don't work too hard," she calls absently, half her brain already focused on whatever mindless dribble is on her phone.

On my way to the front door, I cast another look at the punching bag. My knuckles are a little sore, but it's a good kind of pain. I feel like something in my chest got snapped free.

Dutch better watch out. My energy to fight has just been activated. Maybe I would have considered leaving Redwood Prep before, but because of what he did today, I'll make it my mission to hold on.

I won't ever let him win.

* * *

Jinx: Trade a secret for a secret, New Girl. Were you really sleeping with Mr. Mulliez? And what kind of secret did he want to protect that he was willing to leave Redwood than admit why you were really at the lounge that night?

Chapter Eight

CADENCE

Don't let them see you sweat.

Redwood Prep rises in the distance like a house of nightmares. I half expect shadow monsters to come raging down the stairs.

Fear sends a shiver down my spine, but I tuck my fingers in the strap of my school bag and force myself to keep going.

Brahms' *Wiegenlied* is playing loudly in my ears. My mom wasn't the type who'd ever sing lullabies. Instead, it was Brahms, a dead man, whose melody chased my hardships away and lulled me to sleep.

No matter what they try to do today, Cadence, you will not break. You can handle anything. Don't let them win. They can't win.

The front steps are crowded with students. A few are still pouring in from the parking lot. One of the greatest displays of wealth at Redwood is in that gated yard. Sometimes, Redwood Prep's parking lot looks more like an exclusive car dealership than anything. Tinted windows, shiny paint jobs, fancy rims—the guys in my neighborhood would drool if they ever saw this. I've been here a month and it still takes my breath away.

People are starting to notice me now. I set my foot on the sidewalk and the response is instantaneous. Eyes swing around and train on me. Girls exchange loaded looks. Conversations stop mid-sentence, abandoning whatever juicy gossip was being exchanged.

I turn Brahms up in my ears and let the music drown the disdain dripping from my classmates' rich, privileged faces.

I look down to make sure there are no wardrobe blunders. The button is still there. I sewed it on last night after my shift at the diner.

Now, there will be no more opportunities for cold-hearted boys with hazel eyes to dig their fingers in my shirt and yank me closer.

My hair is brushed and braided neatly down my back. I even dotted a bit of Viola's lip gloss on my mouth. My sister almost snapped my neck in half when she saw me fiddling around in her makeup stash, but I managed to escape unscathed.

A group of girls walk by, laughing and giving me weird glances. I pretend not to notice. With Brahms's soothing lullaby tickling my ears, it almost feels like their intentions are good.

The pointing and gawking comes from all directions once I'm inside and shuffling down the hallways.

It reaches its climax when I stop in front of my locker and see the word 'slut' spray-painted over it.

I glance over my shoulder and notice phones lifted high to take in my reaction.

My lips tremble with rage.

Did Dutch do this?

I grit my teeth and try to keep my face calm as I open my locker. I won't give them the privilege of seeing me ruffled.

Do not lower your head, Cadence.

"Did she sleep with Mulliez?"

"The whore."

"You think he's the only one she screwed to get into Redwood?"

The volume of their laughter is rising and it's drowning out Brahms. My fingers twitch. If I make the song any louder, I'm going to burst an eardrum. Maybe that would be better than enduring their stares and ridicule.

The loneliness hits me hard and fast. I don't belong at Redwood Prep and though people knew it, they didn't care. Now, not only do they know who I am, but they all hate me.

I keep breathing in time to the rhythm of the song. With a patient sigh, I yank my books out of the locker and slam it shut.

When I glance up, I see three tall figures entering the hallway. The Kings all stop and watch, staring at me with pride.

They want to be seen.

They want me to know that they did this.

Dutch is at the front, as he always is. He's standing with his feet apart, hair disheveled and eyes like molten lava. The shirt he's wearing today is short-sleeved and shows the ink climbing over his arm.

Brahms's lullaby ends abruptly as if even *he* fears the cold monster who has me in his line of sight.

Dutch strolls toward me. If I were smarter, I'd turn the other way.

But I'm not afraid of him right now. I'm pissed.

So I storm toward him too.

We collide in the middle of the hallway, neither of us stepping aside. I can feel everyone watching us, but I don't care. I'm boiling with righteous indignation.

"Mulliez is innocent, you bastard," I snap.

He gives me a bored look. "Teachers who meet students in night clubs aren't my definition of innocent."

"It wasn't a nightclub. It was a lounge."

He scoffs as if I'm mentally challenged and he refuses to listen to whatever I have to say. When he moves to sidestep me, I know I'm being dismissed.

Acting on impulse, I slide into his path and slam my hands on his chest. A gasp erupts from the student body.

Zane and Finn arch their eyebrows.

"Keep Mulliez out of this," I snarl.

"Might I remind you," Dutch advances, causing my arms to get squished between his chest and mine, "that you're not in any position to make demands." He bends down so we're eye-to-eye. "Things will only get worse from here. You ready to say goodbye..." his eyes catch on my cell phone, "Brahms?"

"You ready for my fist to meet your face," I snarl, hauling my arm back so I can paint his perfect jawline.

Dutch captures my wrist and holds it in his grasp. "So violent."

I'm not sure, but I think Finn's lips curl up.

Zane coughs into his hand.

I bite down on my bottom lip and try to squirm my hands free, but he's much stronger than me. It's hopeless.

When I realize I'm trapped, I give up and glare at him.

Rage burns through my chest and my heart thumps like crazy.

"Screw. You." I punctuate each word.

Dutch's gaze drops to my lips and he crowds my personal space, practically breathing on top of me. Then he blinks. A wave of something dark crashes through his eyes. His jaw flexes and he tosses my hand aside like it's moldy bread.

"Get out of Redwood before things get worse."

Dutch hikes the strap of his backpack higher on his shoulder, steps past me and continues his royal parade down the rest of the hallway.

Finn and Zane follow on his heels.

I whirl around, my chest heaving and my vision turning red. I did absolutely nothing to those boys and neither did Mr. Mulliez. Why are they trying so hard to destroy us? Is this what rich people do when they're bored? Do they destroy lives for the fun of it?

Before I can think it through, I start rushing down the hallway, fully intending to leave my footprint on the back of Dutch's pristine vest. For Mr. Mulliez's sake.

"Ms. Cooper." A voice calls to me before I can lunge into a flying kick.

I stop abruptly and turn to find Miss Jamieson, the youngest teacher at Redwood Prep, standing in the middle of the hallway.

She glances at me and there's a hint of understanding in her gaze. Then she hurls a look at the brothers. Her eyes narrow. I get the feeling there's a part of her that would like to deliver a flying kick to The Kings too.

"Come with me." She flings her head, indicating the stairwell.

I frown. I haven't been particularly engaged in her

lectures since I've been here and I'm surprised to find out she knows my name.

After a second of hesitation, I follow her.

She leads me down the hallway, her steps swift and urgent. I have no idea what's going on and the secrecy is starting to get to me.

Finally, Miss Jamieson opens the stairwell door for me and gestures for me to walk in first. I pass her by slowly, taking note of her beautiful face.

One of the reasons Miss Jamieson gets the best participation out of all the teachers at Redwood Prep is her immaculate beauty.

She's got long, spiral curls, dainty, pageant-queen-esque features, and a lean body. Her clothes are always professional but stylish and she isn't afraid to wear short skirts or funky blazers on campus.

I've heard more than a few boys talking about how much they'd like to—ahem—experience her.

When she steps in after me and closes the door, she smiles. "I'm sorry for all the cloak and dagger, but Harry really wanted to see you before he left."

"Harry?"

"That's my first name," Mr. Mulliez says, stepping out of the shadows.

Tears press at the back of my eyes when I hear his voice. "Mr. Mulliez."

I fly over to him. His hair is messier than usual and his eyes have dark bags beneath them. Despite the obvious weariness, he musters up a smile for me.

I notice the box in his hands. It's got sheet music, a few awards, and the plaque he hung above the door that says 'music is the language of the soul'.

The moment I see that box, I know what it means.

Guilt springs its mighty claws and rakes a bloody trail from my throat to my spine. I've never experienced a feeling like this before and it *sucks*.

Mr. Mulliez was the first person who looked out for me, gave me a chance and expected nothing in return. Yet it cost him everything.

"No." I shake my head. "You did nothing wrong," I insist. My voice is climbing and the natural reverb in the hallway causes it to bounce back to me. I can hear myself getting more and more unhinged. "You have to stay. You have to fight them. You can't let them win."

"Cadence." He approaches me and stresses my name. "*Cadence.* It's okay."

"No, it's not." I sniff. "I'll go talk to the principal. I'll explain everything. They haven't even gotten my side of the story."

"I'm not leaving because of you."

"Yes, you are," I insist. The world is turning blurry because of the tears that I can't keep back.

"I'm tired of this school, the politics, the way powerful families think they can control everything." He shakes his head. "I've been considering moving for a long time. I'm just glad I got to leave a gem in Redwood before I did."

"A gem?"

"You." His eyes are soft and caring. "I didn't fight for you to get into Redwood just so you could study here. You have the talent to do music and be successful at it. And all the tools that you need to go far are within these walls."

"No." I shake my head. "If they're kicking you out unfairly then I'll—"

"Don't even finish that sentence." He sticks up a finger. "Besides, your contract has a clause that says you'll have to pay back for the scholarship and the termination fee. Do you have that kind of cash?"

I blink unsteadily. I'd completely forgotten about those terms. At the time, I thought completing senior year would be easy. I didn't account for Dutch crashing into my world and trying to burn it to the ground in a week.

Mr. Mulliez glances up. "I asked Miss Jamieson to help me meet you here because I don't think it's the best idea to meet in public, whether inside or out of Redwood. After everything, I don't think it would be proper."

I lower my head. "I'm so sorry."

"Don't be." He pats my shoulder. "Just... try to stay out of the boys' way." Mr. Mulliez pauses. "And don't make enemies with Jinx."

"You know about Jinx?"

He nods. "Try to make friends where you can. That's how you'll stay above their schemes."

The knob on the door rattles. "Why is this locked?" Someone pounds on the door. "What's going on back there?"

Miss Jamieson gives me a frightened look. "Time's up."

"Thank you for everything you've done for me, Mr. Mulliez. I won't let you down."

He smiles and nods his goodbye. In a second, he blends into the shadows and takes the stairs, leaving me behind.

The tears are back again, but they're not from sorrow this time. They're from pure, lightning *fury*. My nostrils flare like a bull and my chest inflates with every breath.

The Kings are going to pay for this.

Dutch is going to pay for this. I just don't know how yet.

Miss Jamieson gestures for me to go out first and makes an excuse to the students about why we were taking up the hallway. I barely hear her over the roaring of my own heart.

In fact, I don't hear anything for the rest of the morning.

It's not until I get to lunch, where the staring, the mean whispers, and the jeers are multiplied, that I come back to my senses.

There's not a friendly face in the cafeteria. Not that I'd want to eat among the pretentious bastards anyway.

I take my tray, keep my head down, and hurry outside to my usual table.

Except someone's already there.

"Welcome, fellow slut." She raises a fist and pumps it against her chest twice. "Mind if I crash."

I blink in surprise, taking note of her jet-black hair, thick eyeliner and leather jacket.

"Aren't you the one I ran into in the bathroom?"

"Am I?" She tilts her head. "Or am I just a figment of your imagination?"

I scrunch my nose.

She laughs and even her goth look can't hide the twinkle in her eyes. "I'm just messing with you. Yeah that was me."

"Nice to formally meet you," I say, setting my tray down at the table.

She sticks out a hand, showing off her long nails with stars painstakingly painted into the gel. "Serena."

"Cadence."

"Oh, I know. You've gotten famous overnight."

"For that stupid rumor about me and Mr. Mulliez?"

"No." She snorts. "No one cares about you and Mr. Mulliez. Teachers and students are a thing here." She peels a banana and makes a big chomp. "It's because of you and Dutch."

My muscles go rigid at the very mention of his name.

Her eyes pore over my face as if she's taking note of each one of my expressions. "You didn't know?"

"Know what?"

"Rumor has it that you were seen being escorted by The Kings yesterday. They even let you into their practice room."

She has no idea. I wasn't being 'escorted' like an important guest of honor. I was being kidnapped.

And the invite to their super-secret private room was just so they could threaten me.

Who's making this stuff up?

Her smile is curious. "And today, Dutch almost kissed you."

"Whoa. That is *not* what happened," I snap. "I'd knee him in the nuts before I let him kiss me."

She laughs. "Eh, don't let the brainless princess zombies at this school hear that. They'd start gathering their pitchforks." She stuffs the rest of the banana in her mouth and talks through the food. "Being seen with one of those guys is the pinnacle of popularity around here. And talking to them?" She rolls her eyes. "A pipe dream."

They sure had a lot to say to me yesterday. I rip the plastic covering my sandwich apart. "Trust me. The rumors are false. There's nothing going on between me and those monsters."

"Hm." She lifts her knee on the table, showing off the ripped jeans under her plaid skirt. "Is that why Dutch and his brothers are sitting at the table directly across from us?"

"What?" I glance up quickly. Like a ghost summoned after calling its name three times, Dutch rises in the distance, flocked by his brothers and a pack of giggling cheerleaders.

I dig my fingers into my sandwich until the cream center globs out of it.

"Whoa. Need a napkin?" Serena asks, opening her bag and rustling through it.

No, what I need is for Dutch to get out of my sight. It's taking everything inside me to stay seated. I owe that bastard a flying kick to the face and it's looking really appealing right now.

Deep breaths barely calm my heart rate. Mr. Mulliez reminded me about the consequences of losing my scholarship. I don't have the money to pay back Redwood Prep, so I have to keep my cool.

Dutch sees us watching. He arches an eyebrow in my direction and offers up a toast with his bottle of water.

His smugness makes my blood boil. It's like he's *aware* of how close I am to kicking his butt and he wants to push me over the edge.

I clutch the table in front of me, jerking my gaze away before I give in to my impulses. The best thing I can do right now is pretend that he's not getting to me. I won't give him the satisfaction of getting under my skin.

"You still expect me to think that nothing's going on?" Serena's finger volleys between our table and Dutch's. "After all that eye-flirting?"

It's more like eye-gouging if you ask me. But we're each entitled to our opinions.

"I'm not hungry anymore," I say, picking up my tray.

She grabs my arm. "Wait. Are you going to throw this away? Because you might as well give me rather than waste it."

"Uh, sure." I give her a funny look and set the tray back on the table.

Serena tears into what's left of my sandwich like she hasn't eaten for days.

I sling my bag over my shoulder. "Enjoy your lunch."

"Oh, I am," she says with her mouth full. Despite my throbbing urge to punch Dutch in the face right now, Serena makes me smile. There's something real about her. A total lack of pretension that makes being around her appealing. Just to see what crazy thing she'll do next.

But it's clear she's a loner and since I am too, I don't see us hanging out too much.

I fling one leg away from the bench and feel a prickling sensation on my back. When I turn around, I see that Dutch's entire table is staring at me.

Dutch, Zane and Finn are wearing hard expressions. But the most ferocious scowls are coming from the cheerleaders. The blonde from the showcase looks at me like she wants to stab me repeatedly.

I'm starting to wonder if she's the one who left the word 'slut' on my locker?

So the kids at Redwood are more offended that I 'might' be dating one of The Kings than that I might be involved with a teacher?

I don't know whether to laugh or cry.

Were rich people always so messed up?

Either way, Blondie has nothing to worry about. There is no way I'm *ever* joining their Kings cult. In fact, I find the way they worship and fawn over Dutch absolutely disgusting. Do they realize who they're rushing to please? Do they know how black his heart is?

Ridiculous.

But if they want him, then they deserve him.

Dutch lifts a hand and crooks his finger at me.

My eyebrow arches.

He nods and then lounges back, like a king on his throne, waiting patiently for me to obey his command.

I scowl, flip him off, and turn around. My steps sink into the grass as I march toward the cafeteria.

I'll spend the rest of lunch practicing piano and trying to forget that Dutch Cross exists. That's the only way I'll survive the rest of this crap-tastic day.

Chapter Nine

DUTCH

Cadence Cooper has the freaking *guts* to ignore me.

Me.

As if she didn't see me beckoning her from across the courtyard. As if those pretty brown eyes of hers didn't recognize what the gesture meant.

"Ooh." Zane taunts me under his breath. "It looks like you haven't broken your toy hard enough, bro."

Finn arches an eyebrow at me. "Maybe you're losing your touch."

"It may take some time, but she's going to learn," I say darkly.

Zane chuckles.

I slide away from the table when a pair of manicured hands latch around my bicep.

Christa looks up at me with her bright blue eyes and the bee-stung lips she got for her sixteenth birthday. Over the summer, she did even more to them. If she keeps going like this, she'll look like an inflatable doll by the time she's thirty.

I shake her off. "Don't touch me."

"Let me handle her." Christa bats thick eyelashes. With a strong gust of wind, those things are going to rip off and go sailing into a tree. "Did you see the little message I left on her locker?"

I wondered who kept painting 'slut' on Cadence's locker with lipstick. It wasn't any of us.

"I'll handle her myself," I growl, not sure why I'm annoyed by Christa's intervention.

The needy little prick pouts and edges up against me. Her hands sliding down the front of my khakis, she whispers hotly, "Forget the trash. She doesn't matter anyway."

My body responds to her not-so-subtle invitation. How could it not? Christa's grabbing a handful. More than a handful.

She laughs deeply in my ear. "Let's do something fun instead."

I'm interested.

But not right now.

Even if I were to drag Christa to the parking lot, yank her on top of me and screw her senseless, it wouldn't wash the taste of Brahm's insolence from my mouth.

She ignored me. Made me look like a fool in front of my brothers. And it deserves a punishment.

Is it my fault she's still got so much of a fighting spirit?

Maybe.

There's a fine art to breaking someone. The best route is to wear them down over time. Grind them into the dust so finely, so completely that there's no hope of rising again.

But Sol's still MIA.

And I need her out of school as fast as possible.

Without an alternative, I ditched the smaller grenades for an explosion that was sure to wrench that unfounded pride from her. And it took Mulliez along with it, which was a bonus.

But this beautiful pain-in-the-butt still has no fear.

It's about time I put the fear of The Kings into her.

"Dutch," Christa whines. Her voice has a hint of desperation in it, as if she can sense that she's losing me, but she doesn't know what else she can do to keep me on her hook.

"Later." It's not a promise so much as it is a way to appease her.

She folds her arms over her chest and stares grumpily at me.

I barely make note of her expression because I'm already stomping away from our table. Serena, one of the many scholarship kids in our class, lifts her sandwich in a toast and dips her head.

I stride right past her, unconcerned by her connection with Brahms. When it comes to allies, Serena was the most likely to chum it up with Cadence.

She's got her own checkered past. Her affinity for flames caused more than a few fire alarms blaring in Redwood. No one's found the evidence to pin the crimes on her yet, which is why her tenure at Redwood hasn't been revoked. Yet everyone seems to know it was her doing. It's caused most to steer clear.

Serena calls at my back, "Nice to see you too, Dutch!"

I smirk.

Two outcasts sticking together.

What a pair.

Brahms is reaching for the door to the cafeteria now, her skirt flirting at a generous rear-end. Unlike the other girls at Redwood Prep who change, customize and redesign their uniforms to within an inch of the dress code, she's wearing the same uniform as yesterday—a too-short plaid skirt that shows off her long legs and a too-tight shirt that looks like it's begging me to unbutton it and put it out of its misery.

That's not a joke. Yesterday, her button popped right off. But that wasn't the most ridiculous part. Seeing that tiny bit of skin made some part of me go haywire.

It was a reaction that I don't understand or particularly care for. The last thing I want to be is attracted to the girl I'm trying to run out of Redwood.

My hand falls around Brahm's wrist and I tug her around so she's facing me. Her long brown braid nearly slaps me in the face and I jump back on reflex to avoid getting whipped.

Brown eyes widening, she gapes at me. "What the hell are you doing?"

"Let me make it clear to you since it doesn't seem to be clear enough, Brahms." I step closer to her, trying my best to ignore the scent of her skin. It's not perfume. Nothing that fancy. It's pure soap, sunshine and something that's unique to her. "When I call you, you run yourself right over to me."

She closes her eyes and lets out a sigh. Without her pretty doe eyes shooting daggers at me, I get a moment to scan her face. Her skin is lily-white, more pale than Snow White. Her nose is long and slender. And her lips…

I keep seeing that redhead when I look at this girl and it's infuriating.

My fingers tighten on her.

She opens her eyes again and lightning flashes at me.

"Are you really that stupid?" Brahms hisses.

My eyes widen. I didn't expect her to say that and it

takes me a second to coach my expression back into a bored look.

"Seriously. Is there something wrong with your head?" She pokes her finger in my chest. "Because you have to be absolutely insane to think what you're doing is okay."

My eyebrow arches.

She steps into me, fearless and sexy as hell. "You listen up, *Dutch*. I am not your property. I do not belong to you. And as long as there is breath in my body, I will *never* give you the privilege of telling me what I can and cannot do."

"I see," I muse, nodding once. "And I totally respect that."

Her jaw drops.

I don't waste a second. Flattening my hand against her torso, I push her off balance and throw her over my shoulder.

The kids in the cafeteria run to the windows to stare at us.

"Put me down!" Cadence shrieks, kicking her legs.

"Keep doing that and you're going to flash every junior in the lunch room," I warn her. For some reason, the thought of them staring at her pert little backside is not sitting well.

Thankfully, Cadence is on the same page because she stops struggling. At least with her legs. But her slender fingers form fists and start pounding on my abs like Zane when he plays drums after a drunken binge.

"Let go," she shrieks. "Get your filthy hands off me!"

"I don't think so," I growl.

"I swear I'm going to slap you so hard that your head spins a full 360."

"Don't flatter yourself, Brahms." I keep moving toward

the tree line. "I wouldn't let you close enough to spin my head in a one-eighty."

"Dutch! Dutch, you better... you better stop. A teacher's going to see you. You think you can get away with this?"

I ignore her. Even if teachers were around, which none of them are, they wouldn't intervene. Not unless they wanted to get sacked like Mulliez.

I can't see Cadence's face, but I can feel the frosty stare she's aiming at my stomach as if she wishes she could drill through flesh and bone and drain my blood until I turned blue.

By the time I get deep enough into the tree line that I'm sure no one in the cafeteria or even the mysterious Jinx can see us, Cadence has accepted her upside-down status and isn't struggling or screaming anymore.

Good girl.

I don't want to take my hands off her, which makes me fling her to the ground a little more roughly than is necessary. She wobbles on her feet, but doesn't fall and slants me a murderous look.

"What the hell do you want from me?"

I turn away from her, wrestling my lust back under control.

Her eyes blaze with fury. "You're seriously doing all this because I didn't run straight to you when you called me? Are you that insecure? Or was I right earlier? Are you really off in the head?"

New Girl's got a lot of fire for someone who has no idea she's poking at a bear. I watch her slam her hands on her hips and wait, angrily, for a response.

When none is forthcoming, she huffs and moves as if she'll walk back to campus.

I grab her by the hips and pull her against me. I thought

my body was wound up from Christa, but I'm not prepared for the way every nerve in my body snaps to attention when her hips connect with mine.

My fingers dig harder into her hip as I hiss.

She whimpers, easing back. Finally. The fear that belongs in her eyes is there.

If only her presence wasn't affecting me as much as mine is frightening her.

I clench my jaw, struggling to make sense of the way she's making my body respond.

"Look, I don't want you around about as much as you don't want me around you. So let's end this quickly, hm?" I can't help the desperation that's leaking out. I don't know if I need her gone for Sol or for myself right now. All I know is that she's messing with my head in ways I don't like.

"Leave Redwood and you won't have to see my," my words falter when she breathes out and her glistening lips part like a temptress on the stormy seas, "my face again," I bite out.

Her chest rises and falls almost violently. "Why do you want me out of Redwood Prep so badly?"

I glare down at her.

Her breathing is still ragged, but she still tilts her chin up bravely. Her voice is soft but firm. "What have I done to deserve this?"

A twinge of guilt eases through my stomach at her question, but I don't let it take root. The only option is for her to go. No other route is acceptable.

She glares at me for a full thirty seconds. "I'm waiting."

"The only thing you need to know is that we don't want you here," I growl, staring hard at her.

She doesn't have the presence of mind to quiver or beg

for mercy. No, she tips her chin up in challenge. "Yes, but *why*?"

"Do you really want to know?" I drop my gaze over her chest, up her delicate throat and finally linger on her lips. Damn. It's shining and pink, like a rose bud just begging to be plucked from its stem.

As I caress her with my gaze, her eyes flash with a mixture of desire and disgust, an intoxicating blend that I feel mirroring in my own chest.

I lift my eyes to hers and let my expression harden again, hiding my attraction to her behind a wall of steel. Her nostrils flare and the little pulse at her neck becomes more apparent.

I'm tired of her back-chatting. Tired of her sass.

"Don't push me any harder, Brahms. Or I'm going to make your wish come true."

"What wish?"

"The one where you leave Redwood Prep in a body bag."

Her eyes narrow and then flare in indignation. "Did you just threaten to kill me?" She's almost foaming at the mouth. "Is that what you're insinuating?"

I flash her a smug look.

She's practically vibrating at this point and I realize that she'd managed to cast a spell on all of Redwood. Because this fiery, beguiling creature in front of me certainly isn't ordinary. And she certainly shouldn't have been able to slide into the background as easily as she had.

A smile edges across my face. She's going to make this a challenge and I really do love a good fight.

"Don't ignore me the next time I call you," I warn. Then I whirl around and stomp through the trees.

I crossed a line.

I shouldn't have threatened her, but it's not like I plan

to do her any real terminal harm. As long as it gets her out of Redwood Prep, I'm willing to do almost anything. Even let her believe the worst of me.

She trudges out of the tree line a few minutes later and I see her fling herself through the cafeteria doors like it's a rooftop and she's got an appointment with the street.

Zane, Finn and the cheerleaders have cleared out from the table. I don't need to call my brothers to know where they've ended up.

I stride to our private room, slip my ID card against the door and step in. The moment I do, I hear Zane pounding the hell out of his electric drums. He's got headphones on, so it sounds like pathetic smacks of rubber tips against rubber pads. But the fact that he's managing to make such a racket without percussions is a telling sign.

I saunter to Finn and accept the water he tosses at me. "What's up with him?"

"What else?"

"Miss Jamieson?" I guess.

Finn shrugs. "He won't tell me what happened, but I'm assuming he tried to get under her skin and she got under his first."

His words send a tightness through my chest. Is that what Brahms is doing to me?

I shake my head quickly.

Nah. What I feel for her is just the thrill of the hunt. What I feel for the redhead, now that's something more akin to what my twin is going through. And it's exactly why I don't want anything to do with the mystery girl.

The farther I stay away from the debilitating effects of love, the less havoc it can wreak on me.

Zane glances up, sees me, and drags the headphones so it's resting around his neck.

I do a chin-up gesture.

He rises abruptly from the stool and saunters over to us. Sprawling in the sectional, he lifts an arm. Finn throws him a water bottle and he catches it out of the air.

"You want to explain what's going on?" I ask.

"Nope?" Zane tips his drink back and guzzles it. When he's done, he peers at me. "Any progress with CC?"

"CC?" My hackles rise immediately. "You're giving her nicknames?"

"You started it. You called her 'Brahms' in the hallway," Zane points out.

"Because it was the song playing on her phone," I snarl. Brahms' *Wiegenlied*.

She didn't strike me as a fan of classical music. Maybe it was the tight shirt that her breasts were practically bursting out of or the short skirt or the lightning in her eyes, but she seemed more like a rocker chick to me.

Not that I care what she listens to.

"Brahms," Finn grips the neck of his bass guitar and plucks a melody on the high strings. "The greatest representative of the musical Romantic movement. Fitting."

"Why the hell is it fitting?"

Finn does that annoying thing where he smirks like he knows something I don't.

I glare at him. "Have you been texting Jinx?"

"This guy." Zane hooks a finger at Finn. "He treats her like she's his girlfriend."

"Information is powerful. And it's through Jinx that I got a lead on Sol," Finn says.

That makes both Zane and I shut up.

I peer at my brother's dark eyes. "What did she say?"

"That the school had his transcripts sent out of the country. Wherever he is, it's not here." Finn frowns.

Zane curses and flops back. "How much did you pay Jinx for that? That's not much of a lead."

"It tells us that going to his house and trying to convince his mother to let us into his room isn't going to solve anything," I say calmly. Folding my hands together, I set it between my thighs and stare at the ground. "It means we have to broaden our net."

"It would be so much easier if he just picked up a damn phone and let us know," Zane huffs. "Damn."

"That can help to narrow the search," Finn suggests. "Wherever he is, he doesn't have his phone."

"You don't think he's, like, dead, do you?" Zane sits up, his eyes wide.

I scowl at him. "Stop talking crap."

"I'm just saying. No matter where he is, Sol would have snuck out or stolen a phone or found some way to contact us."

My knee bounces on the chair. "It feels like we're missing something."

"I can try to talk to Sol's mom again." Zane wiggles his eyebrows. "Try the old Cross charm. It might be too powerful a weapon though. She might fall for me."

"She's more likely to smack your head with a frying pan," Finn says.

Zane scowls at him.

I turn my leather band around and around as I think. It was a gift from Sol. He handcrafted it himself and gave it to each of us. We were around thirteen at the time. He said it was a symbol of brotherhood. From that day on, we made a pact to always have each other's backs.

"We can at least tell her that the school isn't going to hold what happened this summer against him. We got Mulliez out of the way," I say. "And he was the only one protesting it. Once we find Sol, there shouldn't be anyone in our way."

"That's where you're wrong," Finn says, his lips curling up.

I frown. "She's not a problem."

"She's still here." Zane points out. "Even after your brilliant idea."

Finn does another riff on his guitar. I've never seen anyone move as fast as him. It's like his fingers aren't bound by time or physics.

My brother bounces a string. "It not like we can bring Sol back where he belongs even if we find him now."

"Are you doubting me?"

"I'm pointing out the obvious."

"You were the one who insisted on giving her a chance to bow out on her own," I growl. "If we'd broken her without an explanation, it would have been better. But she knows what we want now. She's going to be stubborn."

"All hope isn't lost. Christa's already putting a target on her back," Zane muses. "She wasn't too happy about you brushing her off today."

Both my brothers give me inquiring looks.

I clench my teeth. "I had a mission."

"You had Christa willing to do the freakiest things to you and you turned her down to run after CC."

I glower at Zane for the nickname.

He gives me a smug smile in return. "No mission is that important. Imagine how much Christa's game improved now that her lips are bigger."

"You're not going soft, are you, Dutch?" Finn asks.

"You'll see." I reach for my guitar and play a melody to match Finn's bass line. "Cadence has no idea what she's in for. I'm going to ruin her so badly she never forgets my name."

That's not a threat.

It's a promise.

***

Jinx: Trade a secret for a secret, Dutch. I'm getting all kinds of inquiries about your relationship with New Girl. Access to your private play room. Steamy showdowns in the hallway. Tarzan-style kidnappings. Is there something I should know?

Chapter Ten

CADENCE

I missed the days at Redwood Prep when I was completely invisible. Now, I can't walk down the hallway without people gawking at me, waiting for the next ugly surprise from Dutch and his minions to unfold.

The Kings are as creative as they are cruel. This week alone—apart from getting carted over Dutch's shoulder like a caveman's dinner—my locker got hosed and my books were ruined, my practice keyboard got slathered in honey, and I was locked in the bathroom. Twice.

It's all middle-school level pranking, but it's frustrating as hell.

At this point, I'm looking forward to the weekend so I can have a break from this hellhole.

I shuffle to the music room, frowning at the substitute behind Mr. Mulliez's desk. She's an older woman with greying hair and bug eyes behind thick window glasses.

THE DARKEST NOTE

Most of the time, she seems scared of everyone in the classroom and doesn't do much more than drone on about music theory while the rest of us doze off.

As usual, I take a seat at the back and start gazing out the window, dreading the moment when class is to begin.

It's hard for me without Mr. Mulliez here. There's still a burning in the bottom of my stomach because of how unfair his termination was. Every time I look at the substitute, I'm reminded of Dutch's evil.

For the sake of my sanity, I have no choice but to tune out during class.

I'm counting clouds and trying to figure out how Redwood Prep pays for all that lawn maintenance when the door bangs open.

I glance up along with the rest of the class and then I hold my breath as *they* stroll into the room. Dutch, Zane and Finn are flanked by their groupies in cheer uniforms. Aren't dancers supposed to be hanging on the arms of athletes? Why are they so obsessed with these rock stars?

"Excuse me," the substitute adjusts her glasses, "do you students belong in this class?"

Zane steps forward. His raven hair is brushed back rather than flopping all over his forehead today. Blue eyes sparkle with an incandescent light.

"We're not on the attendance sheet because we've been touring, but we have this class."

"Ah, I see." She adjusts her glasses and bites her bottom lip, clearly charmed.

Ugh. Even grannies fall for Zane's smile. I guess I shouldn't feel too foolish for following him straight into a trap that day in the Cross's practice room.

Just ignore them, Cadence.

I'm trying my best to disappear into my chair when goosebumps start prickling on my skin and waves of awareness charge over me. I look up and notice Dutch glaring in my direction.

He's in black pants and a dark vest today. The black ensemble against his ivory skin and golden-blonde hair is something close to poetry. Amber eyes slice through me, glinting like a predator's.

He's so dangerously beautiful that it's impossible to believe he's around my age. His eyes, his face, his confidence belongs to someone who's experienced far more of the world than any regular eighteen-year-old.

He quirks an eyebrow at me and I know, instinctively, that he's not here to follow the curriculum.

They're here to terrorize me.

My fingers tighten around my pen. I glare at him, refusing to let him see me squirm.

Dutch has got some nerve showing up in Mulliez's class after what he did. I'm sure if someone were to take an X-ray of this guy's soul, they'd find nothing but sulfur and brimstone.

Dutch smirks when he sees me glowering at him. He's taunting me without saying a word.

My heart churns with bitterness. It takes everything in me to stay seated. Storming over and slapping him would play right into his hands, which is why I refuse to give in to the impulse.

It's a well-known secret that Jarod Cross, Dutch, Finn and Zane's dad, has donated generously to the music program and to the school in general. To say the teachers are on the Cross payroll would not be an exaggeration.

The brothers are more powerful than ever now. If

someone was going to do something about Dutch, Finn and Zane, they've certainly been scared back into their holes after what happened to Mulliez.

If I give Dutch the swift kick up the butt that he deserves, he'll have me flying out of Redwood so fast my head spins. The only way to get back at them is to endure. And to do that, I can't give in to my temper.

Time seems to stop while the brothers saunter to their desks. I lower my head, sure that they're not going to sit beside me since all the seats in the back row are already taken.

But they just keep walking.

And walking.

And walking.

Until they get to the desks that surround mine.

Dutch taps his fingers on the table and the student immediately pops up, grabs his bags and hurries to the front row.

His eyes slide lazily down my face when he takes the seat in front of me. "Brahms."

"What do you want?" I hiss. "Why are you here?"

He just smirks.

Christa, the blonde I'd seen at the showcase, sashays past Dutch and stops in front of my table.

She slams her hands on her hips and looks down her perfectly straight nose at me. "Excuse me. You're in my seat."

I am *not* in her seat and usually, I wouldn't hesitate to tell her where she can take her scrawny butt and her prissy attitude, but I'm grateful for an excuse to get away from the Cross boys without it appearing that I'm running.

"Sure." I sling my backpack over my shoulder.

"You stay," Dutch's voice rings with quiet authority.

My nostrils flare, but I pretend not to have heard him. "You can have this seat." I gesture to my desk, sidestepping out of the chair. "I'll find another—"

Before I can blink, long, hot fingers slide around my wrist. Then, in a flick, he tugs me so I lose my balance and fall into the chair again.

Without looking at me, Dutch commands his groupie, "Go sit somewhere else."

Her eyes fill with hurt, but she hides it quickly. Shooting a murderous look in my direction, she turns with a flounce of her skirt and stomps to the front.

"Get your hands *off* me," I hiss, snatching my wrist away from his firm grip.

Dutch arches an eyebrow.

I lean forward and whisper angrily as the substitute starts her boring lesson. "What are you doing here? What do you want?"

"You know what I want, Brahms." He turns slightly so I can only see his striking profile.

It's disgusting the way he doesn't have a single bad angle. A hard jaw line gives way to hair the color of wheat in the summer sun. His nose is straight and his lips are full and distracting.

Why are the beautiful ones always the most evil?

"Is this our weekly check-in?" I hiss. "Are you going to ask me to leave Redwood after every five days?"

"I'm here to remind you that it's not going to get better." He swivels fully and his eyes fall into mine. "Because I'm never going to stop."

A shiver runs down my spine at the threat and at the cold look in his eyes. He means that. Means it with every part of his being.

But why? This obsession with getting rid of me feels way too intense to be a rich kid's escape from boredom. What could I have done to Dutch to make him target me?

I've wracked my brain for days and I still can't figure it out. I'm sure we have never crossed paths in our lives. For one thing, a guy like him—with status and wealth—would have no reason to be on my side of the tracks. For another, I'd remember a face like his.

"Miss Cooper?"

The sound of my name coming from the substitute teacher makes me sit up, alert.

"Is there a Miss Cooper in here?" the sub says again.

Every head swings in my direction.

Nerves tightening in my stomach, I slowly raise my hand.

"I have here," she glances at a sheet of paper, "that you're the only one who hasn't done her practical assignment."

"W-what?"

"According to the office, your assignment needs to be done today." She smacks her lips together and adjusts her glasses. "Come on then."

Fear grabs hold of my heart like a dog with a rag doll. I quiver in my seat. "Mr. Mulliez exempted me from that assignment, ma'am."

"Probably because she was his sugar baby." The statement comes from Christa, who shamelessly tosses her hair over her shoulder and grins at her own brilliance.

An outburst of laughter pours from the classroom and I feel the anger climbing its way up my chest. I'm willing to bet money that Dutch the Douche set this entire thing up.

My legs tremble when I push myself to a standing position. It doesn't help that I can feel Dutch's gaze drilling into me. He slings his arm over the back of his chair and watches me intently as I make my way to the front. One leg is thrown over the other and his expression is smug. He's enjoying this, while I hate it with every breath in my body.

A lump forms in my throat and I approach the teacher rather than the piano.

"Excuse me," I tell her, giving my back to the class, "but I'm not prepared for the practical assignment. A few days ago, my school-assigned keyboard was tampered with and I haven't—"

"It doesn't matter. You can use this keyboard." She points to her own instrument.

"Please. I... I have stage fright." It's embarrassing to confess, but I absolutely *cannot* perform in front of people as myself. The last time I tried messed me up for life.

"It says here that you need to finish the assignment to get the grade," the teacher insists.

"I..."

"Come on, Miss Cooper. Time is wasting." She nudges me toward the piano.

Sweat breaks out on my neck when I fall into the seat. I can feel everyone staring at me, judging me. My heart threatens to explode.

Tapping my foot on the ground, I hover forward and set my hands on the keys.

Come on, Cadence. It's not that different than when you're in costume. Just pretend you're someone else.

My eyes twitch and I struggle to breathe.

It's not working.

"I'm sorry. I can't," I mumble. Lunging to my feet, I sprint past the frightened teacher and away from the sound of cruel giggles. Dutch's heavy stare lingers on my back until the door slams shut behind me.

* * *

Cadence: Were you the one who told Dutch I have stage fright?

Jinx: A secret for a secret, Newbie. I'm the one who asks the questions. You're the one who answers. Are you finally ready to play?

Chapter Eleven

CADENCE

I'm grateful for a weekend away from Redwood. I spend most of Saturday working at the diner. On Sunday, my day off, Viola and I have a spa day and invite Breeze over.

The moment I see my best friend, I throw my arms around her. She laughs awkwardly—Breeze isn't too big with public displays of affection—and tries to pry my arm off, but I only tighten my grip.

I've decided not to tell anyone about what's going on at Redwood. Especially not Breeze. She'll turn up at my new school with a machete, demanding to see Dutch.

It'd be like an ant attacking a giant. Dutch wouldn't hesitate to crush her under his boot.

I don't want my sister or my best friend to be on Dutch's hit list. It's safer all around if I keep my troubles to myself.

But the anger, frustration and helplessness has been boiling inside me and it needs a way to come out. Sometimes, beating the crap out of a punching bag doesn't feel the same as embracing a friend.

"Do you miss me that much?" Breeze laughs.

I nod into her neck.

She pats my back. "What's wrong? You haven't made any super rich friends at Redwood?"

"None as good as you," I mumble. Serena counts as a friend, well, half-friend. Sort of friend? I haven't seen her around since she invited herself to my table.

"What about boys?" Breeze asks.

"What about boys?" I respond innocently.

"Tell me you've gotten some action." Breeze wiggles her eyebrows. "A little under the table activities." She makes a gesture with her fingers. "If you know what I mean."

I smack her hand. "Stop that."

"You think the rich boys at Redwood Prep would go for her?" Viola asks, bouncing into the room.

Her long hair is pulled back into a ponytail that swishes cheerfully when she plops beside me. She's got her arms full of cheap, dollar-store face masks, cucumbers, and nail polish.

"Your sister's got a gorgeous face and a rocking bod," Breeze argues. "Besides, boys don't care if a girl has money. All they care about is—"

I slap a hand over my best friend's mouth. "Boys are not a priority for me right now." I glare at my sister. "And they definitely shouldn't be for you."

Viola rolls her eyes.

I wiggle a finger at her. "I mean it."

Mom got pregnant when she was in her teens. Some vices are hereditary, but I'm hoping like crazy that the 'get knocked up before eighteen' gene skips us both entirely.

Viola is much more boy crazy than I am, which worries

me. I'm working most of the time and she doesn't have anyone else to make sure she's staying safe. 'One thing led to another' is not the kind of story I want my sister to have.

She scoffs. "I'm not going to be a virgin like you all my life."

"There's nothing wrong with being a virgin," I defend myself.

"You know what would be great?" Breeze slings an arm around my neck. "If you found a really cute guy at Redwood Prep to pop your cherry."

"No, that sounds awful," I mumble, thinking of all the pretentious guys I've met.

Breeze laughs. "Are you sure *no* one has been paying attention? I mean, I've *seen* you in that short Redwood Prep skirt. Every time you so much as bend over, you flash a cheek."

"I do not!" I gasp.

Breeze grins. "Unless those guys are blind, someone should have dragged you off into a dark corner by now."

I think of Dutch's hot and heavy hands. The feel of them, as they landed on my upper thighs sent my entire body into flames. What's embarrassing is I'm not sure if those flames were from desire or hate.

"Trust me. There is no guy at Redwood," I say to the floor.

"What if he's not at Redwood?" Viola muses. Taking a small brush, she pours a mixture into a bowl and starts stirring. "What if he's, I don't know, Rick's friend."

"Your hot older brother has a hot older friend?" Breeze gasps. "Why didn't you tell me?"

"Because there was nothing to tell."

"He gave Cadence that." Viola points to the punching bag.

"What the hell?" Breeze's eyes are about to fall out of her face. "That's so sweet!"

"A punching bag is sweet?" I snort.

Viola gets up to grab something from the fridge.

While she's gone, I pull Breeze close and speak in a hushed tone. "Don't misunderstand. Hunter tried to give me money for the electricity, but I turned him down. After that, he brought the punching bag."

"He came all the way here to pay your electricity?" Breeze hisses. "Why haven't you jumped him yet?"

"Because I'm not a prostitute," I whisper heatedly. "Am I supposed to sleep with the first guy who pays my bills?"

"No, of course not." Viola chomps on another cucumber. "You sleep with the second guy who pays your bills."

"Breeze."

"Did you at least thank him for the gift?"

"She didn't," Vi says smartly, returning to the living room.

I cast her a dark look for her betrayal.

Breeze leans back on her slender arms and tilts her head to the ceiling. "I'm so disappointed in you, Cadey. You've spent your entire life taking care of yourself and now that there's a super hot—"

"I never said he was super hot."

"—There is literally no way he can be anything but super hot if he gave you a punching bag." She tosses her blonde hair over her shoulder. "You're going to DM Hunter and tell him thanks."

"No, I'm not."

"Fine. Then I will." Breeze lunges over the sofa and grabs my phone.

"No!" I yell.

Viola holds me back. Locking her legs around me like a wrestler, she yells, "Do it, Breeze!"

While my traitorous sister holds me down, my best friend opens my phone.

I realize she's going to see my messages to Jinx and panic blasts through me. Knocking my sister back with all my strength, I lunge at the phone.

"I'll do it! I'll do it!"

"That's my girl," Breeze says, smiling victoriously.

I take my phone, navigate to Hunter's DMs and tap out a message.

"'Thanks for the punching bag.' See? I sent it." I show it to them as evidence.

"Do you think he'll respond?" Breeze asks.

I sure hope not. In fact, as soon as Breeze and Viola aren't looking, I plan to delete that message.

As if they can read my thoughts, they stare at the phone waiting for a response.

When five minutes pass, I set the phone away. "Look at that. He can't be bothered to respond. Maybe he didn't mean anything by it."

"Or maybe he's not a big social media guy." Breeze thumbs the screen. "He hasn't updated his socials for over a year now."

"Can we please stop talking about Hunter and go back to a relaxing spa day?" I beg. "This is my only time off from work and I don't want to spend it thinking about boys."

Breeze tosses the phone. "Fine. Viola, cucumber me."

We enjoy the rest of our time together. Breeze even sleeps over and helps me get ready for school before taking off with Vi to catch the bus.

I'm so refreshed from spa day that, on Monday,

Redwood Prep's massive buildings and castle-like spires look more like a fairy tale than a haunted mansion.

I even manage to smile at the cheerleaders who pass me in the hallway and glare at me with their icy eyes. They don't get in my way though, which is a small miracle.

The good keeps on rolling when I get to my locker and open it up to see it's free of water, frogs, or any other childish things Dutch can think of.

Speaking of the royal jerk, I don't see him or his brothers for most of first period. I hope they're gone on another tour and won't return until graduation.

Three blissful hours roll by without incident. Feeling good, I bounce into the cafeteria to get my lunch. Since I'm on a scholarship, I have a special meal card. With limited options, I skip over the sushi bar, gourmet burgers and vegan trays and choose a tuna sandwich and a bottle of orange juice.

Satisfied, I turn to carry my tray outside.

That's when a guy wearing a football jacket slams into my shoulder.

I wobble on my feet, gripping the tray while stumbling forward. I barely manage to keep myself, along with my sandwich and juice, upright.

"Watch it, slut," he murmurs.

My temperature rises and I can't hold back. "Excuse me?"

The jock turns smoothly on his feet and stares me down.

I return the glare.

He scoffs, tosses his ragged-looking hair and gives his friends a 'can you believe this chick' look.

"I was having a freaking good day." My voice trembles from my anger and irritation. It feels *so* good to finally lash out at someone. Even if that someone isn't Dutch. "So the least you can do is give me an apology."

"Why would I apologize," he breathes, "to a *whore*."

I can feel the heat climbing in my cheeks. Everyone is watching us and it only makes the humiliation worse.

I tighten my fingers on the tray, wondering if I should bash his head in with it. Then I think of Viola and the sacrifice Mr. Mulliez made to keep me here at Redwood. I think of the money I'll have to pay back if I lose my scholarship.

Deciding this douchebag isn't worth a fight, I suck in my rage.

"Whatever," I mutter. And then I try to walk past him.

He steps into my way. "Where are you going, sweetie?" He shoves me and I skitter back. "Since you're here, why don't you give me the same treatment you gave Mulliez?" He sticks his groin out toward me so I can't miss his meaning.

"Yeah," a voice says, "why don't you get on your knees right here, Brahms?"

Every nerve in my body pulls tight when I hear that raw and silky voice.

It's Dutch.

Chapter Twelve

CADENCE

The cafeteria falls into tense silence. Everyone is holding their breath for fear that the quietest cough will interrupt the drama.

Footsteps thud behind me. I'd know the sound of Dutch's walk anywhere, not only because it usually hints of my coming misery, but because it's a staccato rhythm.

Thud, thud, thud.

Cocky and measured, it inspires a haunting melody. The kind that would play in *Count Dracula* just before the vampire rises from his casket to feast in the night.

He's closer now. I can hear it by his footsteps and feel it by the prickles surging over my skin.

I don't move a muscle when I sense Dutch come up beside me. His energy is crackling with anger, but it's not showing on his face. His gaze is calm, unbothered.

"Go on, Brahms." Dutch reaches for the sandwich on

my tray. He peels the clear plastic with big hands. "We're all waiting for the show."

I twist my head and glare at him.

Dutch arches both eyebrows and tilts his head, drilling in the point. I barely quell the urge to smack him with my tray.

"Or, and here's a better idea," Dutch casually nods at the jock, "why don't you start stripping first?"

"Me?" The jock trembles.

"Who else could I be talking to?"

He stares blankly at Dutch.

Sandwich still in his hand, Dutch walks forward calmly. "You don't want to?"

The jock comes to some kind of realization because he lifts both arms and fearfully backs away. "Dutch, man, I don't want any trouble."

Dutch's stare hardens. His entire face has gone cold.

My eyes volley between the smarmy athlete who's bowing his head and the tatted prince. Dutch hasn't made any moves—he hasn't even lifted his hands—and yet it feels like the jock just got a royal beating.

"See that girl behind me?" Dutch whispers.

The jock's frightened eyes jump to me before swinging back to Dutch.

"You don't mess with her unless you get *my* permission."

A rush of air leaves my lungs, and with it, the bit of gratitude I'd started to feel toward Dutch.

I scowl in his direction.

"Have I made myself clear?" Dutch places his hands on the jock's shoulders and brushes the top of his football jersey.

"Y-yes."

Jaw tight, Dutch strides back to me.

"What the hell was that?" I hiss.

He doesn't answer. Instead, he uncaps my orange juice and guzzles it down. Then he wipes his mouth with the back of his hand, caps my bottle and tosses it back into the tray.

Stupid jerk.

I whirl around, my nostrils flaring as two opposing forces war within me. On the one hand, he did put that jock in his place. Whatever his intentions, he helped me out.

On the other, he claimed me as his 'property' and basically admitted to being the only one who can mistreat me.

Dutch wasn't trying to rescue me. He was just keeping other bullies from tearing into me so he can do it himself. The motives basically cancel the result.

Students move out of Dutch's way as he leaves the cafeteria. The jock scrambles in the opposite direction. His football friends, all looking embarrassed, shuffle behind him.

I stand alone, surrounded by everyone's stares. Once again, I'm the freakshow of Redwood Prep.

With a huff, I toss the rest of my lunch into the trash and storm after Dutch. The door crashes behind me, but when I look left and right, Dutch is nowhere in sight.

Determined, I choose a path and start running. The more I think about what just happened, the more incensed I become.

How dare he 'claim' me in front of the entire school? Do I look like a toy? Do I look like his plaything...

My riotous thoughts come to a screeching halt when I round the bend and spot a sensory spectacle.

Time seems to slow as Dutch Cross strips his shirt off and pours water from the tap all over his head. The muscles on his back flex and my eyes greedily trace the tattoos over his arm and across his shoulder.

There's way more ink than I'd guessed. Not that I'd been able to see anything beneath all the sweater vests. But it turns out, Dutch has transformed his body into walking artwork and it's *the hottest* thing I've ever seen.

He turns, showing off his equally sexy abs and all I can think about is how dangerous it is to be standing here, alone, with him.

I step back, but it's too late. He's caught me. His expression tightens and he stares at me like he can see every dirty thought that flashed through my messed-up head.

I really must be insane if I'm thirsting over the boy who's made my life at Redwood a living hell.

"Like what you see?" he asks darkly.

At his words, the illusion shatters and I'm back to hating his beautiful, tatted guts.

I drag my eyes away from his body and glare at him. "You ate my sandwich and drank my OJ. You need to pay for it."

Amusement flickers in his gaze. His lips curl up a second before he coaches his expression back into its natural 'I don't give a damn' state.

Feeling brave, I tip my chin up. "You've ruined my textbooks, ruined my practice piano, ruined my favorite teacher's *life*. But I will *not* let you ruin lunch for me."

"What?"

"You ate my sandwich. Am I not talking English?"

He studies me for a long moment in which I begin to second-guess every part of this hacked-together plan.

Then he starts moving.

As Dutch crosses over to me, every ounce of bravery I thought I had evaporates.

I start wheeling back.

Dutch is massive. His body is glorious, sure, but it's also a weapon. I saw the way he flung that jock in the cafeteria and the other guy wasn't small. I can't imagine what he could do to me.

Nerves twisting in my stomach, I raise a hand. "Keep your distance, Cross or—"

The rest of my words are trapped in my throat when Dutch shoots his arms out and traps me against the sink. The small of my back collides with the protruding basin. Moisture seeps into my hip, meeting the surface of my heated skin.

I inch back, but Dutch follows me with his head. He's so close, so intense. I battle the crazy urge to scrub my hands over his muscles. Heat bursts up my spine, sending a flush to my neck and face.

Dutch narrows his eyes at me. His hair is damp and hanging limp. I watch a drop of water skate down his strong nose to the top of his luscious lips, curving around it the way my tongue is suddenly begging to.

"I make the demands, Brahms." He leans in a little closer. The pulse in my heart drops to somewhere between my legs. "And I ask the questions." He tightens his grip on me when I try to squirm away. "Ah-ah, little mouse. You followed me here. You deal with the consequences."

"Let me go." I push against him. It's like trying to move a mountain. A mountain that's getting me and my clothes wet.

"Why'd you run last Friday?" Dutch asks, his eyes intent on me.

I stop struggling and stare up at his handsome face, sure I've heard wrong. "What?"

"I thought our sources were off, but you really do have stage fright."

"Sources? You're talking about Jinx?"

This is getting creepy. How did that anonymous number know about my stage fright?

"Remember, Brahms," he grips my cheek to force me to look at him, "I ask the questions."

His grip isn't harsh but it's firm. I shake him off. "Why do you want to know?"

"You're Mulliez's special pick. Why the hell are you studying music if you're scared of it?"

"I'm not scared of music, you buffoon." I glare up at him. "I'm scared of crowds."

I have no idea why this conversation is happening and I especially have no idea why it's happening when Dutch is half naked and soaking wet, but it looks like I'm stuck.

He narrows his eyes and it's clear that he's waiting for more.

Maybe it's stress or maybe I'm still too flustered from what happened in the cafeteria, but the words come pouring out.

"When I was a kid, my mom traded music for drugs. She'd drag me into dens with creeps and crackheads and sit me down at the piano. It was dark, smoky and there was something dangerous about it." I shudder. "Something off about the music I played there. It tainted me. Tainted everything." I huff. "Not that it's any of your business."

He gives me a thoughtful look. I don't know what it means and I, honestly, don't want to know.

Which is why I'm grateful when I hear voices coming our way. A group of students are approaching from the direction of the quad.

Dutch's hands loosen on me as his attention turns to

them. I take the chance to slip his wallet out of his back pocket. By the time he sees what I'm doing, I'm already hopping away with a five dollar bill.

His eyebrows hunker low over his amber eyes. His voice is a deep warning. "Do you really have a death wish, Brahms?"

Before he can pounce, the students see us.

"Dutch, we didn't know you were... occupied."

I can't imagine what a picture we must make. Dutch is shirtless and glaring at me. My entire top is soaked through with water. I'm pretty sure they can all see through to my black lace bra.

"Are... should we leave?"

Dutch makes a sound deep in his throat.

"No, you can stay." I toss his wallet into the sinks and grin when it drops like a rock. "Happy fishing."

"Cadence!" Dutch yells.

It's the first time he's using my actual name, and I don't stick around to hear the words that follow it.

Sprinting away, I skate into the cafeteria and blend in among the other kids.

I hope I ruined his wallet.

I hope I ruined his entire day.

That's just a taste of all the hell I plan to bring on him. Dutch Cross is going to wish he never messed with me.

Chapter Thirteen

CADENCE

The lounge is noisy with chatter, clinking forks, and laughter, but I'm in my own world on the piano. My fingers skate over the black and white keys, wrenching melodies from my twisted soul.

I should be enraptured right now. This week at Redwood was quiet. Mostly because the Cross brothers haven't been gliding down the hallways, leaving havoc and broken hearts in their wake.

Rumor has it, they went to visit their mom. In their absence, my locker hasn't been tampered with. My keyboard's been kept clean and the music teacher has no more bright ideas to force me on stage.

The quiet was supposed to make me feel safe, but it only set me more on edge.

Dutch isn't the type to back off easily. I haven't left Redwood Prep yet which is... obvious. And I drenched his expensive wallet too. He's going to retaliate.

THE DARKEST NOTE

I just don't know how.

Or when.

And that frightening wait has been messing with my head.

I inhale deeply and try to push thoughts of his gorgeous face and even hotter physique from my mind.

It doesn't work and I end up throwing diminished chords into my piece. The music turns choppy, breathing life into my agitation. Or maybe it's my agitation breathing life into the melody. Either way, they feed each other.

The piece is my own now. These notes don't belong to the original composer, but it feels right, so I keep going.

I'm in the crescendo. Eyes closed, swaying, head thrown back. The only place I feel free is here in music. Each note pours after the other. A soothing domino effect. Rain soaking into cracked, dry soil.

I'm so glad I was able to come back to it. I'm so glad the darkness mom brought into music didn't keep me from it.

In the middle of my piece, my skin starts tingling everywhere. I open my eyes and scan the crowd.

The lounge is busy tonight. Wealthy patrons flock to this hole-in-the-wall bar, but it's not for its smoky interior and subtle but elegant decor.

It's for the temperamental chef who's made a reputation for himself.

Gorge's is the kind of place that hands out menus for appearances sake, but they don't expect customers to order from it. In fact, it's always easy to tell the noobs by the way they peruse the booklets.

Gorge is a half human and half supernatural creature. He takes one look at a table and knows exactly what to serve, plus the perfect wine to go with it. There's never been a table that's regretted letting him choose.

Or at least, that's what the manager told me when I started working here.

Rich people and their novelties.

I don't care if the chef's 'super abilities' are a gimmick. I'm here at *Gorge's* because the pay is much higher than bussing. The chef thinks my music 'pairs perfectly with his meals' and it means I get a hefty check at the end of every night plus tips.

Gorge's is safer than being on the street too. The staff look out for me and though customers do walk up to me and try to flirt sometimes, once I start looking uncomfortable, one of the girls steps in right away.

I press my fingers gently on the keys, the notes timid and repressed as I try to locate the reason behind the shift in the air around me.

And then I find him.

Dutch is there, in a booth with Finn and Zane. He's in a faded T-shirt that stretches across his shoulders. His jeans are ripped at the knees. His amber eyes are like a lion's, fierce and golden.

My fingers miss the right key and a discordant, ugly note rings through the lounge. No one seems to recognize the fumble, but I still feel flames shooting to my cheeks. I flunked because he was watching.

Finn and Zane leave the table, their intimidating figures blending into the shadows at the back. Dutch remains seated, his eyes locked on me. His expression is one I've never seen before. It's still intense, but it's not as icy. It's contemplative and a little unpleasant, like he hates the feelings the music is stirring up in him, but he can't turn away if he wanted to.

My heartbeat picks up speed because I don't know what to do with that. Be proud that the god of Redwood Prep is affected by my music? Be sad that it shows he actually possesses a soul?

I sneak another look at him. He's got his head tilted now and his eyes are closed. The slant of his mouth hits the light and it's all I can do to keep playing.

Long-buried restlessness clashes with new anger, like a war of opposing waves.

I'm jerked back to that moment when he trapped me against the outdoor sink, drops of water glistening on his tan skin and his body cut and chiseled to perfection, pressing into mine.

I hate that he can make me feel this way, out-of-sorts and breathless.

Ripping my gaze from his, I finish the song with trembling fingers, closing out an abrupt ending.

The chair legs scrape the wooden platform as I push back. Ignoring the applause that breaks out from the diners, I pounce to my feet and burst through the employee-only doors behind the bar.

I need distance. I need a getaway car. But all I can do is wilt against a wall and try to catch my breath.

"Did you see those models outside?"

"I thought I'd faint. I didn't think people who looked like that existed outside of movies.

"I know right."

The waitresses stop to squeal for a bit.

Then one of them says, "I wish I was Cadence whatever-her-name was."

"I *know*. I'd literally give *anything* to be the girl they're looking for."

Their words stop me in my tracks. Without thought, I stumble toward them. "What did you just say?"

The women give me frightened looks.

"Who are they looking for?" I ask again, my voice tight.

"I don't know. The Asian one came back here asking if we knew some girl named Cadence."

Sweat breaks out beneath my pits and under my shirt.

Jinx strikes again. That's the only way The Kings would know where I work after school.

How does she keep knowing all this stuff about me?

It's a mystery for another day. There's only one reason Dutch, Finn and Zane would be looking for me right after they came back from visiting their mom. And I doubt it's to bring me souvenirs from their trip.

"Do you know who Cadence is, sweetie?"

The waitresses look pointedly at me.

My nerves and fear skyrocket. I didn't give the lounge my real name when they hired me, but I still feel exposed.

"Uh, no. I... no." I blink rapidly.

Way to sound legit, Cadence.

"By the way, what are you doing back here? Your set isn't over yet."

I sling an arm over my stomach. "I'm not feeling well, so I'll change out of this," I gesture to my performance clothes consisting of a bright red tank top, leather jacket and tight jeans, "and leave now."

"Alright, sweetie. We'll tell the manager for you."

"Thank you."

As I leave the kitchen, I keep glancing behind my back to make sure none of the brothers have spotted me.

Since Dutch didn't automatically storm my piano and Finn and Zane were going around asking for me even though I was right in front of them, it means my disguise worked. I'm totally invisible to them.

However, if they keep staring at me, they're going to see

THE DARKEST NOTE

the similarities between this costumed version of me and the one they terrorize at Redwood Prep.

I can't let that happen.

Throwing myself into the dressing room, I slam the door shut. There's a small mirror on the dresser and I catch sight of my reflection.

Do I really look that different?

I lift the glass and stare at my face. Vi does my makeup before I leave for the lounge. She takes it as practice and will throw a temper tantrum if I ever attempt to do it myself.

Normally, when I look in the mirror while she's working, I'll see bronze-colored glops that look like war paint. But by the time she smoothes it all out, my cheekbones look sharper, my jaw looks slimmer and my nose looks like I did plastic surgery.

Makeup is a scary thing.

Paired with the green eye contacts and the red wig, I'm safe. As long as none of the boys see me up close.

My fingers climb to my wig and I start to wrench it off when there's a knock on the door.

"Hey, I'm looking for the pianist? The manager told me I could find you back here," a familiar voice says.

A rush of panic surges through my veins.

It gets ten times worse when I see the doorknob turning.

I have seconds to fix my wig back in place.

Dutch walks in and by now, I should be prepared for the way he fills up the room.

I'm so not.

Without his Redwood Prep uniform on, he looks bigger and taller and more dangerous. I wish I could stop time somehow so I could check him out *and* edge around him, leaving him in an empty room alone.

His hair's flopping all around his face and I realize that I like the messy look. Which is disturbing because he's a menace and a life-ruiner and I shouldn't be liking anything about him.

Appraising amber eyes study me.

I feel warm all over and quickly avert my gaze.

The more time I spend around Dutch, the more I realize why he doesn't bother with macho displays of violence. His *stare* is violent. It's heavy and dark and commanding.

Unnerved, I lower my voice to a husky pitch and ask, "Did you chase me all the way back here just to stare at me?"

His eyebrows quirk and I hope it's not because he recognizes my voice.

Since I was a kid, I've been able to do great impersonations. Just like music notes, voices each have their own unique pitches.

When Viola was younger, she'd beg me to read bedtimes stories for her. *'Voices, voices'*, she'd insist. And I would get into character for her, changing up my tones to bring the fairytale characters alive.

I lean heavily on that skill now, hoping that Dutch doesn't see through it.

He slides a hand into his pocket. "I came to—"

"Ask if I've seen some girl named Cadence?" I butt in.

My anxiety's through the roof. I need to get him out of this room, out of this lounge, out of my *life* as soon as possible.

"I haven't seen her." I turn away from him, hoping he takes the hint and backs away on his own.

But I should know better.

Dutch Cross doesn't leave before getting what he came for.

He lingers in the doorway. His stare caresses me in a way that sets my blood on fire.

As the silence settles, I realize that I shouldn't be so dismissive. Dutch would never tell *me*—the real me—the reason he's so hell-bent on making my life miserable. But he doesn't know this version. Maybe I can pry it out of him while in disguise.

Turning abruptly, I lift my chin. "Why are you going around asking for her anyway. Did she do something to you?"

He takes a step into the room, slowly, as if I'll disappear like a mirage if he moves too fast. His face is set in a thoughtful expression. His strong nose and chin cuts through the shadows.

The silence is oppressive and the temperature rises when he gets close to me. I've never felt such tension before. It's so fragile that one word will make it shatter.

"What's your name?" he asks. The vibration of his voice rattles me in a way that not even music has the ability to.

His body's bigger than I remember, his hard chest stopping a mere breath away from my face. He's my enemy at Redwood Prep. But right now, he's not looking at me like he wants to break me.

It takes me a moment to realize I'm gawking. I slam my mouth shut and shift from one leg to another. "Why do you want to know?"

"Because every perfect song deserves a name."

My eyelashes flicker. Did the broody beast just say something romantic?

As his amber gaze burns into me, I swear my entire

heart flutters right out of my ribs and starts beating like a bat around the room.

I see it then—the interest flickering in his gaze. I thought he came to track me—the real me—down. But he's not. He's back here because he has a thing for my alter ego.

Power surges through my body, crackling like lightning. There have been so many moments at Redwood Prep when it felt like the light at the end of the tunnel was getting smaller and smaller. So many moments when all I wanted was a chance to level the playing field.

I haven't had many opportunities to get back at the great Dutch Cross. Now that a door is open in front of me, I feel bold.

There's no way I'm letting this moment slip through my fingers.

With an unimpressed eye roll, I smirk at him. "Does that line usually work for you?"

A ghost of a smile crosses his face, but it's gone so fast I'm not sure if I imagined it.

"That's usually all it takes, yeah." He shrugs, but the glint in his eyes is anything but casual. "How long have you been playing?"

The interest in his voice takes me by surprise. "A while."

"I've never heard anyone deconstruct Chopin like that. Your piano teacher must love you."

The mention of my piano teacher reminds me of Mr. Mulliez and it makes me greedy for Dutch's pain.

I take a deliberate step forward. "People evolve. I don't see why music can't either. Music is a reflection of us. Of who we are, where we come from and who we want to be."

"It's also a measure of perfection. If we don't play it exactly right, we don't win."

I scrunch my nose. "I think our obsession with holding

on to things, trying to preserve them so they're exactly the way they always were, can keep us from seeing what's important."

His gaze slips down my body. When it slides back up, I realize that this is not a game I can play lightly. "And what is that?"

I dig my teeth into my bottom lip. "Composers are trying to convey a feeling, not a perfect score. It's easier to destroy the classics when I think a few of those guys might be the first to destroy their own work too."

My words earn me a slow grin that sends flames dancing all the way to my toes.

I freeze, hating myself for noticing. This is Dutch—the ruiner of lives and souls. The guy who's made sure that, in the last few weeks at Redwood Prep, I've had something to destroy my entire day.

I drag Mr. Mulliez to the front of my mind and keep my heart on the mission. How do I use Dutch's interest in a way that'll hurt him the most?

I keep chewing on my bottom lip. Since I don't spend most of my time snatching candy from babies like Dutch does, the ideas aren't coming as quickly as I thought.

I need to stall for a while longer.

"You should know how important it is to mark your own path," I say huskily. "After all, you're a musician too."

"How did you know that?" He peers closer at me. "You've been following my band?"

The air freezes in my lungs when I realize I might have given myself away. If I admit I've heard of his band, he might ask me about my favorite song or something. But I haven't actually heard Dutch play yet.

The rims of my nostrils flare as I think on my feet. "I haven't." I reach for his hand and lift it. "You've got callouses on the tips of four fingers, but no callouses on the thumb. It's the mark of someone who spends more hours playing guitar than they do eating and sleeping."

Fear and something else that I don't want to name streaks down my spine as Dutch interlocks our fingers.

He leans over. "I'm going to tell you something and I mean this sincerely."

I shiver. "W-what?"

"I heard you at the showcase and I haven't been able to get that melody out of my head. I've never heard anyone play like that before."

My gaze lands on his. "I wasn't playing for you."

"I know. You weren't playing for anyone but yourself."

I shift forward so our faces are close enough that I can see the dark flecks in his golden eyes. "And who do *you* play for?"

His jaw tightens. A thoughtful look crosses his face. "I don't know. It's more of a habit than anything."

That felt real. That felt raw.

I can't believe Dutch Cross is letting me into his thoughts like this. It feels almost evil to use it. And that just goes to show that I'm not as horrible a person as he is.

I let my gaze linger on his lips. "Music can be so many things, but if it's a burden, it's a sign that something's wrong."

"Maybe."

My chest squeezes, hard.

No, I am not *connecting* with the biggest pain in my butt. He will not become human to me.

Dutch steps closer until his sneakers are kissing my boots. *Bach* he smells like heaven. It's pure fabric softer and sandalwood, and if temptation had a scent it would smell like this.

"I know I'm not the only one feeling this," Dutch says softly, looking both relaxed and intense at once.

"No," I grab his collar. "You're not." Roughly, I drag him closer and smash his mouth to mine.

It's only supposed to be an angry press of the lips, but the moment the warmth of his full lips soak through to mine, all other thoughts fly out the window.

I'm not only kissing my worst nightmare. I'm *enjoying* it. It's sick and twisted and I crave more with a desperation that takes my breath away.

Dutch's fingers brush my cheek and then slide to the back of my neck, pushing me forward and harder against his mouth. It's like he's trying to tell me something. Like he's trying to tell me everything.

The desire inside me twists tighter and tighter. It's a discordant sound. As messy as the notes I played when I first caught sight of him in the lounge.

I should resist it.

I *have* to.

But there's a draw to him, unadulterated and magnetic. The more I want to resist, the harder it is to let go.

He feels the moment I melt because his lips soften above mine, sliding more than attacking. It's so unexpected —that tenderness. A man as big and dark as Dutch shouldn't be capable of such a thing.

But he keeps kissing me like I'm precious and my knees buckle. I slide my hands up his arms, tracing a path over the lines covering his muscular biceps. My fingers thread in his hair and it is every bit as soft and thick as I'd imagined.

He grunts when my nails make their first pass over his scalp and I do it again. His hold on my head tightens in a way that's both strangely sweet and possessive.

I can't help the strangled little sound that escapes my throat when his tongue runs over the seam of my lips.

For a second, the world is full of possibilities.

Then I remember who I'm making out with and my senses return to me, piercing through the bizarrely tenuous energy that sizzles in every interaction I have with Dutch.

I wedge my hands between my body and his massive chest and shove. I'm not strong enough to move him, but with this version of me, he's extra respectful.

Dutch eases back, staring at me through hooded eyes.

I'm overrun with emotions—anger, desire, regret, frustration. There's shame too and with it, the anger surges. On instinct, I lift my hand and smack him hard across the face.

The sound of skin meeting skin reverberates in the quiet.

Dutch's head flies to the side.

My chest heaving, I raise my hand as if I'll slap him again and then I drop the arm. I'm insane. *He's* insane. And this shouldn't have happened, but the least I can do is get an answer.

"You came in here looking for some girl and now you're kissing me?" I accuse in my husky voice.

Dutch's jaw works. He's still staring at the side, his face turning a strange shade of red.

I stab a finger in his chest. "Why were you here tonight? Why were you looking for Cadence?"

"Is it that important to hear the answer?" he growls.

I'm trembling with vehemence. "Yes."

He studies me for a long moment and steps back. When he opens his mouth, I *know* the answer to the madness he and his brothers have been laying on me will finally be revealed.

But there's a knock on the door.

"Are we interrupting?" Zane asks.

I gasp and turn away from the brothers. Dutch may not recognize me, but if I'm under Finn's sharp gaze and Zane's experienced eyes, they might start to pin the pieces together.

"Yeah," Dutch growls.

I catch a glimpse of myself in the mirror and realize that my wig wasn't completely in place. There's a strand of my brown hair peeking from underneath it.

Panicked, I lower my head and brush past the boys.

Dutch grabs my hand. "Wait, where are you going?"

"I have another gig," I lie.

"Stay."

I shake him off, making sure to keep my face lowered. "If you want to talk, meet me at the Crossroads Cafe this Saturday."

Dutch's stare lingers on me when I hurry down the hallway.

I hope he shows up on Saturday, but I have no intentions of meeting him. It would be better if the prince of Redwood Prep left this version of me the hell alone.

Chapter Fourteen

DUTCH

"You want to explain what happened yesterday?" Zane asks, twirling his sticks around. "Or are we just going to pretend that you weren't eye-banging that redhead from the lounge when we walked in?"

I play a complicated riff and hope my brothers take that as a sign that I haven't heard them.

If the mysterious redhead hadn't pushed me away and slapped the hell out of me, maybe they would have walked in on more than an intense stare down and jagged breaths.

The memory of the kiss makes heat swell in my chest and I let an angry note ring. It does nothing to pierce through the haze and rid me of my restlessness.

Mystery Girl did a number on me yesterday.

And I'm not just talking about the slap that almost sent my brain sloshing out of my skull. A slap that came after *she* kissed *me*.

"Just go ahead and smash that guitar into the ground,"

Finn yells to be heard over my thrashing. "It'll be more satisfying."

I whip my head up and glare at him.

Finn is on a high chair, the bass guitar in his lap. Zane is behind the drums, twirling the sticks and giving me a stupid grin.

"We're starting from the second set," I growl.

Then I wait for Zane to tick his drums.

He doesn't.

I try my hardest to ignore both of them, but when my brothers refuse to play, I whirl around.

"We've only got a few days of practice until that stupid dance," I grumble.

Principal Harris has us do 'community service' gigs every once in a while, mostly to punish us for our spotty attendance records. Next weekend, we're going to play for a high school in an area where we'll all probably get robbed or shot at.

"We don't have time to waste," I add, growling.

"We're not the one wasting time, Dutch." Zane points a drum stick in my direction. "You are."

"I have no idea what you're talking about," I grumble.

"What happened between you and the redhead?" Zane insists.

"Nothing."

"Don't feed us that bull," Finn gripes.

"Whatever that 'nothing' was, it caused you to sprint after that chick like you were trying out for the Olympics. Then when you didn't find her, you ran about five red lights before kicking us out of the truck and disappearing who knows where."

I know where.

I texted Christa and told her to get her and that

plumped up mouth out to Fourth Base, the lookout point above the town where almost half our graduating class lost their virginities.

My intentions were to screw the redhead out of my mind. Christa's always a guaranteed good time and I figured I could replace the taste of cherries and innocence with the taste of caviar and rum.

It didn't work.

I was in deep when I realized that Christa was mewling over me and the only reason I was putting any work in was because I was picturing redhead's face on top of hers.

I grit my teeth. "Since when did you two get so nosy?"

"This is my first time seeing you lose your cool in front of a chick," Zane observes, sticking a hand through his raven hair.

Finn agrees. "You looked a little spazzed when you left her."

"She slapped me."

Both my brothers go still.

Finn blinks rapidly. "She did what?"

"And you let her?"

I didn't just let her. I was going to tell her every one of my secrets. Why we were looking for Cadence that night. Why we need her out of school. Why my loyalty is to Sol no matter what.

She had a damn lock on me from the moment I walked into the lounge and saw her behind the piano. There was no spotlight on her that night, but there might as well have been by the way I couldn't take my eyes off her.

Everything about her was so unvarnished and authentic that it made me want to trap her inside me until whatever made her the way she was rubbed against me too.

Hell, maybe that was all it was. The need to feel

someone that genuine under me. I swear I don't go around following girls into changing rooms like a creep. Usually, it's the other way around.

But the way it felt with her, it was almost like I *knew* her. Like we were cut from the same cloth.

"Dutch, what is going *on* with you, man?" Zane demands.

I don't know.

I have no freaking clue why this girl screws with my head. In fact, after the kiss-slap duet, it took me a long time to page through what the hell had just happened to me.

"Are you finally going to chase her down?" Finn asks.

"No."

"That's the only way Jinx will release her information," Zane informs me.

My eyes sharpen on them. "What are you talking about?"

"We tried to pay Jinx for a name," Zane explains. "It was the weirdest thing. She refused to give it to us. Said she'd only release that information to you."

"Why do you think she's playing games?" Finn asks.

"She's always playing games," Zane grumbles. "This time, she's playing hardball."

"Probably because she wants more money," I growl. Whoever Jinx is, she's a good businesswoman. I'll give her that. I can't count how much she's managed to glean from the Cross brothers alone.

"There's something more to that redhead," Finn says thoughtfully. "I can feel it."

I point angry eyes at him. "What exactly are you feeling?"

"Watch it, Finn. Dutch is going to deck you for thinking about his girl."

"She's not my girl." I set my guitar down. "If we're not going to practice, then I'm leaving."

"Why? Your date isn't until Saturday," Zane teases.

I immediately stiffen the hell up.

On the one hand, I want to be smart about this. Whenever I'm around the redhead, my brain goes on the fritz. She's all I can see. All I want. In fact, not even Christa's thirty-thousand dollar lips going to town on me could rid me of the taste of her hot, cherry-flavored lip gloss. After it was over, I couldn't help but wish it was the redhead that I'd had pinned to my steering wheel.

As annoyed as I am about that slap and the Cinderella act she pulled by running away without leaving her name, I know that I'd follow her anywhere.

And that means I'm in *deep*. Way deeper than I'd like to be. I can't lose control and the moment I see her, I'll be putty in the palm of her hands.

Frustrated with my brothers and myself, I sling my guitar over my shoulder in a practiced move and set it back on its stand.

"You bozos practice without me. I'm out."

Zane pouts. "Don't be like that, big brother."

I roll my eyes. I was only ahead of him by a couple minutes, but he'll never cease to milk the distinction.

Finn smirks at me as if he knows they got under my skin.

I grab my backpack and sling it over one shoulder. "What class do we have now?"

"Probably music." He gestures to the drums. "Which is why we're here."

I perk up a bit. Cadence is in our music class. Rather than spend time sulking over the redhead, I can try to make more progress in kicking her out of Redwood.

She destroyed my wallet last week. I can't have her thinking she's escaped my wrath.

My brothers are silent and staring at me.

"Why'd his face light up?" Zane asks Finn.

My brother just shrugs.

Without making them any wiser, I leave the practice room and head to music class. Brahms is getting a little too comfortable with me. Since I'm in the mood, I think it's about time I raised some hell.

Jinx: I couldn't give your brothers a good bang for their bucks, so here's a freebie. Your favorite pair of primped lips has been plotting and scheming for a while now. She plans to strike your girl where it hurts today.

Jinx: What will it be, Dutch? Want to play the hero or the villain?

Chapter Fifteen

CADENCE

Music is my escape.

Until fourth period when it becomes something close to nails on a chalk board thanks to Ms. Eunice, our sub who's sticking around for a lot longer than anyone thought was possible.

Sneaking a peek through the window, I take note of the clouds gathering in the sky. The stormy weather outside perfectly matches my mood. I just want this class to be *over* already.

A glance at my watch gives me some relief. Only one minute until the bell—or the 'end of class chimes' according to my Redwood Prep handbook.

"Um, Cadence and Christa, I'll need you both to come up here after class," Ms. Eunice croaks.

Everyone shifts in their seat to stare at me. Then they glance around to stare at Christa. The loud-mouthed cheerleader who probably has 'future wife of

Dutch Cross' tattooed on her boobs, casts me a smug look.

I have no idea what the smirk is about, but I'm immediately uneasy. The last thing I want to do is walk up there and find out what has Christa so happy.

The chimes go off, indicating the end of the period. With a deep breath, I slip out of my chair and approach the older woman at the front.

I can feel the eyes burning into my back as I make the trek. After my humiliating dash during the practical assignment, my peers have been clamoring to see a part II.

It's no secret that everything I do at Redwood Prep sticks longer in everyone's memories thanks to Dutch's unusual interest in me. My background as a scholarship kid makes this alleged 'love story' even juicer to these rich kids.

My steps slow down and I wrack my brain to figure out what this meeting is about. I'm pretty sure that Ms. Eunice isn't calling me out for another practical assignment.

After that embarrassing day, I tucked my pride deep in my chest and went to speak to her. I explained my phobia and asked if she could allow me to do the practical when it was just me and her in the class.

She agreed and, when she heard me play, she gave me a high score on the assignment.

I don't see her dragging that issue to light again.

The chimes go off a second time, warning everyone that free period has officially begun, but no one moves from their seat. They're too eager to watch the show.

It's no wonder someone like Jinx has such a hold on these rich kids. They love gossip and scandal just as much as the old women in my neighborhood do.

The silence is expectant and heavy.

I pretend not to notice and stop in front of the teacher's

desk. Ms. Eunice doesn't seem interested in chasing anyone out of class. Her dull eyes linger on both me and Christa and her lips are pursed.

She taps the music sheets on the desk in front of her. Then, without a word, she slides her fingers together, sets her chin on them and waits.

At first, I'm confused about why she's showing us our past assignments. Then I take a closer look and my heart drops to my toes.

Our last project from Mr. Mulliez was the Unconventional Music Theory assignment. Before we handed in our song, we were to show our sheet music. I did the homework all on my own since my last attempt at joining a group got me kidnapped, locked in a secret practice room, and threatened by The Kings of Redwood Prep.

But no one would know because the music sheets in front of Ms. Eunice are completely identical. Down to the rests, the crescendos and the rhythm.

I cringe. My first thought is that this has to be a mistake. And then I remember who I'm dealing with and I realize that there's a zero percent chance the similarities are a coincidence.

Dutch is always meddling in my locker. If he's not throwing trash in, he's throwing water and ruining all my books. There's a chance he found my notes, photocopied them and offered them to the dance captain.

"I have no idea how this happened, Ms. Eunice," I say intently, "but I assure you that I didn't copy from anyone."

"Me either," Christa insists.

I slant angry eyes at her. "Stop lying. You know you didn't write this song."

"How can you accuse me when *you're* the one who stole my work." She folds her arms over her chest. Her tone is snooty and condescending. "As you know, we have a zero tolerance policy for cheating at Redwood Prep." Her smile is the definition of evil. "So I'm afraid we'll have to escalate this to the board that my daddy chairs."

Once again, I feel like a tiny bug beneath the boot of a giant. Normally, I'm always in control. Even when things go wrong, I'm the one who pushes up my sleeves and solves it. Mom couldn't. And Viola was depending on me to keep her safe.

Ever since I got to Redwood Prep, I keep slamming against a brick wall. It makes me burn with hatred, anger, and steals all my hope. I've seen the worst of the world, but where I come from, filth looks like filth. It's a junkie, eyes vacant and skin sallow, taking one last hit even if it costs him his marriage, his job and his life. It's that kid on the block who knows there's no other life for him than the one where he eventually gets gunned down trying to line his gang leader's pockets.

Where I'm from, evil looks like what it is.

But in Redwood, the most cruel are drowning in jewels and good looks. They flaunt their status and power. They smirk and make champagne toasts and slap black cards on counters.

I'm nothing like that. And it seems everyone here wants to remind me of my true value. Because I come from nothing, I have no power.

And helplessness sticks.

Christa blinks ridiculously long lashes. The stench of smugness is so thick on her that it would give even Dutch a run for his money.

What bothers me more than this obvious attempt by Dutch to run me out of Redwood is the accusation. Music almost destroyed me, but it ended up saving me and my family in the end. I might become a different person to play in front of crowds, but my music is always honest.

If Dutch wants to run me out of Redwood, fine.

But he seems hellbent on turning music against me, first by taking Mr. Mulliez away, then by stalking out my lounge job last night, and now by lying about my work.

I won't let him win.

Not this way.

If he's determined to become more devious to run me out of Redwood Prep, then I have to up my game too if I intend to stay.

"We won't escalate it then," I say simply. "Let's solve it right here."

Our teacher opens her mouth.

"Ms. Eunice is a substitute. She can't make decisions like this," Christa says, interrupting her.

"It makes no sense to take this to the principal when we can solve it here."

Ms. Eunice lifts a finger.

Christa frowns. "I don't trust you. Anyone devious enough to steal my song would find a way out of it."

I grit my teeth. "I'm not a thief."

"You're poor," she says dismissively, "so of course you're a thief."

I give her a long, dark stare, hoping my gaze alone can intimidate her into telling the truth. But since she's Dutch's current hook up, it basically guarantees that her heart is as black as his.

There's not an ounce of sympathy on her face.

Ms. Eunice smacks a hand on the table. "Ladies, if I may have an opportunity to speak." She gives each of us a sharp stare before continuing, "I know a way to find out who really wrote the song."

Christa's eyes turn shaky. "How?"

Ms. Eunice smiles, allowing her thin lips to stretch over her papery skin. "Let's re-write it."

She slaps fresh music sheets on the desk.

Christa turns pale.

I start grinning hard.

Yes. I can totally do this.

"And then you'll both perform it," Ms. Eunice adds.

My victory crumbles to ash before my eyes. "What do you mean perform it? Like... in front of people?"

"Yes."

I lean forward. "Miss Eunice, I told you I can't... I can't do that."

"I agree. There has to be another way," Christa argues.

Ms. Eunice lifts a hand. "The person that cannot write and perform the song accurately is obviously not the one who wrote it."

Nervous, I pick at the hem of my uniform skirt.

"That's a waste of time," a voice says.

I swing my gaze around and spot Dutch leaning against the wall at the back of the class. At the sight of him, a slow, burning sensation sweeps the bottom of my chest.

Dutch's painfully intense stare bores right through me.

I wish I could run away from it and the memories they inspire.

Instead, I keep staring at his chiseled jaw, the straight nose and the wickedly glowing amber eyes and remember our kiss in the changing room.

The mere memory of his lips burns so hot that I can't look him in the eyes. Not without practically tasting his mouth and the way it teased and then parted mine.

In fact, I can still feel the weight of his kiss.

Like a tattoo.

My hands band around my waist and I hug myself to get my body in check.

Dutch is a hurricane, designed to destroy me until I'm nothing but a stub. He wakes up every morning thinking of the sneakiest ways to inflict pain on me. Sure, he may not have beaten me or assaulted me, but his psychological warfare is ten times worse.

Every nerve ending in my body might be standing up right now, but there's no way I'll allow myself to sink this low.

"We're supposed to be in free period." Dutch checks his watch. "But everyone is still sitting here."

A flush spreads on Ms. Eunice's cheeks. She looks flustered. "I dismissed the class long ago—"

"But they haven't left," he says pointedly.

Ms. Eunice clears her throat and rises. "Everyone leave. Except you." She points at Dutch. "You come here."

He ambles lazily towards her desk, his body moving almost rhythmically. He's a predator on the prowl, totally in control of his side of the jungle. He's the highest on the food chain. What would he have to fear?

Christa gives Dutch a look of blissful relief. The moment he gets close, she wraps her hands around his biceps.

I feel my entire body bristle and I tell myself it's not because Dutch was kissing me yesterday and plotting my ruin with his girlfriend twenty-four hours later. It's only because the sight of him disgusts me. Believe me. That's all it is.

"I *do* expect you both to turn in new assignments. Copying will not be tolerated in my class." She slants a hard stare at Christa. "Even though I'm just a substitute teacher, I can still do this much."

Christa blinks rapidly.

Way to go, Ms. Eunice.

I start to like her a little more.

"And you," she points at Dutch, "since you're so concerned with this matter, I'm giving you the responsibility of helping Ms. Cooper with her stage fright, so if there's a need to handle cases like this in the future, she'll be able to participate."

"What?" My jaw drops. "No, you can't let Dutch help me."

"Why not?" Dutch asks smoothly. There's a cocky smirk on his lips as he watches me.

I point my furious gaze on him. "Because I'd rather choke on a basket of peaches."

"Peaches?" He arches a brow.

I'm deathly allergic to them, but it's not like I'm going to give him or Christa that information so they can try to murder me in the future.

"I heard Dutch and his band are acclaimed in their own right." Ms. Eunice gestures to him. "And since he and his brothers can't be bothered to come to class," her aggrieved look in his direction tells me Ms. Eunice isn't too thrilled about that, "he can contribute to the lesson by helping a fellow student during class."

"No!" Christa stomps her foot. "I object."

"This isn't a courtroom, young lady." Ms. Eunice rises and collects the copied music sheets. "Have the new projects turned in to me by tomorrow."

"Tomorrow?" I squeak.

"Tomorrow?" Christa blanches.

"Or would you like me to go with my previous plan?" She arches an eyebrow.

We both shake our heads.

When Ms. Eunice is gone, I turn and find a furious glare pointed at me.

But it's not from Christa.

Dutch folds his arms over his chest. "Looks like you're my problem now, Brahms."

"You're not seriously thinking about helping her, are you? Eunice is clearly out of her mind if she thinks you can do that." Christa scoffs. "She needs a therapist."

What I need is for the two of them to get out of my face.

"I know you stole my music sheet." I point a finger in Christa's chest. "And I know you," I glare at Dutch, "set her up to it."

His eyebrow quirks and her lips twitch guilty. The confusion on Dutch's face sends doubt skittering through my head. Am I jumping to conclusions here? Did Christa try this stunt on her own?

The moment I start to soften, I shake my head. Whether or not Dutch was involved doesn't matter. He's made his position clear and I'm not going to trust him. Everything he's ever done has been to push me out of Redwood Prep. This time is no different.

"I don't care what you think, Brahms. Just be ready for my brand of therapy."

I think gouging my own eyes out with sharp pencils would be less painful than having Dutch as my therapist.

"I don't think so," I snap.

"It's too late. You already wormed your way into my responsibilities, Brahms." He tilts his head and smirks at me. "It's not a good feeling when you push yourself somewhere you don't belong, right?"

I despise him. From deep down in my soul, to the place where music flows through my veins, it all abhors him.

The urge to punch his smug little face nearly overwhelms me.

Christa grits her teeth and says, "Dutch, can I talk to you? Outside?"

"No you may not." He crooks a finger at me. "Leave. I need to talk to Brahms. Alone."

I snarl at him. "That's not happening."

When I start to walk off, Dutch grabs my hand. The moment he touches me, I feel a zip up my spine. His eyes flicker and he drops my hand as if he felt it too. The look he gives me next is almost disdainful.

Christa lingers, not knowing when to leave. "Dutch."

He ignores her pouting. "Out. Now."

We say nothing while she storms out and slams the door behind her. For a second, our harsh breathing is all that fills the room.

I fold my arms over my chest, not missing the way Dutch's eyes drop there. So much for being so in love with me and my music yesterday. He's wasting no time leering at me now.

His gaze jumps back to mine and he snarls, "If I'm stuck with curing you, then you'll have to do something for me too. I'm not a freaking charity."

"You're out of your damn mind if you think I'm going to follow you—"

I'm cut off when Dutch swoops in and gets so dangerously close to my face that my body turns to jello.

Eyes darkening, he growls, "Then you can pay for my wallet. It's a custom piece worth over five thousand dollars."

"It isn't," I screech. "I don't believe you."

His lips curl up, making him look both dangerous and disgustingly beautiful. "I'll have my lawyers call yours."

My heartbeat picks up. I don't have lawyers. I don't even know a lawyer.

I gulp. "What do you want me to do in exchange?"

"You're going to be my servant until you've paid off the debt." He straightens to his full height.

"I will do no such thing!" I yell, aghast and seconds away from bludgeoning him with my sheet music.

He walks backward, his lips tilting up. "We'll see."

Furious, I can only watch him as he stalks out of the room, taking all the air with him.

Chapter Sixteen

CADENCE

Dutch Freaking Cross is a maniac. I seriously doubt his head works like a normal human being because no one could be this psychotic in real life.

My cell phone chimes at four a.m. in the morning with an instruction from my evil overlord.

Get us lattes before first bell. Double whip. No foam.

Not only is that an inhumane latte order, but it's also a never-going-to-happen order.

It's becoming abundantly clear to me that Dutch really thinks he's a god. Last Saturday, I made sure to remind him that he wasn't... by standing him up for our 'date'.

What did his face look like when he realized I wasn't coming?

I roll over in my bed, dreaming of Dutch's misery, only to wake to another chirp from my phone.

It's a new order from Dutch.

We'd like peach muffins too. The best you can find.

I shudder. He didn't find out about my peach allergy, did he? If Jinx knows that much, I'm going to have to ask Breeze if she's the secret agent who knows all of Redwood's dirty laundry.

At six, I get another message but this time I'm fully awake thanks to Dutch's cruel harassment. It's hard for me to go to sleep when I'm piping mad, which is exactly what this Redwood Prep jerk makes me.

I groggily tap my screen. Dutch's third instruction makes my entire body tighten with fear.

Find this girl.

Beneath the text is a picture of me at the showcase. My red hair looks like it's on fire beneath the stage lights. My head is bowed over the keys and my expression is pure confidence.

One of my first assignments as Dutch Cross's servant is to find myself. And not in the figurative, go on a trip to Italy and kiss a cute foreigner to fall in love way.

My knee starts thumping and I run a hand through my hair, letting my fingers tangle in the braid I sleep with every night. How the hell am I going to get out of this one?

A nervous wreck, I toss the phone away and stumble to the kitchen. I need to find a way out of this restlessness.

By the time Viola rouses from her beauty sleep and totters down the hallway like Frankenstein's daughter, I've got toast, spam and fried eggs laid out on the counter.

Her mouth freezes mid-yawn and she stares at me. Her dark hair's a bird's nest piled on top of her head and there's still a pillow crease under her left eye cheek.

She looks messy and adorable when she lights up. "Is it my birthday?"

"No," I snort.

"It has to be my birthday. Why else would you make all

this stuff for breakfast?" She giddily skips to the small kitchenette table and plunks her pajama-clad legs into a seat. "Whoa. When did you have time to make all this?"

"I got up early," I say simply.

My baby sister doesn't need to know that I was chased out of my sleep by King Butt-hole who's only purpose in life is to squeeze me out of Redwood Prep like an unwanted pimple.

I take the seat across from Viola and share out some eggs.

"I noticed that you've been practicing makeup extra hard lately." Spreading ketchup in a smiley face over her eggs—the way I've been doing all her life, I gently place the plate in front of her.

"Because the freshman homecoming dance is coming up. I plan to do makeup for some of my friends."

"That's so sweet of you, Vi," I say, munching into my slab of fried meat.

"Oh, it's not sweet. I'm charging them by the hour."

I almost choke on my food. "What?"

"The month's almost up and our electricity is due soon. I don't want what happened last time to happen again." Her scowl is dark. "We already know Rick isn't lifting a finger to help us. So much for having an older brother."

"Rick is the reason we can live together even though we're both minors." I set my fork down, alarmed by her bitterness. "Vi, it's not Rick's responsibility to take care of us. It's mine."

"But I can help too."

"You don't have to." I hate the worry crossing her face. She's only thirteen years old. Way too young to be anxious about whether our light will be cut out in a week. "I've been getting more calls to play at the lounge lately. And tips have been especially generous. I can afford the electricity this month. That's not something you need to keep in your pretty head."

She purses her lips. "Are you sure?"

"Yes. Do makeup if you like and enjoy it. Not because you feel pressured to put food on the table." I take her hand and squeeze. "Like always, I've got you."

Her smile is sweet and it makes my heart twist to see the sunshine steal back into her eyes. Vi might have her flighty ways and her rebellious streaks, but she's a good little sister. Way more mature and business-minded than I was at her age for sure.

"Okay." She wraps her fingers around the cup of orange juice. "But I'm still going to charge for the makeup. It can go toward my dress."

My throat tightens when I realize that she'll probably want a new dress to wear. I scramble to think of where I can get the money, but I come up short. There's just no room in the budget for things like that.

Viola shakes her head. "Breeze already offered to lend me one of her outfits. You know she has, like, a bajillion dresses."

Guilt threatens to hold me in a headlock, but I force a smile. "I'm sorry I can't get you a new one, but you can borrow one of mine."

"Ew."

My eyelashes flutter. "Ew?"

"No offense, sis, but you don't necessarily have the best fashion sense."

"Hey!"

"It's a good thing Redwood Prep uses uniforms." Viola lifts a hand. "That's all I'm saying."

I reach over the table and pinch her cheek. "Smart

mouth."

She giggles.

I sit back down.

"Oh, by the way, one of my friends is bringing a date—"

My fingers tighten on the fork. "You do *not* need a date to freshman homecoming."

"I wasn't going to say that, you overprotective nun." Viola rolls her eyes, "I meant..." She takes out her phone and swipes to a screenshot. "This is him."

She shows me a picture of a guy with clear brown eyes and low-cut hair throwing up a street sign. He looks a little too young and scrawny to be a part of a gang, but he's definitely showing off where he comes from.

"Is there a reason you're showing me a pubescent teen trying to look hard online?" I ask, arching a brow.

"Doesn't he seem familiar?"

I purse my lips and look closer. "Not really."

"Cadence!"

"What?" I jump when she yells.

Eyes flashing, Viola swipes her thumb over the screen and shows me another screenshot. This one is of the wanna-be gangster and Hunter.

I gasp when I see Hunter's gorgeous face staring up at me. He's got his arm slung around the kid. The caption reads, 'brothers for life'.

"They're in a gang together?" I gasp.

"I could smack you..." Viola grumbles heatedly. "They're brothers, Cadey. *Brothers.* I found out from my friend who's going with Hunter's brother. Hunter is going to be at the school as a chaperone."

I sigh. "Why is that information I need to know?"

"Hello! You can sign up to be a chaperone too. Then you

can go to homecoming, slow dance with Hunter and fall in love." She smacks her hands together. "It's perfect."

"It's a fantasy that you've built up in your own head. Have you been reading romance novels lately?"

My sister flails her arms like a child throwing a tantrum. "You're no fun."

"And you're going to be late for school if you don't hurry and finish eating now." I gesture to the food.

Hunter might be hot, but I'm not into him like that. I barely know the guy, so there's a chance we can strike a match. Maybe. Not that I'm looking for anything.

A memory of Dutch's kiss flashes through my mind and my body tingles in all the wrong places.

I'm not apathetic towards Hunter because of Dutch.

He has nothing to do with it

In fact, Dutch is the reason I'm against men in general.

He sends my blood pressure rising just by stepping into the room. And every time he makes my life a living hell, I want to smack him. But the moment I see him shirtless, I want to throw my arms around him.

He's dangerous and evil, sure.

But I obviously have a few screws loose if I can't see past his gorgeous face to his ugly insides. My hormones are clearly not a great judge of character.

Sighing, I take the bathroom first and change into my Redwood Prep uniform.

Viola's in her room doing her makeup magic so I just give her a slight wave, which she returns, and make my way to Redwood.

It's always a good day when people don't look at me, look at their phones and snicker. I only release a breath when I see that the gawking and stares are about the usual.

Today's already heading in the right direction.

I stop at my locker and find that everything is dry.

Another good sign.

Maybe I can start to breathe now.

"Hey, stranger," Serena says, popping up by my locker.

I grin over at her. I'm in a good mood and her presence just proves that today is going to be my day. Screw Dutch and his overbearing self.

I'm not anyone's slave.

"Hey." I give her a once-over. "Wow. You look nice."

She's wearing particularly thick eyeliner and it brings out the sparkle in her eyes. Her usual motorcycle jacket is worn over the male version of the Redwood Prep uniform—sweater vest and straight khakis.

"Thanks. I was tired of wearing a skirt so I thought I'd switch it up today." She groans against the locker. "This stupid school won't let us be great and wear jeans."

I chuckle. "Evil overlords. All of them."

Her answering smile makes my heart feel at ease. Although I didn't set out to have friends at Redwood Prep, having Serena as a friendly face really makes a difference.

"I heard about the commotion in your music class." She folds her arms over her chest. "Word on the street is that Dutch saved you."

"He *what?*" My eyes widen.

"After what happened the last time, with you freezing up at the keyboard and running away, crying and screaming—"

"Whoa, whoa, whoa. There was no crying and screaming," I defend.

Unbelievable. No wonder gossip's so powerful and deadly. The story completely shifted after being passed around to the whole school.

"Anyway, he protected you so the music sub didn't force

you to play." Serena tosses her head and the cute raven-haired bob swishes around her cheeks.

"That is so far from what happened it's diabolical." I frown at her, clutching my books to my chest.

"Either way, I didn't take you for the Dutch type." She gives me a once-over. "You seemed more like a Finn-head to me."

"A Finn-head?"

"Yeah. A fan of Finn? He's the quietest brother, but man... those eyes and when he plays his bass..." She stares dreamily into space. And then she shifts her attention back to me. "Not that I notice."

"Totally buy that." I laugh.

She grins and elbows me in the side.

Just then, I spot the Cross brothers sauntering down the hallway.

Oh damn. I turn on instinct, trying to blend behind the students crowding around us.

"What's going on?" Serena asks, looking confused.

"Nothing," I whisper urgently. "I'll see you later."

I hobble around, keeping my back bent and try to scurry in the opposite direction. Too scared to look back, I don't realize that Dutch caught sight of me until I feel a jolt.

My shirt squashes my boobs and I almost stumble. When I peer over my shoulder, I see Dutch, Finn and Zane staring intently at me.

Dutch has his pointer finger in the collar of my blouse and is physically holding me back.

I'm going to kill him today. I have to.

Whirling around, I smack at his hand. "What the hell do you think you're doing?"

"Where's my latte, Brahms?" His voice is smooth and

unhurried. There's a hint of a smirk on his lips that tells me he enjoys the fury rising on my face.

"I'm going to smash your face in," I threaten.

My words seem to bounce off his back like a pebble on a mountain. Dutch doesn't care that I was having a good day. He's here to ruin it.

Screw him.

And screw his gorgeous brothers too.

"What about our peach muffins?" He arches a brow.

"I'm allergic, you bastard," I hiss. "Like deadly."

He tuts. "You could have used gloves."

I glare at him and then turn around.

"Where are you going, Brahms?" Dutch growls.

"Away from you, obviously."

"We need our coffee delivered to the practice room."

I give him a one-fingered salute. My backpack bounces as I stride away from him.

"Okay then." He grunts and, a moment later, I'm airborne. A moment after that, I'm practically kissing Dutch's firm and sexy buttcheek while my legs are spiraling down his chest.

"Dutch, you put me down this *instant!*" I screech. I can feel the blood draining to my face, but that's not the reason I'm getting red. No, it's from white-hot fury. "Dutch!"

He smacks my behind and I yelp.

There's smugness in his tone when he says, "Simmer down, Brahms. If you keep thrashing like that, everyone's going to get a view of your plump little backside."

I dig my teeth into my bottom lip, sure that today's the day it's all going to end.

Today's the day I *murder* Dutch Cross.

Chapter Seventeen

CADENCE

It feels like all of Redwood Prep watches in silence while Dutch basically *kidnaps* me. I hang like a limp rag doll, my arms and hair pointing to the ground and my butt hiked at the ceiling.

My body's tense and my fingers are closed into fist. I'm waiting impatiently for a chance to be put down so I can unleash my fury.

Finn stops in front of the practice room and swipes his card over the scanner. It lights up neon. There's an audible click as the locks slide apart.

Zane gestures to Dutch. "Ladies first."

"What a gentleman," I grouse. My words hit Dutch's rear end, but it's aimed at his obnoxious twin.

Zane laughs, looking handsome and mischievous. Today, his Redwood Prep uniform is a plain white button-down and khakis. The simple look fits him like a tuxedo. It really is no secret why he's got so many followers on social media. His dashing good looks, even from upside down, are lethal.

Dutch takes me inside the practice room. Zane and Finn follow.

The nerve of these jerks. Do they think they can steal an entire *person* and get away with it? Or do they, wrongfully, assume that I've been putting up with their crap because I'm a weak person? Hell no.

I've managed to survive in Redwood Prep this long because I go down swinging. And that's exactly what I plan to do when my feet hit the carpeted floor.

"Now, Brahms," Dutch's muscular arms constrict around my back, "I'm going to put you on your feet now. And I need you to promise me that you're not going to aim for my face."

"That's the money-maker," Zane says.

I stay silent.

Dutch runs a hand over the back of my thigh. "Cadence?"

I shiver, unnerved by his touch, but I refuse to let Dutch's attractiveness get the best of me. Screw my stupid hormones. I'm locked in a room with three big, intimidating rockstars. They can do anything to me and I wouldn't be able to run.

That's not a turn on. That's a dangerous situation.

And these are dangerous people.

Just because they're all sexy doesn't mean I can let my guard down.

"Fine," I grumble.

The moment he sets me down, I launch at him.

Dutch easily snaps my wrist and pulls me into his chest. I'm locked against him, his front to my back. The feel of his body reacting to mine sends a heatwave launching through my skin.

"Brahms, you promised," he says, his tone similar to a parent scolding a child.

Zane chuckles.

"I swear, Dutch, if it's the last thing I do, I'm going to make your head roll across the front lawn like a basketball."

"Ooh. Graphic," Zane teases, taking a seat behind his drums.

Finn's brow quirks exactly the way Dutch's would and it reminds me that even if he and Dutch aren't biologically related, they're brothers.

Dutch is behind me, so I can't see his expression, but I can only assume he's grinning.

I glare at the massive hands bounding me in place. "You better let me go. Now."

"Not before you understand that you don't have a choice here," he insists. "As long as you're enrolled in Redwood Prep, you belong to me. I own you."

Each words sends my temper spiking higher and higher.

He leans down. His lips brush my ear and send a shiver of goosebumps running over my skin.

"There's only one way out, Brahms," he whispers.

"And if I don't take it?" I breathe, turning slightly toward him.

His fingers slide up my arm and settle around my neck. "Then I'm going to show up at your house." He lightly squeezes. "And I'm going to show up at your work. And I'm going to keep showing up in front of you until you know that there's nowhere you can run that I won't hunt you down."

My chest tightens and I realize that, beyond any

shadow of a doubt, I've never hated anyone the way I hate Dutch Cross.

He's a menace here at school, but I refuse to let him and his band of unruly brothers anywhere near my sister. I would die for Viola before I let her face this hellish treatment.

Fighting the urge to bite his hand in case it gives me some kind of disease, I relax. "Fine. I accept."

Dutch startles with surprise.

Finn and Zane exchange looks.

Dutch slowly releases his arms and walks around to face me, still looking suspicious.

"I'll work for you," I spit out the words. "Five grand is about two weeks salary if I'm working eight hours a day. If I'm working twenty-four hours, that's eight days." I lift my fist and he quirks a brow in warning. But I don't swing. Instead, I raise my hand. "I'll pay you back for the wallet."

Dutch narrows his eyes. I can feel him trying to tear me apart, trying to get in front of whatever I'm planning. I offer him a resigned nod and that seems to put him even more on edge.

"You win," I say.

"You're leaving Redwood Prep?"

I scowl. What is his obsession with kicking me out of school?

"No, I'll…" I can't seem to say 'be his servant', "be your assistant until the debt is paid. You happy?"

Dutch grunts.

Finn waves to us. "Now that that's settled, can we practice for the dance tonight?"

"What dance?" I ask.

"None of your business." Dutch fishes in his pocket, produces a wallet that looks like the red version of the one I trashed, and hands me a card. "Get us three coffees from the cafeteria."

"Make mine with foam, please!" Zane adds in his order. The only reason I'm not fuming is because he said please, which shows a politeness that Dutch has not yet revealed to me.

I turn my gaze to Finn. "What about you?"

"Whatever's fine," he says, fitting his bass guitar on his head. Sunlight streams behind him, creating a halo around his brown hair.

I turn sharply. "And you?"

Dutch still looks unnerved. "Extra sugar."

I'm surprised. I thought he'd take his coffee as black as his soul. "Sure."

"Give her a card to get in the practice room," Zane suggests.

Dutch stiffens.

I try to hide my smile.

"Not going to happen," Dutch mumbles. "I'll go with her to the cafe."

"We need to practice before first bell," Finn reminds him.

"Fine." Dutch takes out another card. "Bring it right back in the exact condition."

"I'll think about it," I mumble.

He leans in close and I swear his jaw tightens. "Don't test me today, Brahms."

"Wouldn't dream of it," I snarl back.

His eyes drag down to my lips and a flicker of confusion is in his expression. After it passes, he seems even more pissed off than before.

I snatch the card from him and wave it around. "I'll be right back."

On my way to the cafeteria, I inspect the practice room card and then take pictures of it. There's a guy in my neighborhood who makes fake IDs. Something tells me he'd be able to make a fake pass too.

Standing Dutch up on Saturday wasn't enough. I want him to *know* that the pain that's been inflicted is coming from me.

As I'm walking, someone steps into my way. I bounce against a bony shoulder and glance up.

Christa's in my path, glaring at me. She's in her full cheerleader regalia today, complete with short, flouncy skirt and a tubed top.

"Can I help you?" I ask, not bothering to hide my disdain. I haven't forgotten what she did during music class.

Her eyes drop to my hand and she pounces forward. "What's that?"

"Nothing." I quickly hide it behind my back.

Her gaze slides up to me and her expression twists with horror. "Did Dutch give you a card to his practice room?"

I'm about to deny it vehemently when I realize that this is a prime opportunity. Christa has everything in the world —except Dutch's true affections. Sure, she might screw around with him, but it's no secret that he has no interest in her. Not the way he's interested in me.

Well, the other version of me.

I flutter the card around, making a show of fanning my face with it. "He wants me to have access to him. At *all times.*"

"Give me that." She swipes for it.

I snap it out of reach. "Ah-ah-ah. This is for people who actually mean something to Dutch." I step closer to her and lower my voice. "What do you mean to him, Christa. I mean, apart from being the one he calls when he needs an itch scratched?"

Her face reddens. Trembling with rage, she lifts her hand and tries to slap me.

Fortunately for me, I dodge out of the way just in time.

Unfortunately for Christa, she loses her footing and face-plants against the locker.

The hallway rings out with a metallic bang.

I wince. "Are you okay?"

An ear-shattering scream pierces the hallway.

I cringe. "Guess you're... not okay."

"Christa!"

"Oh no!"

Her dance team minions rush around her, forming a circle. With their help, Christa scrambles to her feet. I gasp when I see all the blood rushing down her chin.

It's coming from a split in her plump lips.

"No, no, no!" She wilts as if she's got a broken leg instead of a minor lip injury. "I paid so much for this."

I'm not surprised by that statement at all and it just goes to show how much Redwood is already changing me.

"You!" Christa's voice is a growl. She crooks a finger at me and, with her pale skin, blonde hair and all that blood pouring down her chin, she looks like a zombie. "You did this!"

"Me?" I stick a finger in my chest.

"You... ow!" Christa cups her mouth and moans pathetically.

Her minions give me sharp, daggerlike looks. They can't seriously believe that I pushed her into the locker, can they? I mean, a part of me wishes I did, but I didn't even touch this girl.

THE DARKEST NOTE

"Christa?" High heels clip against the floor and a soft voice rings out. "What's going on here?"

"Miss Jamieson!" Christa bawls. Big, crocodile tears leak down her cheeks.

The beautiful Lit teacher saunters into view. She's wearing a hip-hugging purple pencil skirt, black pantyhose and ruffled blouse. Her curls are in a high ponytail and her thick coils cascade down her back.

"Christa, what's wrong with your face?" Alarmed, Miss Jamieson hurries over. She inspects Christa for a second and then frowns. "Girls, take her to the nurse."

"This isn't over." Christa's voice is low and muffled due to the giant gap in her bottom lip.

The cheerleading team captain launches an arm around the shoulders of her friends and together, they hobble off. I'm pretty sure a busted lip shouldn't prevent her from walking properly, but I figure exaggerating is right up Christa's alley.

Not going to lie. There's a tiny part of me that feels justified. If Miss Jamieson weren't staring at me, I'd probably high five the locker that's still got Christa's bloody lip print on it.

Eyes stern, the Lit teacher gestures, "Miss Cooper. A word."

Oh no. Am I in trouble now?

I follow her urgently into a classroom. From the writings on the board, I'm guessing she was preparing for first period.

Miss Jamieson closes the door. "Sit, Miss Cooper."

"I really didn't push her, Miss Jamieson. You can check the cameras." I jump to my own defense before I've fully settled into my seat.

"It doesn't matter whether you pushed her or not. The

truth is that you cannot afford to make a single mistake, Cadence. Scholarship recipients are held to a higher standard at Redwood."

"I *know* that." This stupid school would let people like Dutch, Finn and Zane raise hell in their hallways. But the poor, defenseless scholarship kids are the ones who get sacked for the tiniest infractions.

"It might not be fair, but it is what it is," Miss Jamieson says as if she can read my mind. Clear brown eyes sear me. "One bad move and you can lose your scholarship."

"But I didn't do anything wrong."

Miss Jamieson leans dark hands across the desk. "Cadence, Mr. Mulliez had so much faith in you and your journey here at Redwood Prep. He was willing to risk his reputation for it." She swallows. "And although he's gone to pursue further studies in Europe, he still asks about you. I don't want to tell him that you're no longer in school. Do you understand me?"

I lower my gaze. The reminder of Mr. Mulliez makes me feel heavy.

"If you ever need to talk, about anything," she slides a business card with her personal number written on it across the desk, "I'm here." She tilts her head and smiles prettily. "I was a scholarship kid here at Redwood too. So I know a little about what you're going through."

I stare at her stunning face. I seriously doubt she has any idea what she's talking about.

Miss Jamieson was probably the most popular girl at Redwood with looks like hers. And I bet there was no Dutch rampaging her world either.

I smile wearily. "Okay."

"Great." Her eyes sparkle.

Whether she's going to be of any help or not, it's

enough to know that I've got an ally if I need one. It's a relief that she's in contact with Mr. Mulliez too. It feels like he's still here, watching over me.

The beginning of school chimes ring through the hallway and kids start pouring into the classroom.

"Get to class," Miss Jamieson says.

* * *

My phone vibrates while I'm on my way to first period.

Dutch: Are you growing coffee beans? What's taking so long?

I grit my teeth and mime throwing a punch. If only Dutch would walk into a locker and save me some trouble.

"Was that for me?"

I whirl around, stunned to see Dutch approaching. The hallways are empty and his footsteps thud against the floor.

My gaze flickers to his and I see the darkness lurking just beneath the gold.

"Did you follow me?"

"I'm here to make sure you don't spike our coffees with bleach," he says in a totally serious tone. "Zane's got a weak stomach."

"If I tampered with your drink, trust me, you wouldn't be able to tell."

The threat hangs between us, like the eye of a hurricane.

"Might want to be careful with your words, Brahms."

"You might want to not be so paranoid, Dutch. It was a joke."

It was not a joke.

If I'm getting their coffee every day, then you bet I'm going to slip a laxative in Dutch's.

His eyes sharpen on me, but before he can say anything, footsteps clop down the corridor.

"What are you two doing out of class?" a teacher asks, hands on his hips.

"We were just about to head there now," Dutch says. Taking my hand, he drags me in the opposite direction.

I stumble behind him. "My class isn't in this direction."

"We still haven't gotten our coffee yet." His voice is low and steady.

"Are you kidding me right now?"

"One thing you're going to find out, Brahms. We don't kid about coffee."

We get to the cafeteria, which is empty because everyone is in class—as we should be. But I guess the Cross brothers play by their own set of rules.

Dutch leads me behind the counter where the food is kept in warming pans. I notice someone peeking through the window and wait, almost gleefully, for them to scold us.

Instead, the door bangs open and a hefty cafeteria woman barrels out, throws her arm around Dutch's neck and kisses his cheek.

Dutch gives her a soft smile. "Maria, don't tease me if you're not going to leave your husband."

She laughs and scrubs his jaw free of the lipstick stain. "Thank you for what you did for—"

He winks, cutting her off. "Don't mention it. You got what I need?"

"Oh baby." She does a hip roll. "I have *everything* you need, but you were late today. I can't give you any extra love."

"It's okay." He nods at me. "She'll make the coffee herself."

I bristle.

Maria's eyes sparkle at me. "You have a little girlfriend, Dutchy?"

He leans close and whispers to her, "Maria, you know I only have eyes for you."

The older woman swats him firm on the rump and laughs loudly. "Go make your coffee."

Confused and a little disarmed, I follow Dutch into a small room. It's got a counter, black and white frames on the wall, and sacks of premium coffee beans.

"What is this place?"

"Maria's workroom. She makes all the coffee for Redwood Prep." He arches an eyebrow. "Haven't you tasted a cup yet?"

I refuse to tell him that I haven't been able to afford anything outside of sandwiches, water and orange juice.

Instead, I shrug.

He points to the machine, unbothered. "I'll watch."

"You really think I'm going to poison your drinks?"

He levels me a flat look.

I pretend to be offended even though I'd one hundred percent slip a laxative in if I had one.

Dutch stops me when I reach for the machine. "You *do* know how to make coffee right?"

I cut him a sharp glance. "Yes. I used to make coffee for my mom all the time."

"Used to?"

I stiffen and then I clamp my mouth shut.

He leans against the counter where I'm working, his eyes intent on me.

Squirming beneath his scrutiny, I snap at him. "Can you back off? I'm trying to make your stupid coffee."

"Is your mom a touchy subject, Cadence?"

His use of my actual name takes me aback. I blink

rapidly, fighting the unease in my chest with the only weapon I have—anger.

"Tell you what," I lean in to him, my eyebrows lowering, "I'll tell you about my mom if you tell me why I need to look for that redhead."

Flames burst to life in his eyes and though I didn't get to see the disappointment and annoyance kick in when I stood him up on Saturday, this is the next best thing.

His jaw clenches. "You don't need to ask questions. Just do as you're told."

"Are you embarrassed, Dutch? Is there another girl out there who sees you for the despicable human being you really are?"

The flames in his eyes turn to hellfire. It's almost alarming the way I feed off of his fury. It's like the part of me that's broken and numb comes alive when I push his buttons. And maybe that's what happens for him too. The shards in me push into his soft places and make him more monster than man.

His nostrils flare and we stare each other down. I don't shift away as usual. My chest is a whirlwind of emotions. Dutch cracked open that drawer marked 'mom'. It's one I always keep closed for good reason.

The heady mixture of anger and hurt is a tumultuous combination.

Taunting him, I ease closer. "What did she do, Dutch? Did she take off with your car? Or your wallet? Or maybe your black hole of a heart?"

His lips are thinning out and steam is rising from his preppy shirt. Alarm bells go off in my head, screaming bloody murder.

I keep going because, apparently, I love poking angry lions. "Or," my chest brushes his, "did she find out that you're a scared little boy who plays games and trashes lockers instead of having a conversation about what the hell he really wants."

The space between us is suddenly eliminated. Calloused hands slam against either side of me, trapping me in place. I choke on my own breath, the heat in my heart sweeping down to touch my fingers, stomach and all the way to my toes.

I must be disturbed because I don't hate the way Dutch's hard, sculpted body feels against mine. And I don't hate the way he smells either—like sandalwood and sunshine and something dark. Like angsty music.

I breathe in, remembering the taste of him. The explosion of cinnamon. The softness of his hair on the back of my hand. The grunt he made when I raked his scalp.

I want his pain.

But I *need* that grunt again. Need it more than I can say.

I don't know what's wrong with me, but a twisted side is ready to come out and play. It grows stronger the more Dutch glares.

Because the truth is that Dutch Cross owns everything in Redwood Prep, but he can't ever own me. Not the 'me' he really wants. And it's such a power trip that I'm practically tripping out of my skin.

The amber hues of his eyes are like tiny sunbursts, taking on an almost supernatural glimmer. An angry slant to his hot, full lips, he stares me down.

Heat burns in the sliver of space between us, making me sweat. I refuse to touch him, refuse to be the first to give in to the wickedly hot tension simmering between us. Even though I'm throbbing with lust and desire, I will not be the first to cave.

"Who are you calling a little boy?" Dutch presses

forward until his head is right against mine. The big bad wolf getting ready to blow a house down.

The sound of his sharp, rapid breath is all I can hear. It drowns out the thudding of my heart and the roar in my body. It makes my legs tremble like a new-born foal.

Unable to stand, I grab hold of his shoulder when his tongue flickers out against the shell of my ear.

"You want to see fear, Brahms?" he taunts.

I whimper, digging my fingers into his shoulder and arching my back. All the blood is pooling to right between my thighs and it's all I can do to keep myself from bursting into flames.

"Tell me," Dutch presses.

"N-no."

And then he smiles. Evil. Sadistic.

"Keep pushing me and I won't just destroy you," he whispers. "I'll destroy everything you care about."

Immediately, the tension slices in two and I wrench away from him. He lets me go, but the flush in his cheeks and the tightness of his pants tells me I wasn't the only one affected by... whatever that was.

Stumbling on shaky legs, I push past him and hurry to the door. Dutch is my nightmare-come-true, but my body's still roaring for his touch.

I hate myself for being so weak.

Because after everything he's done and all the ways he's ruined my life, I just can't help that I'm drawn to him.

Chapter Eighteen

DUTCH

What the actual *hell* just happened?

To say my body was raging to get under Cadence's tease of a skirt is an understatement.

If I had a little less self-control, I would have pinned her against the counter and had all the coffee cups rattling and shaking with how hard I ploughed into her.

Even now, I have to lean over the coffee machine and grip the shelving hard to keep from exploding. Counting backward from ten doesn't work. Neither does making myself a cup of expresso and draining it.

I can still smell Cadence's perfume—flowery and light. I can still see those brown eyes narrowing on me, burning with anger and lust. She's a twisted little thing. The darkness inside her rose to the surface, clamoring for me. I could see it and it called to me in a way that set every nerve on fire.

I'm losing my patience with her and it's not because I want to break her. I want her under me, sweating, vibrating, groaning for mercy.

Not that I'll give her any. Not that she deserves it.

I shake my head angrily.

I'm supposed to be thinking of ways to kick her out, not dreaming up ways to screw her.

My interactions with the sharp-tongued New Girl always send my blood pressure spiking. But lately, she's been elevating a whole lot more than my temper.

At first, I thought it was because of her resemblance to the redhead who stood me up on Saturday. They share the same height and build, along with the same rosebud lips.

Every time I get a glimpse of Cadence's lips, the redhead blinks into focus. I can't explain it. It's like the girl from the showcase is in front of me. Then Cadence will open her mouth and I'll realize that it's not *my* muse. It's the most infuriating girl in Redwood Prep.

Even so, my body can't differentiate between the two and I keep getting this uncontrollable urge to back her up against the nearest wall and kiss her senseless.

My body's never betrayed me like this. It's frustrating as hell and I can't blame it on the redhead anymore.

Cadence isn't the raw and talented spitfire on the keys. She's a separate person. She's quiet and reserved and shy to the max. But there are moments when she's loudmouthed, brash and fearless.

Every time she pushes my buttons, I find myself going wild. It's as if I'm falling off a cliff and the rope is slipping out of my fingers.

I'm dangerous.

She *makes* me dangerous.

Things could have gone a lot further if she hadn't run from me. And I can't promise that I'd be able to keep a grip on control if she gets under my skin again.

Zane and Finn take one look at my face when I storm to the practice room and they keep their mouths shut.

No one asks me why I left to collect my cards and my coffee from Cadence and came back empty handed. No one says anything to me at all during our first set.

My brothers clear out a minute after our last song, throwing excuses about going to class. I stay back and shred on my guitar until my ears are ringing and my fingers have their own heartbeat.

Then I go find one of the cheerleaders. Christa's not available so I choose someone at random who's willing to open her legs long enough for me to work out my frustration.

She starts moaning and groaning, but it's still not enough for me. I end up cutting things short and send her packing.

The hell is *wrong* with me?

I stalk out of the parking lot and see Cadence in the hallway. My eyes lustfully slide over her long, pale legs in that skirt. I'm crooking my finger and calling her over before I've thought it through.

She grips her schoolbag tight and marches toward me.

"Hand over the cards," I bark.

She slants angry eyes at me and shoves the cards in my direction. Even the brief contact of her fingers on my palm sends me reeling with lust again.

"Go get a table in the cafeteria. Make sure it's nice and warm by the time I get there."

She grits her teeth, her body tensing with quiet rage,

but she doesn't talk back. Stomping through the hallway, she disappears around the bend.

I feel two presences beside me.

A moment later, Zane speaks up. "Did you two fight again?"

"No," I growl.

"It looks like it," Finn grumbles.

Zane rolls his eyes. "You're the one who's supposed to be getting under her skin, Dutch. It shouldn't work both ways."

"I'm sticking to the plan," I snap at them. "I'm running her out of Redwood."

"Why does it seem like she's the one running you?" Finn observes.

I shoot him a dark look full of warning.

His answering look is unbothered.

Heels click against the floor and at the sound of it, Zane perks up. He looks eagerly behind him. His face drops in disappointment when he sees it's not Miss Jamieson trotting toward us.

"Why do you keep falling for that?" I grouse. "You know she ducks into another hallway if she sees you up ahead."

"He's right," Finn agrees.

"Why don't you move on?" I ask my twin.

"Why don't you ask Jinx for that redhead's number and find out why she ditched you on Saturday?" Zane accuses.

"I'll handle it my way."

"Which is what?" Zane taunts. "Hoping you stumble on her in another bar?"

"I heard she quit because you were hounding her," Finn says.

"No, she didn't," I grumble. According to the lounge manager, she was planning on leaving that job anyway.

"If you don't take care of... whatever's going on in your head, you're going to screw your way through the entire senior class and still not feel any better."

"You should know right?" I hiss.

Zane's eyes go dark. "Yeah, man. I do know. It freaking kills me that I'm like this. But I know that woman is too good for me and I know I'd ruin her, so I'm doing my best to stay away."

Both Finn and I look at Zane in surprise. He's not usually this self-aware.

"Damn. I don't think you've ever been that honest before," Finn mumbles.

"Maybe if she heard you talking like a grown-up instead of a horny teenager, she'd take you more seriously," I say.

"And maybe if you didn't sneak up on that chick and kiss her like a crazed fan, you wouldn't have gotten slapped and stood up. Look at that," Zane says. "We both learned something today."

Finn chuckles.

My lips twitch. Count on my brothers to help me take a ridiculous situation and make it feel doable.

At that moment, my phone buzzes.

My blood drains when I see the message.

"What is it?" Finn asks, picking up on my shift in mood right away.

"It's Jinx," I say, looking between my brothers. "She says she's close to getting a location on Sol."

Jinx: Not all heroes wear capes. What will I get for finding the fourth member of your band, Cross Boys? I don't think money is going to cut it. How about a trade. A secret for a secret? Dutch

can start by telling me why he and Stage Fright were caught getting hot and heavy in the coffee room?

Chapter Nineteen

CADENCE

"You sure we're not going to get shot?" Zane mumbles from outside my dressing room.

"It's a high school homecoming," Finn barks back, but his voice shakes as if the idea has crossed his mind too.

"You think freshmen aren't packing? Or their older brothers aren't? Have you heard the term 'drive-by'?"

"He's got a point," Finn says with a hint of nerves.

"You're both being ridiculous," Dutch growls.

I stiffen at the grit in his voice. As usual, he sounds irritated and growly. I don't think it's because of his brothers though, since he tends to lighten up around them.

No, he's been broody and dark ever since he laid eyes on me after school. Today's the day of their performance—the one they still haven't told me much about.

We spent a couple hours in the practice room before he and his brothers whisked me away from Redwood Prep to get ready.

I'm particularly exhausted today and don't really want to be here. I'm missing out on Viola's first homecoming and will have to satisfy myself with the pictures Breeze takes on my behalf.

Not that Dutch cares. My evil overlord's been on my case ever since that staredown in the cafeteria.

Every day, without fail, he forces me to get coffee and makes me drink his first to test if it has bleach in it. Then he instructs me to carry his books to class. Then I *have* to appear at his beck and call for whatever stupid errand he needs done. Then, as if he wants to make my life after school a living hell too, Dutch has me practicing with them until sunset.

But not on the piano, no.

He has me playing the triangle.

I know this is revenge. He's trying to make sure that the undercurrents between us never surface again.

If his goal was to make me resent him more well, then... mission accomplished.

I go home every night and slap the crap out of the punching bag, pretending that I'm rearranging Dutch's chiseled jaw.

"Wait." Their words register and I shove the dressing room door open. "Did you just say your band is playing for a freshman homecoming?"

No one answers me. Probably because they're all busy staring.

Zane's jaw clops open.

Finn arches both eyebrows.

And Dutch... Dutch looks angrier than usual.

Nervous, I slide a hand over my dress. "What?"

When we left school today, Dutch drove straight to a warehouse in the heart of the 'money district'. It's our town's equivalent of Rodeo Drive where all the stores are overpriced and pretentious.

A well-kept woman met us at the door and escorted us all the way upstairs. There, the boys disappeared into their own changing rooms and a clerk presented me with a silky black dress and platform goth boots to wear.

I went along with it because the boots looked amazing with all its straps and dangling chains. Plus a dress this expensive has never touched my skin before.

Dutch is the first to look away. His jaw flexes and he curls his fingers into fists.

Zane hops out of the sofa. "Damn, Cadence. Way to show up."

Finn nods his approval.

My lips curl up a little. "Thanks."

Dutch swings around. His dark stare burns into me.

I can see the desire flaring to life in his eyes. He averts his gaze, but it's still there in the tenseness of his jaw, the flare of his nostrils, and the agitated hand that he slides into the pockets of his dress pants.

All the boys look like gothic princes in dark trousers and button-downs, but there's something about the way Dutch's sleeves are folded back to reveal his ink that sets him apart as the most dangerous and most likely to wreck your soul.

His blonde hair has product in it so it's not flopping around on his forehead. This put-together style makes him look even hotter.

Wicked thoughts spark to life in my head, starting with how his hands would feel slipping against the silk on my dress and ending with how muscular his body would be without that shirt on.

I lick my lips slowly, taking note of the way Dutch's

gaze latches onto my mouth as if he wants to trace the path himself.

The tension between us hasn't eased up. Not since the almost-kiss in the coffee room.

It's torture to be so close to him. To want him and hate him at the same time. Now that I've admitted to my dark craving, I can't look Dutch in the eyes. Just in case he figures out that I'm more messed up than he is.

Because for him, it might be a simple matter of attraction.

But for me... I should know better.

Mom's track record of bad decision-making has to skip a generation. Dutch Cross isn't the kind of guy who'll promise a future and actually deliver. He's the kind of guy who'll take a woman's mouth and virginity and then vanish into the blackness that he came from.

I don't want to see what a mess he can make of my heart. I won't ever give him that opportunity.

"Why am I wearing this?" I ask.

"You'll find out," Dutch says cryptically.

I have a bad feeling about this.

First of all, Dutch's band will be playing at my old high school. Which means he'll be playing in front of my baby sister.

Viola already has a huge crush on Zane. Thanks to Breeze, she's now a fan of The Kings. She'll approach them for sure and if she sees me with them, she's going to act as if we're all friends.

I don't want these worlds colliding.

"I'm not going," I say.

The three handsome brothers stop midway to the door.

Bending over, I pretend to have a stomach cramp. "Suddenly, I'm not feeling well." I fan my face. "I think I might have eaten something with peaches in it."

"Did anyone feed her peaches before we came?" Dutch growls at his brothers.

They exchange looks.

"No," Finn says.

Dutch frowns at me. "I didn't see you eating anything since lunch."

"You don't know everything I've done since lunch," I shoot back.

Zane looks amused. "Is there something we should know about?" He arches an eyebrow at Dutch. "Brother?"

"Stop screwing around," Dutch warns me.

"Stop thinking you own me," I answer back. "You don't."

"Get in the damn car, Cadence."

"No."

Finn glances at me in concern. "Did you really eat something with peaches? Dutch mentioned you were allergic."

Shoot. I need to spin another lie to make this one more believable. I slam a hand on my hip. "I might have been making out with a football player this afternoon. I think he might have eaten peaches for lunch."

Dutch moves like lightning across the room. When he stops, he's closer to me than my next breath.

His eyes drill into me and his hand falls on my lower back. A little sound escapes from my throat, and it seems to bring out the beast in Dutch because his eyes darken instantly.

The sight of him bearing down on me has desire pounding through my veins.

I can't kiss him right now.

His brothers are watching and I need to keep a clear head so I can keep him away from Vi.

I lift my hands to push him away.

Instead, his fingers latch onto one of my wrists. I don't miss the way we both take a sharp intake of breath.

Dutch recovers quickly. Turning, he drags me out the door and down the steps.

My body buzzes with fury and I push at his fingers. "Let me go."

"Keep fighting and I'm going to *carry* you into that homecoming dance. Over my shoulder." His eyes are dark and I know he's good for the threat because he's done it twice before.

"Screw you," I hiss.

His smirk is sinister and makes my body throb in the worst way.

"You keep begging for it and I just might, Brahms."

I stop struggling immediately.

Dutch juts his chin at the car and I huff before climbing in. His brothers join me and we're off.

The silence is broken only by my aggravated breaths. I glare a hole into Dutch's head, ignoring the way Finn observes it all.

Zane clears his throat. "Cadence, I heard this was your old high school."

"Don't engage her," Dutch scolds him.

What? Are they supposed to treat me like I'm not even here? I slant another dagger look his way and answer Zane haughtily. "Yes, I attended that high school."

"Is that why you acted like you were sick? Because there's something there you don't want to see?" Finn asks.

"Or someone?" Zane turns around in the passenger seat and wiggles his eyebrows.

The car suddenly lurches to a stop.

Finn almost smacks his face into the headrest.

Zane grips his seatbelt tight.

I grab the door handle and am spared from whiplash.

"Dutch, what the hell? What kind of driving is that?" Zane yells.

"There's a red light," Dutch grumbles.

Finn gives his brother a narrow-eyed look. And then he turns to me so our knees are almost touching. "Is it an ex?"

"I—"

"What the hell is this? An interrogation?" Dutch growls.

"We're just asking questions," Zane says.

"Don't ask a damn thing. She's not going to be around long enough for the answers to matter anyway."

I wish I was sitting behind Dutch so I could kick his chair.

"He's right. I don't see how that's any of your business," I say pertly.

Finn just grins.

Dutch turns the radio on. "No more talking!"

"Bossy," Zane teases, but he kicks his legs up on the dashboard, beats out the rhythm of the song on his thigh and doesn't ask me anymore questions.

I'm plotting on ways to avoid my sister when Dutch pulls his luxury car into the parking lot of my old high school.

I stare at the chain-link fences. They have to lock up everything or junkies will break in, use the bathrooms and ransack the place. The buildings are rundown with peeling paint.

I know from memory that inside is no better. We have to bang on our lockers to get them to open up. Our cafeteria serves mystery meatloaf instead of sushi and gourmet burgers. And most of our teachers look like they've given up on life already.

It feels like getting dunked with a cold bucket of water to be back here after spending almost two months at the fancy and luxurious Redwood Prep with their in-house gym, fully heated indoor swimming pool, tennis court, sprawling gardens and elegant decor.

"So this is how the other side lives," Zane mumbles, looking almost excited to be here.

Dutch tosses a bag at his brother. It's round and large, so I assume it's carrying the cymbals.

Zane opens his hands and catches it just in time.

"Carry that. They said we should set up through the back door."

I start to take out a guitar.

Dutch snatches it from me.

"What are you doing?"

His gaze lazily snakes down my dress to my shoes. "You shouldn't be carrying anything." Before I can start to think that he's grown a soul overnight, he adds, "You might trip and fall and then our equipment will be ruined."

So much for being a gentleman. Dutch is pure evil. I'm sure of it.

"Let me take it inside." I grab for the equipment.

He narrows his eyes and drags it out of reach. "Are you going to pay if anything gets broken, roadie?"

I scowl at him.

He glares back, refusing to break eye contact.

"Can you guys go eye-stab each other over there," Zane says with a hint of mischief in his tone. "We need to unload the truck."

"Don't tell me what to do."

"Shut up, Zane."

Dutch and I speak at the same time. When we realize we've actually agreed on something, we both huff in disgust and move out of the way.

Despite my insistence and a few sneak attempts, the Cross brothers get the equipment unloaded without me. Dutch keeps a sharp eye whenever I get too close and faithfully chases me away.

I'm already ready for the night to end when I hear a voice sing-song, "You're *here!*"

My best friend comes streaking down the school's steps. She's wearing a tight blue dress that falls over her stunning body. Her blonde hair's piled up on top of her head.

She stops short when she sees me. "Cadence?"

"Breeze." Panic locks on my head and clamps tight. "W-what are you doing here?"

"I told you I was on the planning committee this year. They asked me to help out with the freshman dance."

She probably did tell me that, but I can't remember. Though it does explain why our old high school would insist on booking The Kings instead of a regular DJ like they always do.

Breeze's gaze volleys between me and the three gorgeous rockstars who are standing next to me. "What's... this?"

This is a very long story that I have not yet shared with my best friend.

"We're Cadence's friends," Dutch says.

I give him a look so full of poison it's a surprise he hasn't dropped dead yet.

Dutch ignores my glare of doom. Stepping forward, he offers his hand to Breeze. "And you are?"

"I'm whatever you want me to be," she says, giggling and twirling her hair.

Dutch gives her a charming smile and I swear I didn't think his face was capable of making that expression. His eyes are sparkling, his lips are relaxed and he seems like an actual human being instead of a cold god.

"I'm Dutch," he says. "This is Finn and Zane."

"Hey." Zane waves.

Finn gives her a nod of acknowledgment.

Breeze almost faints. "Wow, it's... it's so great to officially meet you. I'm so psyched about tonight."

"So are we." Dutch arches a brow. "Where can we start setting up?"

"You can go through the side door there." She points.

"Great." Dutch gives her another heart-melting smile. I have no idea where this sweet guy act is coming from. He's been an absolute hellion to me, yet he's propping himself up as someone who'd never hurt a fly.

"Great," Breeze says dreamily.

Dutch winks at her.

I almost throw up in my mouth.

The band members pick up as many instruments and equipment as they can carry and disappear into the school. The moment they're out of ear shot, Breeze attacks my arm.

"How. Could. You. Not. Tell. Me?" She punctuates each word with a smack. "When were you going to mention that, not only do you know The Kings personally, but they know your name and take you along on gigs."

"That's not what's happening."

Breeze steps back and her eyes widen. "And what is this dress? Is it designer? Oh my gosh! Did they buy it for you?"

"No. I mean, sort of."

"Your voice just went up two octaves, hon. If you want to lie to me, try a little harder."

"It's not what you think."

"What do I think?" She challenges.

"I'm not *with* them. We're just... doing a project together."

"Perfect!" She throws her hands up. "Because if you were with one of The Kings, I'd totally go back inside and tell Hunter not to hold his breath."

"Hunter's here?" My breath hitches.

Viola told me he would be, but I didn't expect him to actually show up to a freshman homecoming. He didn't strike me as the PTA big brother type.

Dutch jogs down the steps of the school, brawny arms free of his guitar and speakers. His brothers aren't flanking him, which means they're still inside setting up.

His gaze tangles with mine and even in the darkness, it's hypnotic. I force my gaze back to Breeze.

"It'll be awkward dancing with Hunter. Ever since he came by that day, we haven't spoken. Plus, he never responded to my DMs."

Dutch's back muscles flex as he reaches for something in his truck. His movements are slow and measured, even though he's in a rush. So I know he's listening intently.

Breeze watches his lean, athletic body and drool slips down the side of her lips.

"Breeze," I say.

"Huh? Oh right. You. Hunter. This dress." Her eyes snap to attention and she grabs my hand. "Cadey, he has to see you in this dress. There's no way he'll think of you as just his friend's little sister again."

I start to stumble behind my best friend when I feel a

strong set of fingers encircle my other wrist. Blazing heat radiates from his touch as he tightens his grip on me.

Breeze looks at us both with wide eyes.

"What are you doing?" I snap.

The scowl crossing his face tells me he doesn't appreciate my tone. "We need you on stage."

"On stage?" I hiss. "Why?"

"You'll see." His lips curl up and I'm reminded of a lion again. Dutch peers intently at me. "I have other plans for you tonight, *Cadey*."

Chapter Twenty

CADENCE

"No, absolutely not."

Dutch and I are standing in the hallway on one side of the gym while Finn and Zane are on the other.

I thought Dutch was dragging me with him to get in one last argument.

Assuming Dutch wouldn't be scheming of ways to make my life miserable was my first mistake.

Letting him drag me here while Breeze watched was my second.

"I'm not getting on stage," I hiss at him.

"You said you'd be my assistant. Twenty-four seven. That's the deal." His brows hunker low over his amber eyes. He's seems extra impatient tonight. It's weird. Dutch is always in a mood. But this feels different. It feels... volatile.

"*You* play on stage. The screaming fans. The bras that get thrown at you. That's your thing," I snap.

"Bras?" The storm in his eyes softens a bit. "Cadey, this

is a high school dance. If I pick up any bras here, that's half a felony."

"I don't care. I'm not going on stage."

Dutch shoves his hands in his pockets. "We need you in our set."

"Because the triangle is *so* important to the overall sound?" My voice rings with sarcasm. "I seriously doubt it."

My gaze cuts from Dutch to the exits. I wonder how much brute strength I would need to push him off and make a mad dash for the highway.

I'd rather take my chances with the gangbangers on the street than climb on top of that crudely built platform with the decorations that are already falling off. The only way I'd even consider doing such a thing would be if I had my red hair, makeup and stage name.

"I heard your sister attends this school." Dutch steps closer.

"How do you know that?"

"Jinx sent a picture." He smirks. "Viola Cooper. Big brown eyes. Nice smile. Wants to be a makeup star."

My shoulders stiffen. "Don't even *think* about talking to my sister."

"Then get your butt up there." He juts his chin at the stage.

My stomach froths with nerves and I break out in a cold sweat. "I can't."

"Yes, you can."

"Why are you doing this to me?" I moan. Even though I know. It's because he hates me.

"You need to get over your stage fright."

"Dutch, I *really* can't."

He leans down, meeting my gaze. "Don't think of the crowd. Imagine it's just you and me, hm? Beat that triangle the way you want to beat my head in with a hammer." He pauses and seems to think about it. "But beat it to time."

"I refuse."

"Not an option, Brahms." He shakes his head.

Outside, the MC is announcing the band. A cheer goes up from the freshmen.

"It's time." Taking my hand, Dutch drags me toward the stage.

"Can you just drop it?" I grip his shirt, twisting it for dear life. I never thought I'd be begging Dutch for anything but here I am. Practically on my knees.

"Since when did you back down from a challenge, Brahms?"

I focus on his stubborn gaze. "This is different. I haven't played on stage as myself since I was twelve."

This time, the hand he closes around me is patient. Slowly, Dutch rubs circles on my wrist as if to calm my racing pulse.

"Don't look at them, Brahms." He leads me through the door. "Look at me. Keep looking at me." He glances back. "Because if you run, I'm going to find you and you're not going to like what I do to you."

My eyes narrow in distaste, but I can't snap at him because we're already stepping on stage.

The instruments are set up. Guitars. Drum set. Multi-colored lights. Big balloons are held back by a net canopy. And then there are the eyes.

A sea of faces sweep before me, all dressed beautifully and shrouded in shadows. I can't see Viola but, honestly, I can't see anything beyond my own haze of fear.

I think I'm going to throw up.

Dutch releases my hand and I make a move to run off

the stage when Finn steps into my path. He's got a bass guitar slung over his shoulder. His eyes are intent on me.

I give him a desperate look. "Finn, please."

He shakes his head and juts a chin at the triangle.

Zane is sitting behind a set of impressive looking drums. His raven hair falls into his face and he shakes his head to toss it out of his eyes. Smirking at me, he points a drumstick in my direction.

I'm hollowed out by fear and confusion. Why are they doing this to me? Do they want to see me choke? Is this their final plan to push me out of Redwood Prep for good?

"Sit there." Finn points to a chair that's all the way at the back of the stage.

I race over, my heart hammering in relief and my trusty triangle tucked close to my chest.

As I get comfortable, Dutch nods at me. I hadn't realized he'd been waiting for me to sit down. That little hint of thoughtfulness makes something shift in my chest.

I nod back and watch as he grabs his guitar from the stand and swings it over his head with effortless grace. He looks so at ease. The bastard.

My entire body's on fire and I'm trying hard not to hyperventilate. The last time I stood in front of a crowd, I was twelve, crying, and afraid.

I squeeze my triangle tighter. *This is different. You're not behind a piano.*

The self-talk helps. I start to calm down a bit. Dutch is here. So is Finn and Zane. And though they've been awful to me, at least I'm not alone. I'm tucked all the way at the back, safe and sound, playing an instrument that has no weight in the performance.

Just breathe, Cadence. Just breathe.

Dutch is facing the crowd. He wraps long, slender

fingers around the mike. His voice booms through the auditorium as he introduces the band and I see several girls swooning. Poor things are already under his spell, which is no surprise. Dutch is tall and beautiful under the lights.

Staring at him is better than getting lost in my head. I notice his cocky smirk when he unhooks the mike. He prowls the stage while Zane starts playing a catchy drum beat. His head bobs and he unleashes another confident grin. This is his world and he owns it.

Zane stops playing.

Then he lifts his sticks and counts down.

One, two, three.

I'm so close to the drums that when Zane bangs on the cymbals, I almost tear out of my own skin. Finn comes in with a funky riff on the bass and Dutch matches it on the electric guitar beat for beat, his face tense in concentration.

I gasp in astonishment when I hear Dutch play. He's using music like a weapon, tearing apart everything I thought I knew about him and building it all back again.

The roars get louder as the sea of freshmen grin and bounce in excitement.

I'm at the back, so all I can really see is Dutch's profile, but it's powerful enough to keep my attention. Sharp cheekbones. Strong jaw. Pouty lips. He rips through the guitar piece the way I pour my soul into a piano, like this might be his last night and nothing else matters but this moment.

It's a thousand degrees on stage, but my arms sweep with goosebumps.

Dutch's lips part, his hair flopping as he keeps his attention on the guitar. He's got us all spell-bound, waiting.

And then...

He puts his mouth on the mike and a note trembles through the air.

The screams that pour from the crowd nearly shatter what's left of my eardrums.

Dutch sways from side to side, giving himself totally to the song. It's a side of him I've never seen before and it's appealing as hell.

I love the rasp in his tone and the realness that he brings to his performance. It's raw and vulnerable, even if the tempo is upbeat.

His confession the other night trips through my mind. *I don't know what I play for.* It's hard to think that he's struggling so much when he's so good at it.

The Kings begin their first song and the kids erupt into cheers.

I'm reminded in an instant why music is so universal. It doesn't matter that Dutch has way more in his bank account than any of these students could dream of. It doesn't matter that he drives a fancy car or lives in a mansion or has a famous music legend for a dad. Right now, in this moment, he's speaking the language that everyone understands.

I bob my head to the rhythm, connecting with every line, every verse and every chord. Not because they're perfect but because the singer isn't giving me a choice but to come alive.

Eventually, I graduate from head-bopping to dancing in my seat. Sometimes, I even forget where I'm supposed to play the triangle.

Towards the end of the set, the band erupts into a music break. Dutch plays a complicated solo on his guitar. Finn pounds out a rhythm on the bass and Zane goes to town on the drums, getting the biggest reaction from the high schoolers.

I see Dutch gesturing to me.

My eyes nearly bug.

I keep shaking my head. *No.*

He juts his chin at me as if to say *you're next*.

I shake my head again.

He nods again.

We do the bobble-head routine for a minute until Zane slams his sticks against the cymbals and, while the golden disks are ringing, he points to me.

I swallow hard. The crowd comes into focus and fear chews me alive.

"You're up, Cadence!" Zane warns as he finishes out his solo.

Heart in my throat, I struggle to my feet, lift my triangle and slam the stick against it. The ring blasts over the air and Dutch immediately wraps a melody around the note so it feels like something new.

The freshmen go wild, trashing their heads and dancing.

I jump up and down in excitement.

I didn't... pass out.

I did it!

I find Dutch's eyes and give him a big smile. He dips his chin in approval. Sweat is running down his face and his hair's a mess, but I've never seen him look more captivating.

He turns away and sings the chorus again. The guitar screams beneath his fingers. We're gearing up for the end.

To my surprise, Dutch swivels around and gestures for me to come to him.

I wag a finger.

He tosses his head in a 'come on' gesture.

I walk to the front, my knees shaking.

Amber eyes sparkle at me and though Dutch's not saying anything I can feel him asking *you ready for this?*

I whip my head back and forth in a desperate 'no'. Not that he cares. Dutch rakes his guitar pick over the strings and Zane pounds the drums. It's time for the big finish.

I hit the triangle in time.

Once.

Twice.

I mimic Dutch and whip my hair back and forth.

The final blow of my triangle is met with applause and screams. Dutch plays a final chord progression before letting the note ring.

It's over. There's a buzz running through my entire body. I can't believe I just did that. I got on stage and played that triangle as myself.

Me.

Cadence.

No wigs. No makeup. No stage name.

I've always been honest with my music, but this is my first time in years being honest with who I am when I play it.

Tonight, thanks to Dutch, I broke that mold.

Without thinking it through, I close the distance between us and throw my arms around his neck just as the net breaks and balloons come raining down above us.

Chapter Twenty-One

DUTCH

My arms encircle Cadey's waist and I breathe in her scent.

I want the hug to last longer, but she pulls back and a conflicted look passes through her brown eyes. Then, as if she's made up her mind about something, an uncomfortable grin touches her lips.

Her hair slaps me in the face when she whirls around and throws her arms around Finn next. My brother exhales in surprise, his eyes shooting to me.

Cadence releases him and goes to Zane. I scowl in my twin's direction, watching carefully to make sure his hands don't slide down any further than they have to.

The possessiveness takes me by surprise. So what if Zane hugs Cadence? It doesn't matter to me. *She* doesn't matter to me.

I rip my eyes off her although everything in me wants to keep looking. Kneeling next to my guitar, I turn down the volumes.

Normally, I'd wait for the event to be over before I start taking down instruments, but I jump straight to the mixer board, mute the other guitars and start unplugging wires.

Cadence hops off the stage and I pretend not to notice.

"Dutch, what are you doing?" Black and white sneakers fall into my line of sight. They're pristine, which means they belong to Finn. He's a sneaker head and treasures his vintage shoes like trophies.

"I'm taking down the instruments," I mumble. It should be pretty freaking obvious.

"Where did Cadence go?" Zane asks, joining me at the front of the mixer board.

"How the hell am I supposed to know?" I growl.

There's a fine line between harmless ribbing and fight talk. I know I'm spinning out closer to starting a fight than anything.

But Zane doesn't look annoyed. He just looks amused.

"What's got your panties in a twist?"

I roughly bend our wires so they can fit in our travel case. "I flunked on the last riff."

I got nervous with Cadence standing beside me and my fingers didn't bend the strings right.

My brothers nod because they know how seriously I take music. What they don't know is how much of tonight's music I enjoyed simply because Cadence was there with her stupid triangle.

My head's a mess and it's all her fault. When I saw her walk out of the changing room wearing that silky black dress, her mouth all glossy and pink...

I nearly busted a vein.

Then she threw her arms around me after the performance tonight.

It was just a squeeze, as basic and innocent as vanilla cream, but my pants got so tight I'd thought they'd pop off.

Every nerve in my body is alive from her touch.

Finn looks at me like he knows the real reason why I'm restless. I need my brothers to get out of my face as soon as humanly possible.

"Oh, I found her." Zane nods in the direction of the crowd.

I look up almost eagerly. And then I scowl when I don't see Cadence anywhere.

"By *her*, I mean her hot best friend." Zane winks at me. "Who did you think I was talking about, Dutch?"

"Screw you." I flip my brother off.

Finn scrubs his chin. "Any of you guys feel like we've seen her friend before?"

"Who? Cadence's friend?" Zane clarifies.

Finn nods.

"I don't know." Zane takes the mike cords out of my hands. "What I do know is Dutch isn't allowed to take down our instruments tonight."

"What? Why?"

"We'll take care of this."

"I got it." I reach for the music cord.

Zane blocks me. "We spent a crazy amount on these wires and you're bending them wrong. If they stop working in the middle of a set, I'm blaming you."

"Go spike the punch or something." Finn slaps me on the back and retreats to his bass where he carefully sets the guitar in its case.

"You boys need any help?" A nerdy-looking teacher wearing glasses approaches us. But he's not really looking at us. His eyes dart around like he's on the search for stowaways.

I start to notice how empty the front of the stage is. We usually get lots of girls coming up to us after a set. By the looks of the teachers hovering around us, I'm guessing the lack of interaction is intentional.

I drag a hand through my hair and peruse the crowd again. It's dark and almost impossible to make out any individual faces, but I locate Cadence anyway by the shimmer of her dress.

Hell, I spent most of the drive over to the school trying not to think about her in that dress but I failed. Big time.

Everything about her affected me.

The way her rack spilled out of the top.

The way she chewed on her glossy mouth when she realized where we were going.

The way she kept playing with her earrings.

I shouldn't be thinking about her.

But there's...

I don't know. There's something there.

In the distance, Cadence stumbles back as a tinier girl pounces on her. It's too far to tell, but I'm guessing that's her little sister. The other girl is wearing a frilly dress and big hair.

Looks like Cadence comes from a family of huggers.

Zane motions to me. "Can you put this in the truck?"

"Yeah." I accept the mixer from him, glad for an excuse to leave the gym.

When I return, Cadence is standing closer to the stage.

And she's with some guy.

My hand curls into fists when I see how close the other guy is to her. She laughs at something he says and her hand lands on the sleeve of his jacket.

The sight makes me livid.

I've felt a ton of dark feelings in my life, but the ones

that are currently thrumming inside me are the most frightening because I have no right to them. Not with Cadence.

I roughly grab my guitar case and stalk outside. The night wind does nothing to cool my fury. I bend over the backseat, tensing my shoulder muscles and doing my best to keep still.

Say I do walk in and cut off that guy from talking to Cadence? Then what?

I don't want her for myself.

She's not the girl I care about.

She's the girl I need to run out of Redwood.

I curl my fingers into fists and pound the chair. It's like I'm being torn from the inside.

The connection I feel with the redhead is real. Every time I think I've got a hold on myself, I hear her play and she wrenches something out of the deepest, darkest parts of me.

But I can't pretend that Cadence isn't getting under my skin too. Even now, I want to drag her into one of the empty classrooms. I'd run my hands down her body, over her curves. I'd swallow her throaty moans to keep her quiet so we don't get discovered by the chaperones.

Because once I get a taste of her, I sure as hell won't stop for anything short of a hurricane.

I rake my hands roughly through my hair, breathing hard and fast.

Need is pounding in my veins.

I scrub a hand down my pants.

A long groan escapes. I sound like a tortured mental patient.

Approaching footsteps warn me that my brothers are coming. I straighten up and scowl at them.

Zane is carrying a drum piece in a padded case. The school provided a fully-equipped drum set, but my twin never plays without his own snare.

"You ready to head out?" Zane asks.

I look behind him. "Where's Cadence?"

"She's staying," Finn says.

My nostrils flare. "Who's taking her home?"

I picture that guy offering her a ride, reaching over the stick shift, setting his hand on her thigh—my temper spikes.

"Why do you care?" Zane challenges.

I stare him down. "I don't."

"Then let's hit the road. There's no reason for us to stick around." Zane throws an amused grin over his shoulder. "The admin want us gone faster. They think we'll fall for jailbait."

My feet are rooted in place. Leaving Cadence here to flirt with some jerk chaperone makes me want to smash my fist through a window.

But I don't have a reason to stay.

At least not a good one.

Forcing myself to turn, I follow my brothers to the car.

"Wait!" A girlish squeal rings out, causing us all to stop.

The girl who hugged Cadence earlier comes leaping down the back steps. She's huffing and puffing by the time she gets to us.

"I'm..." She pants. "Voila... Cadey's... sister."

I arch an eyebrow, taking note of the family resemblance. Viola isn't as tall as her older sister, but she's got that same delicate beauty. I can see the family resemblance in their eyes and in their smiles. Although I don't have much to compare it to since Cadence rarely smiles at me.

"Hey, Viola," Zane says.

Finn does a chin-up.

"I know you're busy and I didn't come here to fangirl over you." She straightens after catching her breath. There's a flush to her cheeks and a sparkle in her eyes. "Don't get me wrong though. I totally would because I adore you guys. You were amazing tonight."

"Thanks." Zane flashes her his signature grin.

The poor kid almost faints.

I step forward. Cadence started getting in line when I threatened to show up in front of her house. Which means she's trying to protect something close to home. Her sister.

"We got time." I ease closer to her.

She blushes.

"Do you play piano like your sister?" Zane asks in a friendly tone.

"No, I don't. I kept begging Cadey to teach me, but she's always working late." Her giggle is self-conscious. "So I kind of found my own thing."

At the mention of Cadence working hard, I get a prick in my chest.

"Anyway," Viola waves a hand, "I wanted to thank you for helping my sister get over her stage fright."

"There's still a long way to go," I warn her. Playing the triangle in the background is a far cry from being able to play alone in front of crowds.

"Yeah, but you have to understand, Cadey would *never* get up on stage before. She'd break out into hives, throw up and..." She shudders. "It was awful."

"When did the stage fright start?" Zane asks.

Viola chews on her bottom lip and it reminds me of her sister. "Mom wasn't always... in her right mind. Sometimes, she'd take Cadence to places that weren't safe and forced her to play."

Finn looks disturbed.

Zane curses. "What kind of mom would do that?"

"One who has a drug problem," Viola confesses.

My heart sinks to the pit of my stomach.

"When our mom died," Viola's eyes get misty, "I thought that Cadey would never play again. But then she got her scholarship to Redwood and she met you guys and now she's having fun. Mom might be gone, but it's almost like she's still here, watching over us."

"Sorry about your mom," Zane says quietly.

"She wasn't that great of a mom to be honest," Viola admits, her eyes on the ground. "Cadey was the one who paid the bills and took care of me. She never really got a chance to be normal." Viola must realize she's sharing too much personal information because she suddenly cringes. "Oh my gosh. Do *not* tell her I told you all of that. She'd kill me."

"Your secret's safe with us," Finn says sincerely. Just then, his phone chirps and he glances down. His expression shifts instantly. It's enough to set me on edge.

"What's up?" I ask my brother.

Finn clears his throat. "We need to go. Now."

"Viola, it was great meeting you," Zane says, trotting toward the truck.

"Let us know if you ever need anything," I tell her, backing away.

She brightens. "Totally."

I climb into the driver's side and wait for my brother's doors to bang shut. Starting up the engine, I glance at Finn.

He lifts his phone. "It's Jinx. She got a location on Sol."

* * *

Jinx: No good deed goes unpunished. Since The Kings were kind enough to bestow their royal presence on kids from the southside, here's my gift to you. You'll find your buddy Sol here. Location attached. But be careful. Not every caged bird can be freed.

Chapter Twenty-Two

DUTCH

The quiet is stifling when we storm into the lobby of Holy Oaks Training Facility.

Finn looked it up on the way here. It describes itself as boot camp lite—somewhere between a military training camp and a psychology center for troubled teens.

I've been sick to my stomach since I learned this was where Sol's family stuck him after he got kicked out of Redwood Prep. Far away from his family and friends, he's probably been suffocating back here.

"Can I help you?" A man with a buzz cut, dull eyes, and thin lips stares us down from behind a receptionist desk.

"We're here to see Solomon Pierce," Zane says calmly. Finn and I decided to let him do the talking.

I'm too on edge to fake pleasantries and Finn always jumps to the point, no matter where he is. Since sweet-talking women and authority figures is Zane's cup of tea, we're keeping our mouth shut.

Buzzcut glances at me and then at Finn. "Visiting hours are over."

"You see," Zane leans against the desk, "we drove all this way to visit our dear friend."

He points to a sign. "Make an appointment and come back tomorrow."

I curve my fingers into fists. There's three of us and one of him. If we get him out of the way, we can go storming the facilities looking for Sol.

Finn stretches his hand in front of my fist. His eyes flash on me and seem to be saying 'calm down'.

How the hell am I supposed to calm down?

Sol is in here because of me. He's been here for damn near two months without any contact from us at all.

After taking the rap like that, we shouldn't have left on tour. We should have made a better effort to keep in touch. Then maybe none of this would have happened.

Zane clears his throat and lowers his voice. "Mr..." He glances at the guy's nametag, "Dusty, Sol is like our brother. I'm sure he's mentioned us. We were all a part of a band together. The Kings."

"Ah, you were the punks who got him in trouble and then ran out on him."

I stalk forward.

Finn grabs my arm and locks me in place.

Zane laughs tightly, but I can tell that even he's starting to lose patience. "Things got out of hand and we haven't been able to get in touch with Sol for a while. Since you're aware of our situation, I'm sure you can make a little exception for us to work things out."

"Since I'm aware of the situation," he rises to his full height, "I won't be approving any visits from the lot of you.

When Sol is released, he can choose to contact you, but we will not be facilitating it."

"But—"

"Leave. Now." He folds his arms over his chest.

Zane walks back to us, his lips tight.

I lean in. "We can take him."

"Getting arrested won't lead us to Sol faster," Zane answers.

Damn. When Zane is the voice of reason, I know I've officially lost my mind.

Desperation makes me stubborn. I was the one who told Zane that I'd get his suspension revoked. Things have spiraled out of control, but I can't let him down.

My brothers flank me on either side as we walk out of the lobby. I can feel the tenseness in their shoulders and I don't know if it's because they're afraid I might try to jump Dusty or if they're battling guilt of their own.

As we're passing the security booth, I get an idea.

Zane slams the car door shut. His lips twisted in a scowl, he mumbles, "I say we come back with a ladder and some blow torches."

"You plan to burn the place down?" Finn asks.

"If we create a diversion—"

"Damn it, Zane. We're not arsonists," Finn reminds him.

"You have a better idea?"

Finn rubs his temples. "Maybe if you'd be quiet, I could think of one."

Zane scowls at him.

Finn glares back.

I turn to them and start the car.

"Where are you going?" Zane accuses. "Are you just gonna give up?"

"No," I say.

"Well?"

I don't feel the need to explain further and my brothers know me well enough to leave me alone when my brain is percolating.

Our truck zooms through downtown as I stop at every ATM I can find. When I'm done, I've got a duffel of bills.

Zane eyes the bag at his feet. "You think Dusty would fall for this?"

"He doesn't seem like the type," Finn says.

Again I don't answer.

When we get back to the boot camp, I check my watch.

"Guys, wait for me," I tell my brothers.

"You don't need back up?" Zane asks, a hand on the door handle.

I shake my head, grab the duffel and head out into the drizzling night.

After a few minutes with the security guard, I hustle back to my brothers.

Zane grins at me. "I see you came back empty handed?"

"Not quite." I flash a security pass at my brothers.

Finn's eyes widen and he snatches it. "Who's Orville?"

"The security out front." I glance between the two of them. "He said he's going off duty in ten minutes. The other guy is always late, so we've got about five minutes to get in."

"Which is where this comes in I assume." Zane wiggles the pass.

I nod. "Sol's in room 201. We can't be long or they'll figure out he let us in."

"Dutch, you genius." Zane smacks my back.

Finn smirks at me. "Impressive."

"I'll bathe in your praise later. We've got to hurry."

My brothers file behind me as we sneak through the back door and move carefully up the stairs. It's late and there's no one moving around in the hallways.

"There!" Zane whispers, pointing to Room 201.

I look both ways and charge across the corridor, my heart pounding. I open the door and let my brothers in first before I slip inside.

"What the hell?" Sol bellows from his perch on the bed.

"Sh!" Finn quiets him.

"Hey, man." Zane's grinning broadly. "Long time no see."

"Sol," I say.

Our best friend gazes at us with wide brown eyes. Then he leaps off the bed and attacks Finn and Zane in a two-armed hug.

"Bastards," Sol says, his voice cracking.

Finn thumps him on the back.

Sol releases them and glances at me. His bare feet press against the floor as he takes a few steps my way.

I avoid his eyes. "Sol, man... I... I'm sorry."

"Shut up, Cross." Sol sweeps me in a hug.

My bottom lip starts trembling, but I firm it like a man and refuse to get emotional.

Sol leans back. The light shines in his face. He looks thinner than usual, his cheekbones are hollowed out and his eyes are a little sunken. His skin, which was always a healthy tan, is pale.

"Like the beard," Zane says, making a motion over his own chin.

"Yeah." Sol smiles sheepishly. "I figured, since the ladies here aren't anything to look at, I'd try it out. You're lucky you came today. A few months ago, you would have seen it in the weird, straggly phase."

We laugh, but it's hollow and empty.

Silence creeps in when the chuckles fade. It's like we're standing in a pool of regret. I'm up to my knees in it and I don't know how to get unstuck.

"How did you find me?" Sol asks, whirling around and taking his seat on the bed again. "These psychos don't let us use our phones or laptops. And the internet is heavily supervised."

"That must be fun," Zane quips.

"Unbelievably." Sol tugs at the hem of his pajama top. It's an awful greenish-brown color with standard buttons and wide-legged pajama pants. He catches me looking at it and grins. "They force us to wear uniforms here. Even when we sleep."

"Sol, man, we're gonna get you out of here," Zane says. I look at my twin and his expression is more serious than I've ever seen it before.

Finn nods. "You shouldn't have taken the rap by yourself that night."

"Nah." Sol shakes his head. "What's done is done."

"That's not good enough for us," I declare firmly. "We're getting you back into Redwood Prep. Where you belong."

His eyes flicker to me before dropping to the ground. "Forget it, man. I've already missed two months of school."

"That's not a problem."

"Why do you think I'm here, man? I *wanted* to go back to Redwood Prep, so I acted up at every school my mom tried to shove me into. Didn't last more than a week here or there. That's why she stuck me into this hell." He glances at the ceiling. "And that's how I know that if I don't get into a school soon, I'm going to have to repeat an entire year."

"How soon?" I ask urgently.

"Two weeks. Max." He lifts a shoulder in a half-hearted shrug.

Two weeks? The deadline ricochets through my body.

Finn gives me a pointed look. "Two weeks isn't a lot of time. We've been trying to find a way for you since we got back to Redwood but..."

"But what?" Sol asks, wide-eyed and innocent.

Zane rubs the back of his neck and shoots me a loaded look. "We haven't been successful."

"It's alright." He sighs, resigned.

"We'll figure something out. I promise. You're getting out of here one way or another."

"Unless you *want* to join the military?" Zane asks with an uncomfortable grin.

"No, no, man." Sol chuckles. Then he flops back on the bed and stares at the ceiling. "I want to eat mama's *enchiladas* with the sauce that's a family secret. I want to drive to school with my friends and act like a sound engineer even though I know jack about music."

Zane laughs softly.

Finn smiles.

I stare at the floor in guilt.

Sol's voice gets low and vulnerable. "I want to feel normal again."

At that moment, an alarm goes off.

Finn fishes for his phone and swipes it off. He gives Sol an apologetic look. "We have to go."

"Five minutes are up already? Damn." Zane shakes his head.

"Thanks for stopping by, guys. Sorry I couldn't offer any refreshments or anything."

"Make it up to us next time." Zane offers his fist.

Sol bumps it.

Finn gives him a two-fingered salute.

"I'll see what I can do about your mom's enchiladas," I tell Sol firmly.

His lips curve up in a half smirk. "Don't get my hopes up, Dutch. I'm starving already." As if to prove the point, he rubs his belly.

Sol's pajama top lifts at the corners and exposes his skin. I catch sight of weird jagged scratches tearing into his lower stomach.

My eyebrows tighten.

Sol glances down and quickly drops his shirt. "You should leave. I don't want you to get caught. Dusty's gonna ban you for life."

"Come on." Finn tugs me when I don't move. "Someone's coming."

I hurry behind my brothers.

The footsteps get louder and we jump around the bend, holding our breaths while the sound of a door creaks open.

"I heard talking," someone says.

Sol's voice answers back. "I was talking to myself, Pete. It gets lonely in here at night."

There's a sinking feeling in the pit of my stomach and I don't know if it's out of guilt for what I've already done or for what I'm about to do.

Chapter Twenty-Three

CADENCE

My phone's been quiet since the dance last night.

I stumble out of bed, groggy and confused. Normally, Dutch is blowing up my cell with instructions.

Get coffee.

Buy strings for my guitar.

Print my homework.

He's like a deranged eighteen-year-old boss from hell.

Today, nothing.

Instead of feeling overjoyed at getting a break, I feel uneasy.

What is wrong with me? Why do I care that my biggest tormentor is choosing to take a day off?

I take out the ironing board and set it up near my bed. Yesterday, I forgot to wash my uniform and had to do it when Hunter dropped me and Viola back home late after the dance. Now, the fabric's still damp. I'm hoping that steaming it will help it dry faster.

"Knock, knock!" Viola sings from the door.

"Hey." I smile when she dances into my bedroom. Her hair, as usual, is a mess. "Vi, I've told you a million times to braid your hair at night so it's not a hassle to comb it later."

"Who has time for that?" she squeaks. When she sees me with the iron, she runs straight to me. "Let me help."

I eye her suspiciously. "What did you do?"

"Nothing."

I frown. "If you're trying to get out of school today, it's not happening."

"I'm not." She scrunches her nose. "Although I think it's totally ridiculous to host a dance on a *Thursday*. After partying all night, they really expect us to get up and go to school? Idiots!"

"I think that's exactly what they want, yes."

When I was at the dance yesterday, I noticed the way teachers were keeping the girls from flocking to Dutch, Zane and Finn.

Since the teenaged pregnancy rate is so high in our neighborhood and young girls are constantly dropping out of school, the board must be doing everything they can to keep the kids on the straight and narrow.

"So..." Viola looks up with a wickedly mischievous grin.

"So what?" I shoo her away to continue ironing.

She plops on my bed and props her hip up in a sexy pose. "How does it feel to have not one, but *two* boys chasing you?"

"What are you talking about?" I laugh.

"Hunter is so much cuter and nicer in person. Admit it. He was into you."

I think back to our short conversation at the dance yesterday. Hunter's brown eyes were warm as we both laughed over how I'd DM'd him the day he took a detox from social media.

"He was not," I insist.

"Then why did he offer to drop us home?" Viola undoes her bun and runs her fingers through her dark hair.

"Because it's on the way," I tell her.

"I know for a fact that it is *not* on the way," Viola argues. "And he barely spoke a word to either me or his brother. He was just staring at you the entire ride." She nudges my hip with her foot. "And you liked it."

"It's called being polite."

"You didn't have to accept his ride," my sister shoots back.

"Yes, I did."

There was no way I could get back in a vehicle with Dutch after playing together.

"Well, if you don't like Hunter... do you like Dutch?"

I almost burn my hand with the iron. It's only my quick reflexes that cause me to jump out of the way when the hot plate teeters off the board.

Viola shrieks. "Cadey, are you okay?"

"I'm fine." I brush my hair behind my ear and stoop to pick up the iron. Thankfully, it's not broken.

"Breeze thought you two were dating."

"I talked to Breeze and cleared that up." Before we left the dance, I took my best friend aside and explained as much of the situation as I could. She swore she wouldn't forgive me for not telling her I was 'friends' with The Kings, but eventually we hugged it out.

Breeze still has no clue about Dutch tormenting me. And she doesn't know about me toying with him as my alter ego either. I'm not telling her all that until I have to.

"No, I don't like Dutch."

At least not the Dutch that got Mulliez kicked out.

Or insinuated that I was sleeping with a teacher.

Or ruined my locker, destroyed my keyboard, and treated me like absolute crap.

But the Dutch that stood up for me in the cafeteria and pushed me to face my fears is... well, a different story.

I'm not *against* that Dutch.

I'd actually like to see more of that Dutch around.

"Oooh. Are you thinking about him right now?" my sister teases.

"You're distracting me." I shoo Viola out of the room. "Go get ready for school."

"Fine. But for what it's worth, I'm Team Dutch."

My eyes bug. "You don't even know him."

"I know he kept looking at you when he was playing yesterday. And you were looking at him too."

My mouth opens and falls shut.

"I know he's the one who helped you get over your stage fright."

"That's... it's not what you think."

"I like him," Viola says again. "But what matters more is that you like him too." She smiles at me and then starts singing, "*Dutch and Cadey sitting in a tree...*"

I grab a pillow and aim it at her head.

The door squeezes shut before it can get to her and my sister's maniacal laughter rings through the house.

Still no message from Dutch.

I open my locker and reach for my textbooks. Glancing

over my shoulder, I check both ways, wondering if Dutch has gotten to school yet.

"What are you looking for?"

"Ah!" I yelp and turn to face a smiling Serena. "You scared me."

"Sorry." She tosses her black hair. Today, her face make-up's a little lighter than usual, but she smeared her thin lips in black. The motorcycle jacket's back along with the school blouse and skirt.

"You look nice." Serena bumps me with her hip.

"Uh, thanks." Before I left this morning, Viola insisted on doing my make up.

'You've got two guys trying to get with you. You're popular now. You can't be running around without eyeliner.'

I forced her to keep it light, but I do kind of look nice.

"I heard you shredded it with The Kings yesterday."

"Let me guess. Someone texted Jinx for information?" I sigh.

"No." She snorts. "It was all over social media. The Kings have their own hashtag you know."

"Oh."

"How does it feel to be the newest member of the band?"

"I'm not the newest member."

"Aren't you?" She drops an arm around my shoulder. "I thought you were Sol's replacement."

"Sol? Who's Sol?"

"The only guy allowed to sit with the Cross brothers during lunch. He quit Redwood at the end of junior year though. No one knows why, although some say it's because he got kicked out the Cross brothers' good graces for not being rich enough." She lifts a hand and says, "And before you ask, no. I haven't asked Jinx. That was just a rumor too."

"What's up with that Jinx thing anyway," I ask, thinking of all the texts she's sent. She hasn't let up at all.

"No one really knows. She buys and sells secrets. Sometimes, if she's feeling nice, she gives out secrets for free." Serena's eyes sparkle. "But we all know one thing for sure. If Jinx gets in touch with you, it means your life is about to be insane."

I frown at her explanation.

Just then, I see Dutch entering the hallway. As usual, Zane and Finn flank him on either side. Today, he's wearing a hoodie up over his face.

Immediately, I sense that something's wrong. His eyes are darker than usual—less amber suns and more of a solar eclipse. His steps aren't measured. They're heavier, more urgent. Like he's a mercenary, marching to eliminate his next target.

I can't put a melody to it.

The crowd makes way for them, but I remain in place.

Dutch catches sight of me and, for a second, it feels like I can't breathe. Then he drags his gaze away and keeps walking right past me as if I don't even exist.

Zane and Finn give me pitying glances, but they don't talk to me either.

My heart cracks, but I force the hurt off my face. After last night, it felt like we'd come to some sort of understanding but, obviously, I was wrong.

"I guess you're not Sol's replacement after all," Serena says woodenly.

A melody blasts from the speakers in the hallway.

It's time to get to class.

"You okay?" Serena asks.

I nod absently. "Yeah, I'll see you later."

I wrap my fingers more tightly around my books and put one foot in front of the other. Dutch can pull a cold-shoulder all he wants. I mean nothing to him. And from now on, I'm going to make it clear that the feeling is mutual.

Chapter Twenty-Four

CADENCE

My goal to get over whatever weird thing was happening between me and Dutch is tested at lunch.

"You want *me* to come to your party?" I gawk, staring at the invitation.

"People actually give out paper invitations these days?" Serena asks.

We're seated around our usual tree on the Redwood Prep lawn. The guy in front of me is a football jock with a nice smile, dark skin and bright hazel eyes.

"It's a retro party." He nods at the typewriter script on the page. "It should be fun."

"Uh... I'm not really the party type," I admit.

"Anyone who hangs with The Kings is the party type." He winks. "Besides, I think you're cool and I'd like to see you there."

"Oh."

With another camera-ready smile, he walks off.

I blink in confusion. "What just happened?"

"You got flirted with, for one. Second, you got your first official invite to a Babe Gordon party." Serena actually sounds excited. Which is rare for her since she views everything with a pessimistic lens.

"Okay, but *why?*"

"Probably because Dutch dissed you this morning." She points at the leftovers that I packed this morning. I stole some finger food from the dance so I could save money on my meal card.

"You gonna eat that?" she asks.

"No..." Before I can finish, Serena snatches my plate from me and inhales it.

I laugh. "Slow down."

"Sorry." She sets the dish down and licks her lips. "Why do you think Jinx has so much power? Our school runs on secrets and scandal. Ever since that tension-filled moment in the hallway, people have been whispering that you and Dutch broke up. You're free game now."

"We were never together," I grumble.

"Doesn't matter. In their minds, you were with the god of Redwood Prep. And since he was close enough with you to let you play in their band yesterday, people are assuming you're the one who rejected *him.*"

"Do people have nothing better to do than gossip?"

"Rich people? No." She shakes her head.

I slide the invitation toward her. "You want it?"

"Only if you come with me." She pouts. "I have a pair of vintage pilot pants that I got at a thrift store and I haven't found a place to wear it yet."

I look over her dark eyeliner and black lips. "You'd really go to a party? Voluntarily."

"You think I can't?"

"No, I mean..." I frown. "I don't mean to offend."

"You didn't." She laughs. "I go for free food and drinks. Duh."

I laugh.

Serena grins at me. "Have you ever *been* to a rich people party?"

"Not really." Breeze was always hopping from one rager to another, but I doubt our neighborhood parties are anything like a Redwood Prep bash.

"I've been to a few. I always take plastic containers and empty water bottles. If I organize well, I can have bomb lunches for an entire week."

"Serena..."

"Hm?" She licks her fingers.

I want to ask her why she never has food for lunch, but I decide not to go there. We're friends who hang out, but we haven't gone that deep yet.

"Nothing."

She grabs my hand. "You'll come with me, right?"

"Just to get some food and go?"

"Absolutely. Did you think I'd actually spend time there?" She sticks out her tongue as if it's a disgusting thought. "I've been with these snobs for four years. They only get more obnoxious when they're drunk."

I think about it. I have the night off anyway and I was planning to spend it with Breeze. But I know my best friend would kill me if I didn't take an opportunity like this.

"Okay."

"Yay!"

"Just in and out, right?" I clarify.

"Just in and out."

* * *

I regret it the moment Serena slows her beat-up motorcycle in front of a mansion. Lights are on in every window. Music's blasting. People are spilling out of the front lawn holding red cups.

They're all dressed beautifully in retro hairstyles and dresses. The guys are in oversized tuxedo jackets. The girls are wearing boa feathers and long gloves.

"I'm starting to regret not putting more into my costume." I look down at the silver dress that Dutch bought me. I'm wearing it because I have literally nothing better in my closet. I paired it with a fake ostrich feather coat that I borrowed from Viola's closet. I'm also wearing a headband across my forehead.

"Oh, no one will notice." Serena waves me off. "We're not here to stay anyway."

"That's easy for you to say," I mumble. "You look incredible."

She's wearing a fluttery pirate shirt with her vintage pants. Her hair's in a bob and long pearl necklaces fall to her chest.

"Thanks." She fluffs her hair. "Now let's go."

She drags me into the house.

It's surprisingly chill given the volume of the music. Most of the students are either dancing, standing around talking or drinking in the kitchen.

We walk deeper in. My eyes jump from the vaulted ceilings to the expensive paintings to the lit up pool through the glass balcony. The only thing more dazzling than the decor are the costumes. I have to give it to the rich kids, they know how to dress for a themed party.

"You ready?" Serena grins and holds up her giant purse. Inside are empty food containers.

I start to nod but freeze when I spot Christa and her

dance minions in the kitchen. We haven't crossed paths since she crowded me in the hallway. She's been out of school 'recovering' from her split lip.

If she sees me tonight, I know she'll make trouble. Her minions have been snarling at me every time we pass in the hallway.

I have a feeling they've been holding off on their retribution because of Dutch. Since he told off that jock in the cafeteria, people have been keeping their distance. But now that everyone thinks I dumped him, I'm free game.

"What's wrong?" Serena asks.

"I think I'm going to wait outside," I tell her.

"Outside? Why?" she yells to be heard over the music.

I jut my chin in the cheerleaders' direction.

"Oh." She bobs her head in understanding. "I'll come find you."

While I'm weaving through the dancers in the living room to get as far away from Christa as possible, I feel a hand on my arm.

It's Babe.

"Hey, you look great," he says in my ear.

"Thanks." My first instinct is to brush his hands off me, but I stop myself. I'm squarely in the 'try something new' mindset tonight. It's step two of my plan to burn whatever stupid bridge I thought I'd built with Dutch.

"You look good too," I add, leaning in close.

He really does. His hair's combed out into a big afro and he's wearing shiny disco clothes.

"Thanks." He does a little turn and shows of his sparkly jacket.

I smile because his grin is infectious. He really is cute.

"Wanna dance?"

I shake my head. "I don't know. I don't really..."

But he's already leading me to the dance floor. "Come on. You know you wanna dance."

What the hell. We only live once, right?

I follow him without protest, glad that he takes me into the middle of the crowd so it doesn't feel like everyone is watching me.

The music has a funky beat and the singer croons about 'good loving'. It's not what I usually listen to, but I appreciate music in all its forms.

Bobbing my head, I let my body move to the beat.

"That's it, girl." Babe encourages me when I start to feel a little stupid.

He does a Micheal Jackson move, complete with a leg kick.

I laugh and we come together again. Babe places his hand on my hips and it doesn't feel uncomfortable.

I sway my body from side to side and he dances right against me, matching me rhythm for rhythm. When the beat gets faster, I move my fingers, mimicking the notes as if a piano's in front of me.

Wow.

This is actually fun.

I turn around to tell him that when Babe's face stiffens. He drops his hands from around my hips as if I'm poison.

Stunned, I look in the direction he's staring in and see Dutch glaring at us. He's got a cup of beer in his hand, but he's not drinking from it. In fact, he looks a few seconds away from splashing it in our faces.

My fingers curl tighter around Babe's hands. I raise my chin in defiance. "Don't worry about him."

"Sorry, sweetheart. You're not worth getting mixed up with The Kings."

Well damn him.

THE DARKEST NOTE

I refuse to stop enjoying myself even when Babe slinks away to go grind against some other brunette. My reason for coming to this party was to take a whole bunch of food back home to Viola but now? My mission has changed. I'm going to have a great time on this dance floor and I'm not going to leave until I'm good and ready.

I give Dutch my back and keep dancing. Whether I look crazy or not dancing by myself, I don't care. Music is in my blood and I might not be the greatest dancer in the world, but I understand rhythm and I understand a brush off when I see one. I hope Dutch does too.

I hear his heavy footsteps padding toward me even above the music. My body coils with tension as I imagine him glaring a hole in my back.

Everyone in the crowd backs away, watching and whispering. I stop dancing as exuberantly because I'm pretty sure I look like an idiot at this point.

Dutch bends over and whispers in my ear, "Come with me."

Heat spreads up my neck and face. I probably look redder than a tomato right now.

We're close. Way too close. My senses are overwhelmed by him. The subtle spice in his cologne, the heat of his body, the sound of his gravelly voice—it all goes straight to my chest.

The music from the speakers shifts to a souls song and I feel the tension in Dutch's body tighten.

He grabs my arm. "That's not a request, Brahms.'

"In case you haven't noticed, I'm busy. So screw off."

Gasps go up from the crowd.

I glance up and see Dutch clenching his jaw. He nods once and marches back to where he was standing. His brothers are there, both of them watching with conflicted expressions.

Dutch shoves his cup at Zane. When he turns around and faces me, his expression is thunderous. I shiver in fear. He looks *pissed*.

My alarm bells start ringing and I back up a step.

Dutch goes straight for me.

My heart bucks when I read his intentions.

"Don't you dare, Dutch."

But I might as well have saved my breath. The big oaf catches me by the arms and bends at the knees. I'm up and over his shoulder in less than a blink. The party goes completely silent except for the singer crooning from the speakers.

I squirm, trying to right myself. After being turned over his shoulder so many times, you'd think I'd have found a way to straighten up by now.

At least I'm not wearing a Redwood Prep skirt and flashing my butt cheeks at everyone tonight.

As we're passing the kitchen, Serena stumbles out holding two plates full of wings. Her eyes bug and she looks torn between wanting to save me and wanting to go nowhere near this mess.

I wave her away, knowing better than anyone that she shouldn't get into Dutch's path right now. His sick, twisted mind might try to get revenge on her and I don't want my friends in the crosshairs of this war.

Dutch carts me up to the second floor, kicks a bedroom door open and barges in.

The two people currently occupied on the bed squeal and try to cover themselves up.

"Get. Out."

Two naked blurs streak past us, carrying their clothes

and shoes with them.

Dutch kicks the door shut with his boot and throws me unceremoniously on the bed.

I squeal like he tossed me into a tub full of live octopi. Ew. I know *exactly* what was going on in this bed a second ago and I don't want any of it touching my skin.

Fuming, I pop to my feet. "Who the hell do you think you are?"

"Don't you remember, Brahms? As long as you're at Redwood Prep, you belong to me."

"I belong to *no one*."

"That's where you're wrong, *Cadey*." His amber eyes are glowing. "You. Belong. To. Me."

"Sorry to burst your sadistic little bubble, Dutch, but I'm not your property. You don't get to just," my voice climbs as my temper explodes, "boss me around."

"That's exactly what I can and will do," he says stiffly.

"What the hell do you want from me?" I surge toward him. "You've been icing me out all day and then you get pissed off when you see me dancing with someone else? Choose a freaking side and stick to it!"

His brow tenses. Dutch is usually so good at holding in his emotions, but I can see it all bubbling right under the surface tonight. He's not just angry. He's seething with it. A rage so dark and turbulent it can't be controlled. It's like a part of him is coming unhinged.

I should be scared. He's big enough and strong enough, to break me in half. But I realize something when I see his emotions laid bare.

He's fallible.

Vulnerable.

Human.

He's fighting with me, yeah, but he's really fighting

with himself. The scars are all over him from the vein bulging out of his neck to the flare of his nostrils.

He's not the cocky god of Redwood Prep.

He's like me, torn up and conflicted and broken as hell.

I smile and it seems to set off a flame in him. His stormy gaze locks on me. "You think this is funny?"

"I think you're pathetic," I spit.

His lips press together, flattening into thin lines.

"You act like you own all of Redwood Prep, but you're so afraid of me. So afraid to tell me what I did to you. Why do you hate me so much?"

He turns away, his jaw flexing.

"Do you really think you're impressive for tormenting someone like me? You run around making my life hell and for what? What could a poor girl like me possibly have that the big bad wolf of Redwood Prep has to take from her?"

He grabs me by the shoulders and drags me close to him. I can feel his heartbeat banging against his chest.

"You know what I want," he grinds out.

My eyes fall on his lips. There's something more behind his obsession with kicking me out of Redwood Prep. I can feel it.

"Why do you need me gone?" I whisper intently.

Instead of answering, Dutch stares me down. His eyes are tormented. It's like I'm watching him being torn in two.

I press up on my tiptoes, my lips an inch away from his. "Tell me, Dutch."

He growls low in his throat.

The heat between us isn't unfamiliar to me, but it's different tonight. The temperatures are rising, slow, steady, like the notes before the climax of a song.

My breathing deepens when Dutch steps closer to me, penetrating my personal space. "Stop testing me, Cadey."

I'm so caught up in him that it takes me a second to realize I've got my hands under his shirt. He captures my wrist, his jaw flexing.

I've felt this surge of desire before—in the dressing room when he kissed me and when we had that moment in the coffee room. Both times, I was able to pull myself back, but I don't know if I can now.

Dutch looks like a bad decision in the making. His shirt is black and so are his pants. He's darkness in motion, imposing and yet incredibly magnetic. When he watches me, it feels like I'm naked. Like there's nothing I could hide from his eyes.

This connection, in all its pulsing brokenness and sharp edges, is what I want. Just like the music that filled me when I was downstairs, I may not have experienced it before, but it's familiar to me. To my body. To my soul.

I crave it.

More of it.

My skin comes alive as I feel Dutch's strong fingers sliding beneath my coat and slipping it down my arms. Fake feathers tickle and caress my skin before pooling into a puddle at my ankles.

Still watching me, Dutch presses a hand against the small of my back. Silk meets hot flesh and a surge of air hits the back of my lungs. He draws me close in a rough motion, smashing me into his sculpted body.

"Why are you wearing this dress?" It's not a question so much as it is a berating.

I don't have time to think about an answer when his lips drift on top of mine. The heat inside me swells, throbbing with its own pulse and sending signals of desire through my body.

I slide my hands around his waist and push into his

back, nudging him closer to me. Close enough that I can feel *everything*.

It's new and thrilling. I've never let any boy as close I let Dutch get to me. We're breathing each other in, drowning in each other. There's not enough oxygen to stay alive.

The song from downstairs crawls beneath the slit in the door, filling the room with a sensual rhythm. I lap at his mouth, wanting to taste more of him.

This kiss is different than the one we had in the changing room.

That time, I wasn't myself—my *real* self.

And Dutch was gentle with her. The other me.

Tonight, he's not. He's pushing up my dress and rubbing his hands all over me. Then he's squeezing me. Hard. I moan and he growls at me before dragging the sleeves of my dress down my shoulder and sliding his tongue across my chest.

I dig my fingers into his shoulders. Hot, desperate sensations whip through me, too fast for me to contain. Too much for me to handle.

His name falls out of my lips and he surges up, smashing my head into the wall with the force of his kiss. Maybe I see stars. Or maybe I hear fireworks. I don't know. I just kiss him deeper and he sucks at my bottom lip, making my knees buckle.

Without warning, Dutch picks me up and drops me on top of the vanity mirror. His lips don't leave mine for a second.

I'm already too far gone to stop this. I slipped off the edge of the cliff long ago. Now, I can only fall, waiting for the inevitable, painful crash to the bottom.

Only it's not painful. The fingers that land on me leave

prickles of pleasure everywhere they touch. His caress is hot and patient as he palms my inner thighs.

My heart is hammering against my ribs. I push my legs further apart. I've never slept with anyone before. Never went past second base. But if Dutch stops touching me, I think I might die.

"Dutch," I moan.

His eyes suddenly burst open and he looks down at my face as if searching for something. When he doesn't find it, the beast that never strays too far rises from the depths, right before my eyes. His icy expression returns and he pulls his hands back just as they were about to...

"Damn." He curses. "I've had enough of you in my head." He backs away from me, his shoulders tense. "I've had enough of you in my school. I've had enough of you at Redwood, Brahms."

I quickly close my legs, ashamed at the need that's burning in me even now, beneath his fiery disdain. Beating out those flames with a quick stomp, I jump off the dresser and glare at him.

"Bastard." I adjust the straps of my dress and stalk across the room. Humiliated tears are burning in my eyes and I don't want him to see.

"Stop."

I don't want to, but my legs freeze on command.

Dutch stomps in front of me. His eyes are still dark with desire and one look at his pants tells me fighting is the last thing he wants to do right now.

I don't know if I'm glad he stopped us or if I should have barreled on and got it out of the way. I only know he drives me crazy and I want him out of my head just as much as he wants me out of his.

Dutch whips a check from his back pocket. It's got a crazy number of zeroes on it and my eyes bug.

"What the hell is this?"

"It's yours," he says darkly. "Not only that. I talked to a friend of my dad's. Once you leave Redwood, you can enroll at a new school."

"Is this what I think it is?" I scoff. "Are you trying to pay me off, right now?"

Dutch scowls at a point just above my head. "I know your situation, Cadey. I talked to your sister—"

I grit my teeth. "You talked to my sister?"

A dangerous feeling builds in the middle of my chest—warning me that I'm on the verge of committing murder.

"You need this money. I know you do. Your pride isn't worth proving a point to me." He lets out a breath, his chiseled jaw clenching and unclenching.

"I hate you."

His eyes burn. "Is that why you were whimpering my name three seconds ago?"

A crazed laugh pours past my lips as it all starts to kick into place. "So that was the plan, right? Lure me up here to take my dress off for you? Have some fun with me before you pay me off?"

He turns around and gives me his back. "Everyone has a price. People like you *always* have a price."

His words set off my anger.

"Because I'm *poor*, you think I'm desperate enough to let you screw me and then accept your money?" I arch both eyebrows. "Who the hell do you think you are?"

"Cadey."

"Don't freaking call me *Cadey!*"

"I don't know what kind of fantasy you've built in your

head about me, but I'm not some freaking Prince Charming."

"No, you're the villain."

And I'm an idiot.

The biggest one on the planet.

Silence falls as we glare at each other.

My chest swells and contracts.

His eyes dip there and he forcibly glances away.

"Even if I screwed you tonight, it wouldn't have meant anything," Dutch says as if he needs to clarify to himself more than me. He turns around to face me. "I'm trying to end this before it gets worse. Believe it or not, this is mercy."

I want to take off my heels and bludgeon his head with it. Show him what this mercy feels like.

Stalking up to him, I hiss, "You can take your money and shove it. I'm not leaving Redwood Prep. Ever."

His eyes narrow on me.

I wrench the door open and stalk out, leaving my shredded heart and my stupidity behind.

Jinx: Trade a secret for a secret. Want to tell me what happened between you and Dutch at the party tonight? Inquiring minds want to know. Be careful with your silence, Cadence. If you don't get ahead of the story, the story will crush you.

Chapter Twenty-Five

DUTCH

I grip the headboard as it slams hard and fast into the wall. Every thud is louder than Zane's drum when he's mid-solo.

I'm surprised the headboard doesn't crack the plaster, and while I should be more engaged with the girl who's currently under me, making faces that shows she's having a real good time, my thoughts are stuck on the strength of the wall grout, so I don't think about the girl who's really on my mind.

Or girls. Plural.

Because I've got a freaking bug for the both of them.

Whatever the hell that means.

"Your turn, Dutch," Christa murmurs. I glance down and try not to cringe. Her bottom lip has a big stitch in it, which hasn't stopped her performance at all. At least so the rumors have said.

I should be excited about finding out for myself, but I'm not.

Just a few minutes ago, Cadence was in here screaming bloody murder at me.

And a few minutes before that, she was whimpering my name like a damn tease.

Maybe it was a bad idea to bring Christa into the same room.

"I'm done."

Stunned eyes meet mine. "But..."

"Out. Now."

She goes still.

"Do I need to repeat myself?" I growl.

Christa rolls to a sitting position. I found out earlier that her lips aren't the only fake things about her. The two giant melons currently rolling around her chest snag my attention.

I couldn't care less about them.

She scoffs. "What the hell is wrong with you?"

I glower at her.

"You're no fun anymore!" She pouts and it draws my eyes even more to her stitched-up mouth.

"You want to have fun? Go downstairs."

The party's in full swing. The music's changed to a disco track and drunken whoops are rising all the way to the second floor.

"Dutch." Christa crawls on the bed toward me like something out of a horror movie.

I glare at her. She must have the memory of a fish. Did she conveniently forget my instruction to get the hell out?

"You're never like this." Christa drags her manicured nails over my chest.

That much is true.

I don't punk out on a good game.

Which tells me that Cadence has me more messed up in the head than I'd thought.

Damn.

I scrub a hand over my face. When I saw her on the dance floor, something inside me went dark. I hauled her upstairs to give her the money. I told myself I wasn't going to kiss her. Wasn't going to touch her. Guess what? I kissed her. I touched her. And I wanted more.

But I can't. She's a distraction. And the longer she's around, the more it hurts the people I care about.

It's bad enough that while Sol was in the freaking slammer, I was traipsing through Redwood Prep, backing Cadence up against coffee machines and worrying about her stage fright. Now that I know how desperate his situation is, I can't hold back anymore.

It's why I didn't chase her when she stalked out of the party tonight. It's why I didn't turn Christa away when she latched on to me downstairs, rubbed herself all over my jeans and whispered that we should go somewhere private.

I thought I could screw Cadence out of my system. But every time I close my eyes, it's her face that's tattooed behind my eyelids.

Not Redhead's.

Not Christa's.

Hers.

I'm royally screwed.

"You can't seriously be into that scholarship kid." Christa gapes.

Damn. If she won't leave, then I will.

Sliding off the bed, I grab my jeans and step into them. Christa watches angrily, her arms crossed and her head twisted to the side. She looks like a toddler throwing a tantrum.

"You'll regret this, Dutch," Christa warns.

Hell, I already do.

I walk down the stairs and out to the pool. Girls in bikinis are playing chicken, squealing and laughing. The splash of water is louder than the music.

"That was fast," Zane teases, a grin on his face. Two girls are nestled in on either side of him. He's cupping one between the thighs and the other is practically licking his ear off.

Finn is in the pool 'teaching' a girl how to swim. It looks more like she's grinding against him underwater though.

I grab the beer my twin offers and chug it back.

"How was Christa?" Zane, nosey as he is, interrogates me. "Did all the," he gestures to his mouth, "fillers make a difference?"

"Not really," I growl.

"Bummer." He shakes his head and sighs.

Through the balcony doors, I see Babe—the host of this party—with his tongue deep in some girl's throat. That girl isn't Cadence, but it still pisses me off.

The way he was grinding all over Cadence tonight made me see red. She looked like she was enjoying herself. Her expression was one I'd never seen on her before and the fact that she was looking like that *with him* made me act without thinking.

I'm glad my reputation precedes me. If the jock hadn't backed off on the dance floor, I would have given him a reason to.

Something about her makes me break all my rules.

Zane glances in the direction I'm watching and smirks. "He and Cadey looked good together. Maybe we should let *him* talk to her next time. They seemed to have hit it off."

I stare him down, my expression alone daring him to say one more word.

Finn climbs out of the water to join us. I toss him a towel and he accepts it with a nod of thanks.

Zane kisses each of the girls on the mouth and then shoos them away. When we're alone, he leans forward. "What are we going to do now? We've only got a couple days to save Sol."

I glare at the hills in the distance.

Finn rakes a hand through his hair roughly.

I don't have an answer that they'll want to hear. "We're going to have to turn it up a notch."

Finn flashes me a worried look.

Zane looks uneasy.

It's not like we have a choice. What's the freaking alternative? Let Sol rot in that boot camp while Cadence skips around, unhindered, at Redwood?

"My loyalty is to Sol, always. But you heard about her home situation," Zane says. "Her mom was screwed up in life and she's probably left even more of a mess in death. After Viola dropped those hints, I did some digging. You don't want to know the kind of people her mom was getting involved with before she died."

"Maybe we should stop here," Finn says.

I hear the plea in his voice for me to not cross any lines.

But I shake my head. "If she was smart, she should have taken the money. She's being stubborn now. We've got no choice but to get more drastic."

Finn scowls at me. "She probably didn't want to take the money from you." He frowns. "I told you we should have sent Zane to talk to her instead."

"That was the plan until our resident caveman here backed her upstairs." Zane rolls his eyes at me.

"I saw an opportunity and went for it."

"Nah." Zane takes a sip of his beer. "You saw another man touching her and you lost it. There's a difference."

I hate that he can see right through me.

"You guys have any bright ideas then?" I snap.

"We keep trying with Principal Harris," Zane says. "Get dad involved if we have to."

"We burned that bridge." I sneer.

"Which one?" Finn asks.

"Both of them. If they see we're desperate, they're going to give us the run-around on purpose."

My brothers go quiet again.

I tap my fingers on the arm of the beach chair. Cadence's eyes when she told me off tonight are burned into my head. I have no freaking clue when she started getting to me, but it's in a different way than Redhead.

I willingly gave that pianist a piece of me. With Brahms, I didn't want her to barge in. Didn't ask for it. I'm fighting it with every breath in my body. Every muscle, every nerve. Every vein.

I slouch low in my seat. My brothers' anxiety is feeding into my own. I hate that we don't all agree about how to handle this. But I can't let their fears or my own emotions shake me.

I owe my loyalty to Sol. His sadness was palpable that night. He got entangled in a situation that wasn't his own doing and yet he took the rap for it. He's the one suffering all the consequences.

I need to get him out of there.

No one is getting in the way of that. No matter how much I want her.

"We don't have time to deliberate this," I tell my brothers. "She needs to get a cold hard brush of reality. Quick."

Finn gives me a sobering look.

I arch an eyebrow. "Are we in agreement?"

Zane glances at the ground.

Finn pulls his lips in.

"It doesn't matter if we are." I push to my feet. "I'll handle it one way or another."

Sympathy has no place in this war. My brothers might have fallen for Brahms's spell, but if I'm the only one standing, so be it.

I'll burn it all down to end this.

Even if I that means I have to burn myself down with her.

Chapter Twenty-Six

CADENCE

A note slips out of my locker at school on Monday.

Meet me at the pool before first period.

It's in a masculine scrawl and it's signed simply 'Dutch'.

I glance around, looking to see if he's watching. Weird. Leaving a note in my locker isn't usually Dutch's style. He'd either text me or show up out of nowhere and cart me over his shoulder like a Neanderthal.

Pulling out my phone, I shoot him a text.

Why do you want to meet me at the pool?

There's no response.

The smartest thing would be to totally ignore this message, but I have a feeling that if I do, whatever revenge Dutch is planning will be ten times bigger and ten times more public.

The school is already buzzing thanks to him dragging me up to the second floor at the party. I don't even want to know what kind of rumors are going around about us now.

Best to deal with him away from prying eyes so this madness ends quietly.

The pool is all the way on the opposite end of the school where the football field and gym are located. The hallway is empty when I pass by.

My footsteps thud. It feels like my breath is bouncing off the walls. I wonder where everyone is until I notice an under construction sign.

That explains it.

As I approach the pool, alarm bells start ringing in my head. I never learned to swim, so I keep a healthy distance from this death trap.

Giving the water a wide berth, I glance around. Pale blue reflections dance on the walls. The bleachers are empty and a fine hint of dust lingers in the air. Dutch is nowhere to be seen.

I turn in a circle. Something doesn't feel right. Deciding to listen to the voice screaming in my head this time, I don't linger.

I take a step toward the door when a shuffling sound comes from behind me. Before I can turn around, two hands slam into my back. I scream and tumble forward.

On instinct, I throw my arms out, struggling to keep upright.

But I can't regain my balance.

I hit the water with a smack, sinking fast. Panic fills my body. I claw my arms through the water, fighting to reach the surface.

My kicking and thrashing produces a ton of bubbles, but it doesn't push me up. Instead, it feels like I'm sinking faster.

Deeper.

Deeper.

I can't breathe.

My lungs are burning.

Save me. Someone save me.

But there's no one around. All the signs would keep people from even venturing near this place. I was the idiot who believed Dutch. I was the one who put myself in the middle of his dangerous game.

Please.

The fight in me starts to weaken. I'm feeling more and more exhausted. Although I'm putting all my effort into flailing my arms and legs, it's just not working.

The truth hits me in the face.

I'm going to die.

Here.

At Redwood.

Alone.

My only thought is of my sister and who will take care of her when I'm gone.

I'm sorry, Vi.

I wish I'd never come to Redwood.

Darkness steals over my vision, robbing me of my anger and the last of my breath.

DUTCH

"Move!" I yell, blasting through the crowd that's scattering in front of me. Kids turn and give me wide-eyed stares.

The hell?

Don't they understand the words coming out of my mouth?

"Out of the way!"

I sprint down the hallway, knocking aside anyone who's foolish enough to stay in my path. Hurling through the back door, I take a shortcut to the athletics area.

She has to be okay. She has to be okay.

It's the only line in my head.

I was driving to school when Cadence's text came in. At first, I thought it was a joke, but there was this feeling inside. Something telling me to check it out.

That's when a video of Cadence falling into the pool lit up my cell phone. Before I could even think about what I should do, I was already running like a maniac away from my brothers.

"Cadence!" I roar. My voice bangs against the wall and echoes back to me.

Without stopping, I pump my arms at my sides and dive straight into the water. The shock of cold hits my skin, but I barely feel any of it. Whipping around desperately, I freeze when I see Cadence still and floating in the deep end.

Her hair curls on top of her head as if a part of her is still reaching for the surface. Her eyes are closed and there are no bubbles coming out of her nose.

Damn it. Damn it.

Swimming over to her, I hook a hand around her stomach and propel us both back to the surface. I explode out of the water, taking a deep breath. Cadence's head lolls.

I don't think she's breathing.

Carrying her limp body to the edge, I set her down gently and jump out after her.

I set a finger under her nose. Only a shallow puff of air hits my skin.

She's barely breathing.

"Cadey. Come on. Wake up!" I push down on her chest,

calling on my faint memories of CPR that I did a few summers ago.

I hear the panic in my voice. It's bouncing against the walls like a game of ping pong. But screw it. I don't care what this fear deep in my stomach is saying about me, saying about what I feel for her.

I don't care about anything but seeing her big brown eyes open and knowing she's alright.

"Cadey. Wake up," I growl. "That's an order." Clipping her nose, I press my mouth to hers.

A moment later, she chokes up water.

I hold her upright, patting her back while she gets everything out. Her eyes are hazy and her skin is pale.

"Cadey, are you okay?"

She doesn't answer. Her body goes limp again and she falls into my chest.

That's not a good sign.

Footsteps thud in the distance. My brothers charge toward the pool. Their eyes bug when they see me, dripping wet and holding an equally drenched Cadence.

"What the hell happened?" Finn explodes.

"I'll explain later. I need to get her to the nurse."

"Here." Zane whips his jacket off and hands it over to me. "Her lips are blue. Her body might be going into thermal shock. You gotta keep her warm."

I snap the jacket from him and dip it around Cadence's shoulders. She's trembling. Even though her eyes are closed, her teeth chatter loudly.

Damn. It breaks my freaking heart.

"It's going to be okay," I whisper. Pushing my arms beneath her, I hoist her up from the cold tiles and cradle her limp body against my chest.

I almost slip when I run to the door. Recovering quickly, I keep up the pace and tear through the exits.

My brothers rush after me.

I don't speak to either of them. My fingers curl into Brahm's body, giving her as much warmth as I can while running like hell.

When I see the infirmary up ahead, I kick down the door.

The nurse yelps and shoots to her feet. I know how this must look. Me—soaked through to my skin. Cadence—covered in Zane's jacket, pale, blue and lifeless.

"She needs help!" I bark. Stalking across the room, I gently deposit Cadence on a hospital cot while, behind me, the nurse rushes into action.

"Stand back," she says, pushing me away so she can inspect Cadence.

I want to snap at her, tell her to work around me, but Finn grabs my arm. Zane takes the other.

My brothers physically restrain me so the nurse can rush around Cadence. When I keep staring, she pulls the curtain so I can't see anything.

"Shut up," Finn hisses in my ear before I can protest.

"Let her do her thing," Zane advises me.

I pace the length of the infirmary. It's a small space with a couple framed certificates on the wall. Fake plants line the desk. Sunshine bounces through cottage-like windows. It's way too freaking cheerful for what I'm feeling right now.

Zane sticks a hand into his pockets. He slides me a demanding look. "Was this you?"

"The hell?" I scowl. "Why would I arrange for her to drown and then save her?"

"Last Friday, you said you were going to get drastic," Zane recalls.

THE DARKEST NOTE

"Is this what you meant?" Finn hisses.

Both my brothers look at me like I've lost my mind.

I curl my fingers into fists. I've done some messed-up things, sure. I'm not going to deny that. I'm no saint. But I've never straight up tried to murder anyone.

Before any of us can say another word, the nurse whips the curtains aside. "She'll be okay."

The relief that sweeps over me almost collapses my chest.

"But she was very close to danger. If you hadn't rushed her here," her expression sobers, "it might have been a different story."

"Does she need to go to the hospital?" I ask urgently.

"Her body temperature is rising slowly. I'll give her something warm to drink when she wakes up. I'll keep monitoring her until then. You can all go to class now. There's nothing more you can do."

I stalk forward. "I need to see her."

"She needs rest—"

"I know that." My voice is rising and I cringe. Lowering my tone, I say, "I won't wake her up."

She purses her lips, thinks about it and then nods.

Finn and Zane gesture for me to go ahead.

"We'll wait out here," Finn says.

"Don't you have class?" the nurse insists.

Zane cranks out a smile that has her blushing. "Can you give us a minute more? We'll leave as soon as we're done here."

She clears her throat, still looking flustered. "Five minutes."

"Thank you so much," Zane says huskily.

I grip the curtain that's hiding Cadence from view. Just before wrenching it back, I hesitate.

What the hell is wrong with me?

I'm not supposed to be the dutiful hero of the story. I spent all weekend freaking plotting all the ways I could bring her doom. She's in my way. She's in *Sol's* way.

Maybe I should have left her in the water.

That thought alone is messed up. I don't deserve to pull aside the curtain, but I do anyway because I break all the damn rules, even if they're my own.

Cadence is lying flat on her back. Her hair's still wet and seeping into her pillow. There are several blankets piled on top of her. I note that her rose-bud lips are starting to return to their normal, pink color.

It's unnerving how beautiful she is even without makeup. Most girls pile it on, needing it for the confidence boost, needing a mask. I'm not against it. Redhead and her fiery red lips star in my dreams most nights... when Cadence isn't taking over the fantasy. But there's something about Cadey's fresh-faced beauty that makes her look innocent and fragile. Like something to be protected.

Something to be protected?

What. The. Hell.

I can't do this. I can't get soft on her. Not when the stakes are so high and the clock is counting down. We have less than ten days to get Sol back into Redwood.

Even if she's got a crappy mom and a tough home life, it's none of my business. She's not where she belongs. That much hasn't changed.

Despite the eloquent arguments, I still don't leave Brahm's makeshift room. Spying some towels on the shelf, I take one down and gently smooth it over her hair.

If the point is to keep her warm, then her head should be too.

I work quietly until most of the clumped strands are

dry. Then I lift her head, gently, and slide a fresh pillow beneath her.

When I return outside, I hear the nurse asking Zane, "Is there any family we can alert?"

"No," I growl out.

The nurse arches an eyebrow.

"Her mom died. Her younger sister shouldn't be worrying about this crap." My fingers flex and curl back into a fist.

"O... kay." She looks taken aback.

Zane chuckles, doing what he does best—smoothing over a tense moment with charm. "Could you let us know when she wakes up, beautiful? We'd really appreciate it."

"I'm supposed to contact her family only—"

"Just let us know," I cut in brusquely.

"We'd really appreciate it," Zane says, turning up the charm a few notches higher.

She gives him a tight nod.

When we leave, my brothers flank me on either side.

"Who do you think was behind this?" Finn asks, his arms swinging rigidly.

"Only one person would be this stupid." I fish out my phone from my pocket and show them the video. If it was just about Cadence, they wouldn't have sent a video. Someone wanted to make a point to me too."

"Christa," Zane hisses.

Finn clamps a hand on my shoulder, trying to stop my march down the hallway. "Let's go to the practice room. Figure out our next step."

"I already know what my next step is."

Zane looks worried. "What are you going to do?"

"Don't worry." I toss a cold glance over my shoulder. "All I'm going to do is talk."

"We'll come with you."

"Don't bother. I'll take the rap for this one alone." I jut my chin at the opposite hallway. "Principal Harris will be on our tail if all three of us miss any more classes. You two are late because of me. Don't give him another reason to screw us off."

Finn shakes his head.

Zane doesn't move a muscle either.

I huff and nudge my brothers in the opposite direction. "Go."

They leave reluctantly. I watch to make sure they're not going to double back and sneak up on me like they did at the pool. Even though I was grateful for the assist earlier, I really don't want them interfering this time.

Storming down the hallway, I stop in front of first period Lit. Miss Jamieson is at the white board, talking about Shakespeare. I knock on the door out of respect for her and then I barge in.

She stops talking abruptly. The big brown eyes that Zane took one look at and fell hard for blink up at me.

"Mr. Cross, can I help you?"

My eyes sweep the room until they land on Christa's smug face. She's wearing a pink shirt under her sweater vest and a stupid looking beret.

"The principal needs to see Christa," I say through gritted teeth.

Usually, I would just growl out what I want and most teachers wouldn't care enough to stop me.

But I know better than to try that with Miss Jamieson. Even if it did work, she probably wouldn't stick around Redwood Prep if she thought she'd lost the respect of her students. And then my twin would kill me.

"The principal?" Miss Jamieson raises both eyebrows, as if she's not sure she believes me.

I nod. "Yeah."

"Okay." She makes a go ahead gesture. "Christa, you may go."

Christa and her friends exchange knowing looks and giggles as she climbs to her feet. Grabbing her purse, she swings it at her side and follows me out the door.

"What's going on, Dutch?" she asks, but her voice is a little too giddy for the question to sound casual.

I say nothing.

We're still too close to the classrooms. I can feel Miss Jamieson's eyes on me through the windows. She's a smart lady and she likely smells my BS a mile away. It's probably why she was able to smell Zane's too.

Christa smirks up at me. "Enough walking, Dutch. What's so important that you would pull me out of class?"

I look both ways to make sure we're in the camera's blindspot. Then I whirl on her, unleashing the full breadth of my fury in a narrowed gaze.

"What *the hell* did you do?"

Christa's eyes widen and she shuffles back. "Dutch."

I show her my cell phone, trying hard to keep my cool. If Christa were a guy, I would have thrown a punch. But since a physical fight is out of the question, all I can do is warn her to never cross me again.

"What is that?" Her voice drags and she puts on an expression of fake concern. "Oh my gosh. Is Cadence okay?"

"I know you're the one responsible for this little show." I bend over her, keeping my voice low and calm. I've found that it's scarier when someone is emotionless than when they're loud and obnoxious.

I lost my cool with Cadence yesterday and she saw right through the anger to what I was trying to hide.

"Me?" Christa presses a hand into her chest.

"I know you're the one who sent the video."

"I didn't." Her eyelashes flutter so hard it's a miracle they're still attached to her face.

"No?" I nod brusquely. Pulling the cell phone back to me, I call the anonymous number that forwarded the video.

A phone rings from Christa's purse.

Her face drains of blood and her mouth opens in an 'o'.

I didn't think anyone could be that stupid, but I highly underestimated Christa.

When she realizes she's cornered, her expression crumbles and big, crocodile tears come to her eyes.

"Dutch, I don't know what came over me. I was just so mad and I wanted to scare her a little." She sobs.

"She almost *died*, Christa. You could have killed her."

Genuine horror fills her eyes. She latches onto my hand. "I didn't think she'd drown. I mean, who doesn't know how to swim? There are, like, thousands of ways to learn."

I bite down on my bottom lip to keep from unleashing my frustrations at her. She's not worth another second of my time.

Flinging Christa's hand off, I march away.

"Dutch." Christa launches at me and slides her arms around my waist, hugging me from the back.

"Let. Go."

"I can get her out of Redwood," she sputters desperately.

My entire body goes still.

"I've been talking to my dad. Wearing him down. You know he's the chairman of the board, right?"

When I still say nothing, Christa inches around me so

she's staring into my face. Her eyes are still shimmering from the tears. Mascara is running down her cheeks.

"If you say the word, Dutch, I'll call my dad. He's got the ear of everyone on the school board. I'll make up a reason to kick her out of Redwood Prep for good."

Chapter Twenty-Seven

CADENCE

"Are you okay? I haven't seen you around school lately," Serena mumbles. "At first, I thought you were just ditching me because of what happened at the party, and then I didn't see you the next day and I wondered if Dutch had finally run you out of Redwood."

I adjust the phone to my other ear while I stir a cup of hot tea. "No, I didn't get kicked out of Redwood."

She makes a sound of pure relief. "What happened then?"

I shrug the blanket tighter around myself and sink into the couch. "I got sick."

Turns out, getting shoved into a freezing pool and can weaken a body. After waking up in the nurses office, I found out I had a fever. She sent me to the hospital and by that time, the fever had turned into raging flu symptoms. I got a doctor's note saying I can't rejoin society for another three days.

"Oh my gosh. Are you okay?" Serena asks.

"I'm fine." I smile when Breeze emerges from the bathroom, sees me making my own tea and slants me a thunderous look.

My best friend stomps over to me and wrenches the cup from my hand. Pointing a finger at the couch, she mouths, "*Sit. Now.*"

I stick my tongue out at her but obediently take my seat.

Serena sighs. "You're being totally understanding, but I already prepared my speech so I'm going to go for it anyway."

I laugh softly and nestle into the corner of the couch, watching as Breeze brings a flu pill along with my tea.

"At Babe's party, I tried to follow you up the stairs. Zane and Finn were standing there like two bodyguards. They wouldn't even let people onto the second floor. I told them my friend was in there. They said Dutch would drop you home."

My eyes bug. I had no idea Zane and Finn were right outside the bedroom door. Did they hear us that night?

Heat flares in my cheeks. "It's okay. I, um, I got home okay."

She doesn't need to know that I was so ticked off, I walked almost a mile on my own before I realized I was completely lost. At that point, it took me another half-hour to hike to a bus stop. Apparently, buses don't run in neighborhoods as fancy as Babe's.

"So did you make up with Dutch? I heard he ran through the hallways holding you in his arms like he was shooting a scene from *The Notebook*." Serena laughs. "Are you two back to being the golden couple of Redwood?"

I hack out a cough, pretending that I'm choking on something.

She yelps. "Yikes, that sounds bad. I'll let you get some rest."

"Thanks. I'll see you at school later."

When I hang up, Breeze gives me a pointed look. "The old cough-hack maneuver. She fell for that?"

I accept the pill, set it on my tongue, and chase it back with the tea.

Breeze plops into the chair beside me, observing me intently.

"I appreciate you ditching school to take care of me," I say, shifting away from her. "But you really didn't have to."

"Yes, I did. You barely tell me anything anymore. Now that there's nowhere for you to run, I want to hear everything."

"Everything?"

"You think I buy that weak excuse you gave me at the dance? I *saw* the way Dutch watched you when you were talking to Hunter that night. He looked like he wanted to rip Hunter's head off."

"Trust me. If he wanted to rip someone's head off, he would've."

Breeze purses her lips. "Even the kids at Redwood are whispering about you two. Are you seriously going to keep lying to your best friend?"

I grab a pillow and pull at the tattered strings. She's right. I can't trust anyone if I can't trust Breeze. It's time I come clean.

"Dutch has been trying to kick me out of Redwood."

Her eyes bug. "*What?* Why?"

"I have no idea. He won't tell me."

"What's he done?"

I scrunch my nose. "Remember that scandal with the teacher a few weeks ago?"

"Yeah." She bobs her head.

I give her a pointed look.

She gasps loudly. "No! They were talking about you?"

"That's not the only thing. He destroyed my locker, my keyboard and..."

Breeze pounces out of her chair.

"Where are you going?" I call.

"To kill him. Duh!" She shoves up the sleeves of her shirt and turns toward the door.

I chase after her and drag her back to the couch. "Breeze. Wait."

"Why should I wait? Why is his head not on a freaking pike?" Color flushes her cheeks. Her voice trembles, but it's not because she's scared. It's because she's enraged. "Who the hell does she think he is to try and ruin your life?" A humorless laugh falls past her lips. "And here I thought he was such a catch for helping you with your stage fright. I didn't know it was an act."

"That's the thing." I chew on my bottom lip.

She whips her hair around, her eyes on fire. "What's the thing?"

"I don't... know if it was an act."

She frowns at me. "Explain that."

"I know this might sound crazy but... a few weeks ago, he stood up for me when this jock tried to shame me in front of everyone in the cafeteria. And when I got pushed into the pool, I heard that he was the one who saved me."

"Okay, so he's not a total douche. Are we forgiving him for everything he's done?"

"Of course not," I say vehemently. And then, less vehemently, I tack on, "But it's complicated."

She thinks about it and then nods. "You think a guy who likes you is going to treat you like crap? Sweetie, how many girls have we seen in our neighborhood who end up getting hurt thinking like that?"

My chest pangs in pain. "You're right. I know you're right. The thing is…. I should hate him. And I did. At the start, I wanted him to die a painful death, but now—"

"Now you're falling for him?"

"Absolutely not."

"Good." She sweeps her hand up my back. "Forget about, Dutch. He may be hot and rich… and gorgeous and talented…and—"

"Can you not?" I frown at her.

"But," she smiles, "you don't need a guy who swings hot and cold. Besides putting any kind of hope in Dutch *choosing* you out of all the harems of girls who fling themselves at him is just wishful thinking. You deserve a guy who's more down to earth. Someone who only has one or two girls after him, instead of a horde."

"Interesting way of thinking."

"So let's talk about Hunter." Breeze grins.

I groan. "Breeze, can you stop pushing Hunter at me?"

"Is it not clear that I'm Team Hunter by now?"

"I've *barely* spoken to him. And he's several years older than me."

"Age is just a number, honey. And you're not going to be a minor for much longer."

"Yeah, but—"

"I know for a fact that he wants to speak to you more often." She points at my phone. "Didn't you say he slid into your DMs?"

"All he said was 'hey'."

"Exactly! That's basically a love confession."

I roll my eyes. "Now you're just being ridiculous."

"I say forget about Dutch and move on to Hunter. The man gave you a punching bag." She shoves a hand at it. "A punching bag. If that's not boyfriend material, I don't know what is."

"You're right."

"So what are you going to do?" she asks.

"About what?"

"About Hunter?"

"I don't know."

"Text him back," she says, swatting me.

"Ow! Ow! I'm injured," I bawl out.

"Ooh. Sorry." She soothes my hand.

I sigh heavily. "Maybe I'll consider texting him back. Just to be friendly."

Breeze blows me a kiss. "Atta girl."

I smile as she fusses over my pillows and then turns on a movie. But my thoughts aren't on the rom-com. It's on a certain blond guitar player with a penchant for scowls and tattoos.

I know Breeze is right about Dutch being too difficult to deal with. And I know I should probably take her advice. Mom didn't turn into a raging drug-addicted narcissist overnight. She started by falling for the wrong guy at the wrong time.

But there are flashes of moments when Dutch doesn't seem like the wrong guy. Especially when he's goofing off with his brothers or charming old cafeteria ladies.

I think about the day he stepped in between me and the jock in the cafeteria. The day at the dance when I was able to have fun on stage, surrounded by an entire freshman class, just because he was by my side.

More than that, I saw flashes of the real him when he was with my other self.

After everything that's happened, I can't deny that there's something dangerously volatile between us.

Especially when I'm in costume and I can *feel* that he's interested in me.

Whether it's as myself or as someone else, Dutch is the one I keep running back to. And whether he cares to admit it or not, there's a part of him that keeps running back to me too.

One day, when we collide, it's going to destroy us both.

What scares the hell out of me is that I don't think either one of us will be able to stop it.

* * *

After the movie, Breeze leaves. As I'm walking her out, I notice a letter in our mail box.

My eyes bug when I take it inside and read it.

Behind on mortgage payments?

I blink and blink, waiting for the words to change.

They don't.

Sure that this must be some mistake, I call the bank to verify.

"It says here that a Mrs. Cooper withdrew the funds herself," the perky bank worker says.

A chill runs down my spine. I dig my fingers into the cell phone.

"Will there be anything else?" she chirps.

"No. Nothing else."

I sink into the couch, my head spinning. A feeling of dread slithers down my back.

Don't panic, Cadence.

First things first. I need to find a way to pay the bank. If not, Viola and I might be homeless. Rick only agreed to sign the guardianship papers because of mom's last request, but he won't take us in. Breeze doesn't have enough space for the both of us.

There's no way I'll allow my sister to sleep on the street. Throwing my blanket off, I throw on a pair of jeans, sneakers and a T-shirt and show up to the diner. It's so busy that the manager allows me to work my shift as long as I keep a mask on.

Later that night, I get a call from the lounge inviting me to do an impromptu event.

"It's in an hour. Do you think you can make it?"

"Yes, I'll be right there."

Viola comes home when I'm about to leave.

She takes one look at my outfit and frowns. "Why are you wearing the wig? Did you do your own makeup?"

"Yeah. Does it look okay?"

"I guess." She frowns. "Are you going to perform?"

I avoid her question. "There's a burger from the diner on the stove. You just have to microwave it." I hop on one foot and zip up my boots. "Make sure you do your homework before you play on your phone."

Viola grabs my hand. Her big brown eyes peer into mine. "Cadence, you're sick."

"Thanks, sis," I say dryly.

She frowns. "I meant physically ill. You shouldn't be going anywhere right now."

"I don't have time for this, Vi. I need to leave."

"No." She wraps her fingers around me.

"Vi, let go."

"You're going to work yourself to death if you keep going like this."

Her insistence is the match on my powder keg of a stress ball. After getting pushed into a pool, almost drowning, and, now, realizing that we're going to be evicted, I snap.

"Can't you see I'm doing this to take care of us!" I yell.

Hurt pools in her clear brown eyes.

I instantly regret snapping at her. My shoulders sag. I scrub my forehead with my hand. "Vi, I'm sorry. I shouldn't have yelled. I'm just... there's a lot going on."

"You think I don't know how hard you work? You think I'm not grateful?" She shrieks. "I'm just worried about you. There's only so much you can do, Cadey. Eventually, you're going to break and I couldn't survive that."

"Yes, you could. You're stronger than you think, Vi."

"No, I'm not," she insists. "Mom's gone and if you go too, I'm going to be all alone. I'd fall apart without you."

My heart twists painfully. I think about the letter in the mail and my call with the bank. There's so much at stake right now. I can't let her tears sway me.

"Vi," I swallow hard, "I'm feeling much better. You don't have to worry."

"The doctor said you should rest for three days. It has not been three days, Cadey. If you go out there and faint or something for a few bucks—"

"I won't faint. I really need this job and I really need to go, okay?"

She sucks her tears back in and nods.

I'm halfway to the door when I turn back. "And Vi?"

"Huh?"

"Lock the doors tight behind me. Don't open it for anyone."

"Why do you keep telling me that. I'm not a child," she huffs.

I think about the letter from the bank. "Not for anyone okay?"

"Okay."

Heart in my throat, I throw the door open and run down the stairs.

* * *

Jinx: How long are you going to resist me, New Girl? Or should I say Cadey? Redhead? A rose by so many names doth smell as sweet. Will your petals finally be plucked tonight?

Chapter Twenty-Eight

CADENCE

The last thing I expect to see at the pop up event is my brother, but Rick is circling around the stage wearing a black T-shirt with the words 'SECURITY' on it.

I duck my head, tugging on my red wig in case he recognizes me. It's a pretty futile adjustment.

It's not like I'm invisible. I'll be in front of him, playing the piano the entire time. At that point, there will be nowhere to run.

Still my heart thuds until I successfully sneak past and climb on stage.

The pop up event is being held in the park. Stars twinkle overhead and a gentle breeze teases my red hair. Out on the sprawling green lawn, the lounge places fancy tables and black chairs, inviting guests to sit and sample wine.

Gorge's has never done an event like this before and I'm a little surprised that they would call me in. The chef tends to hold grudges and he wasn't happy when I handed in my resignation letter. I was sure that my business relationship with the lounge was over.

My boots thud against the wooden steps. Behind me, string lights decorate a beautiful arch. It's fitted with vines and flowers in bloom. From the beautiful fragrance sailing to the piano, I'm sure those petals are real.

It's a beautiful set up. Well-thought out. So I'm not sure why Gorge's waited until the last minute to ask me to play. Maybe their hired pianist bailed?

I lift the case and set my hand on the black and white keys. The first note shatters the air around me. People who were in their own worlds get drawn into mine, lured by a sound that speaks to something in their souls.

I don't look up, but I can feel their inquisitive stares. It makes me antsy. I'm not in my element, here in the spotlight where the entire park can see and judge me, but I feel less nervous than usual.

My chin tilts higher as I shift to another note.

My heart is calm instead of beating like crazy.

Is it because of what happened at the homecoming dance with The Kings? I played the triangle in front of a crowd of fourteen-year-olds. Maybe it affected me more than I thought.

With a deep breath, I glance up.

And it doesn't freak me out.

I glance at the piano again and then look up again.

My stomach doesn't clench. In fact, it's a little exhilarating to see how much people are enjoying my music.

It's a victory. And after the week, no after the weeks that I've had, I needed one.

I'm okay.

For the first time since I can remember, I smile when I

play. My fingers run over the keys, dancing to a rhythm that no one else understands. I close my eyes and let it flow how it wants to.

Music welcomes me. Envelops me. It's a tide that sweeps over my entire body. Rough on the surface, fragile underneath.

I didn't have time to prepare a hip-hop backing track or plan a concert that flows smoothly. This is just me. My blood. My heart. My everything. Like I shoved a hand into my chest and pulled out my intestines.

When I'm done, I hear applause. The pop up event is alive with movement. Waiters dip in and out of tables. Couples of all ages sit, entwined, facing the stage. Not a single table is free. In fact, there's a line of customers watching and waiting beyond the velvet ropes that cordon off the event.

The shame returns, fierce and crippling. It's worse this time because I know what it feels like to play as myself. The liberation. The authenticity. The wig and makeup feel even heavier on me now than they did before.

I hurry off the stage and nod at the two violinists who walk up next.

The manager of the event is underneath the drinks tent. He gives me a thumbs-up. I wave awkwardly in return.

My phone chimes.

I glance down in surprise when I see they deposited more than the agreed upon amount in my account. Since when did Gorge pay right after a performance instead of three days later?

I'm not going to complain. This will go a long way in putting something towards the rent.

"Hey."

At the sound of my brother's voice, a bucket of cold

THE DARKEST NOTE

water splashes over me. After mom died, I gave him so many chances.

He'd just found out his mother was a drug addict and he had two half sisters who were just as poor and messed up as he was. It was probably a lot to take in. I understood.

But he didn't reach out to us for weeks. And then, when we asked him for help, he told me to jump off a cliff. Maybe he didn't use those exact words, but it was clear we were nothing but a burden to him.

I swore to cut him out of my life and pretend he never existed, pretend mom never told us he existed.

So why is there a part of me that wants to get a hug from him?

Keeping my back to him, I cough. "What?"

"I just wanted you to know that you play really... well..." He steps in front of me suddenly and his eyes widen with amazement. "Cadence?"

"How did you..." I realize I just gave myself away and redden. Terrified, I glance around, noticing all the waitresses giving us a weird look. Did they hear us?

His eyes bug. "It *is* you."

I look up into my brother's face. We first met a day after I received mom's suicide note. He came to the house wearing dusty jeans, a stained button down and old sneakers. His hair was thick and wavy and he didn't look anything like me or Vi.

If it wasn't for the angry tears in his eyes and the way his voice broke when he demanded, '*is she really dead*', I wouldn't have believed he was my brother.

Today, Rick's wearing a nice T-shirt and jeans without any rips or holes in them. His shoes are shiny black and his hair is nicely combed.

Rick frowns at me. "Why are you wearing a wig?"

"Not here." I grab his arm and drag him away from the tent.

He stops me. "I can't go anywhere. I have to work."

"Where's your post?" I whisper.

"That way." He juts his chin at the edge of the park.

I follow him there, keeping my head down and walking swiftly. When we get to the cluster of trees, he stops me. "I can't go any further than here or my manager might rip into me."

A thousand thoughts are ripping through my head. How did he know it was me? Where has he been? How has he been? Why didn't he help us when we needed him?

I force my tone to steady, refusing to look like an unhinged child in front of him. Despite my wig, green eyes and weird get-up.

He catches my eyes and his own well with a strange emotion. "You look just like her."

"Who?"

"Mom."

Immediately, guilt and anger set in. It's a weird mixture that concocts in my heart and sends a burning sensation straight to my lungs. To be associated, in any way, with my mother is like a punch to the gut.

"She came to visit me one time." He kicks at a rock. "Dressed like that. With the red hair. Didn't know it was her at the time. She never introduced herself to me."

I cross my arms over my chest and force air into my lungs. "Guess that answers how you recognized me."

"Aren't you too young to be playing in wine bars?"

Gorge's never asked about my age or my real name, which is one of the reasons I loved working there.

"Aren't you too busy with your own life to care about what I'm doing with mine?" I shoot back.

His eyebrows wrinkle and a flash of guilt passes through his brown eyes. He hides it quickly by ducking and laughing.

"You've got a temper just like her too."

"Stop comparing me to mom," I snap. "You barely knew her."

"Oh, I wish I'd *never* known her. Trust me. If she'd stayed out of my life the way she always had, things would have been simpler." His deep scowl makes me wonder if he knows more than he's letting on.

Annoyance needles my skin. "Don't worry. We're not going to crash into your life and disrupt it like mom did. Are we done here?"

It's hard to look at him right now. He's complaining about knowing mom for a few months while I've been dealing with her crap for *years*. Knowing that, he still hasn't shown any bit of care. He turned his back and left me to deal with the fallout.

It's fine. I've never seen him like a brother anyway. But sometimes, having hope and getting disappointed instead is worse than never having it at all.

"No, Cadence. We're not done here," he says with a huff.

Emotions are starting to burn the back of my eyes. "What do you want from me?" I scream.

Yelling is the only way I'm going to keep the tears from spilling. I'm exhausted. Physically and mentally stretched to my limits.

"Look, I know you hate me right now. And to be honest, I don't particularly like you or what you represent. You look so freaking much like her and it messes with my head."

I scrape at an angry tear that falls down my cheek.

He looks down at me, red in the face, like he's fighting

tears of his own. "But I've had it hard. It's not because I want to shut you out, okay?"

"*You* have it hard?" I hiss. "Try being seventeen and going to the fanciest school on a work scholarship. Try staying back to clean classrooms and then running to the diner to work a shift. And then playing music in a lounge at night because you need rent money. Oh, and speaking of rent money, try getting a notice in the mail saying you've defaulted on a loan!"

His eyes widen and he takes a step toward me. Hands on my shoulders, he croaks, "You got a mail saying *what?*"

"Get off me." I shrug his arms away.

Still looking dazed, Rick drags a hand over his mouth. "There's been a mistake. You weren't supposed to get any letters."

I freeze. His words bounce around in my head, but they're not making sense.

He pulls his lips into his mouth, looking defeated.

"You're the one who's been paying the bank." The puzzle pieces come together as I speak. "You—of course. Mom wouldn't have been responsible enough to work anything out with them. It was you who's been paying our rent since she..."

"I didn't want to tell you. But I lost my job and I had to scramble to get another one. This gig," he gestures to the security uniform, "is so I can make enough to cover both our rents. But I keep falling short every month. I haven't been able to keep up with the payments."

Shock ripples through me. No wonder he snapped at me when I asked why he didn't take care of the electric bill like he promised. He'd already been extending himself trying to cover our loan.

Mom never left anything for us. Her last act as our

mother was to dump the responsibilities on her children's shoulders.

I turn around because it hurts to hear the truth. There was a part of me that thought she'd changed at the end. Maybe she'd really done something selfless for once.

It's a blow to learn I was wrong.

It's a blow to learn that my half-brother has been taking care of us while I've been resenting him.

It's a blow to learn that so many things I thought I knew were lies.

My head pounds.

"Cadence."

"You won't have to take care of our rent anymore," I finally spit out.

He steps toward me.

"Don't." I wrench my arm back before he can touch me. "We really have been a burden to you. I get why you resent us. If I'd known, I would have taken care of it sooner." My nostrils flare. I'm talking big, but I don't have a way out. I feel like I'm drowning. Everything inside is pulling so tight that I can't even breathe.

Mom just keeps throwing me surprise after surprise, except all her 'gifts' blow up in my face. I'm not sure how many more of her secrets I can take.

"Wait." Rick puts his hand on my shoulder.

"Get your hands *off* her," a voice hisses through the night.

As I'm feeling the most fragile and battling a screaming chaos in my head, Dutch steps into our line of sight.

I watch him and the broken shards that linger in the depths of my soul, scattered from years of living with pain and heartache, comes alive. A snake rising from smoke.

The chaos in me gets louder. Wilder.

I'm out for blood tonight.

And I'm going to take that pound of flesh from Dutch.

* * *

DUTCH

She's wild. Fiery. Mine.

Mine.

That certainty clicks into place when I see Redhead standing close to a security guard.

Cadence has been messing with my head and tearing past my defenses. I've got a thing for her and it's stronger than even I would like to admit. But it's nothing like this.

Damn. When I heard Redhead play tonight, it wasn't just my pants that tightened. My heart, my lungs, my fingers, everything responded to her. She's what music is supposed to be. Everything my music isn't.

Now, standing so close to her, it's like a switch has flipped.

Again.

But this time it's firmly locked on Redhead.

I'm doing everything I can to control myself. Because my hand is begging me to inch over her waist and drive her into my side. It's not just a physical thing. It's more than that.

I need her on my skin like a balm on a burn victim. Need to breathe her in until whatever she's made of is what I'm made of too.

My steps are long and angry. I don't stop until I'm right beside her.

"Who the hell are you?" the security guard warns. He's about my height with broad shoulders and brown eyes.

There's something familiar about his face, but I'm too angry to place it.

"Me?" I nod at Redhead. "I'm her number one fan."

She snorts. "He's my stalker."

"You've got a stalker?" The security guy takes a threatening step forward.

I square up, ready to take him. It's been a hell of a long week. Cadence has been out of school and Christa's been bothering me everyday, asking if I'm ready to pull the trigger.

With one phone call, she can end it.

I just have to find a reason to get Cadence on the board's radar.

Easy.

One and done.

It's the answer I want.

The answer I need.

But I've been hesitating to take it.

Insanity.

Sol's waiting for me to break him out of prison. There's no time to be wavering. I needed to get my head out of my butt crack. Fast.

Which is why I asked the lounge's manager to do me a little favor.

I'm surprised Redhead took the bait.

She looks up at me with her fierce green eyes. I stare right back. She's Cinderellaed me way too freaking much. Tonight, I'm not letting her go until I get what I came for.

Her eyes flick to the guard and she waves him away. "I got this."

"We're not done talking." The guy has the audacity to put his hands on her *in front of me.*

I stalk forward, ready to slam his face into the next century.

Redhead beats me to it. She smacks his hands away and steps right into his space. "Leave us alone. We'll take care of our own business from now on."

He opens his mouth as if he'll call to her, but I stare him dead in the eyes. Whether it's the warning in my expression or the finality of her tone, but something convinces him to back the hell off.

Redhead is already a good distance ahead of me. I have to lengthen my stride to catch up with her.

"How did you know I was here?" she asks, not slowing down.

"I paid the lounge to set this up."

She stops in her tracks. The eyes she pins on me are dark. There's something wild about her tonight. I heard it in her music, when her fingers were banging on the keys like she had something to prove. And I see it right here, in the wrinkle between her brow and the tension in her lips. If anything, the music was only a glimmer of the chaos inside her. The chaos I feel in my own chest.

"So you really are a stalker."

The words aren't said in fear.

I take courage from that.

"Like I told that guy back there—" The guy who I really hope isn't her boyfriend. Because, as I stated earlier, she's mine now. "I'm your number one fan."

"Thin line between that and a psycho." She turns the bend, heading toward the parking lot.

Her fire makes something deep inside me come alive.

I need her.

It's less of a thought and more of a physical reaction.

"Do you generally go around kissing psychos?" I ask, hot on her tail.

Her heels skid against the pavement. Her red hair swishes around her cheeks. She's wearing a regular white blouse and black pants. Simple. Elegant. It reminds me a little of Cadence—

I shake my head to loosen the thought.

I'm here with the girl I want. The girl who moves me.

Nothing and no one else matters.

She purses her lips. "Is that what you're doing? Getting revenge?"

"Why'd you stand me up that night?" I ask, getting closer to her. The fragrance of her perfume floats to me. It's subtle and sweet. Like sunshine and vanilla. Like Cadence.

I press my eyes together and punch that thought in the face.

This is Redhead.

Redhead.

Not Cadence.

"What night?" she asks, tilting her head and batting her eyelashes innocently.

My insides light up in anticipation. She wants to play games? Fine. I'll give her as much trouble as she's giving me.

"You owe me a date, sweetheart."

She rolls her eyes. "I don't owe you anything."

"Then I'm the one who owes you."

Her eyebrow quirks.

"I always repay my debts." I lean down, getting close to her frustratingly sexy lips. "Can I show you how I plan to repay you?"

She turns it over in her head. I can see her thoughts churning.

"Come on." I slide my hand to the small of her back. It feels familiar. Feels right. Like I've touched her a million times before.

"I'm not getting into a car with you."

"Because I might be a psycho?"

"Haven't we established that?" she returns cheekily.

I laugh. Everything about her delights me. I can't explain it. Can't even begin to make sense of it. But I would change everything about myself, become something entirely new for this girl.

"I figured you'd have your reservations. Which is why no cars are involved." Jutting my chin at the building across from the park, I whisper in her ear, "Tell me what you want to do."

She trembles slightly.

I breathe over her neck, right there against her collar bone. "If you accept, I'll never show up in front of you again."

"And if I don't?"

"I will chase you to the ends of the earth."

Her lips curl up. "A threat?"

"A promise."

Her eyes flicker to my mouth before she juts her chin down. "Fine. But no names. No questions."

"A mystery. How exciting."

"A safety measure. I don't want you chasing me anywhere."

I extend my hand to her. "Come with me, Redhead."

Her eyes dart away for a bit. I watch her hesitate, but I don't move towards her. This has to be her choice.

When she finally puts her hand in mine, relief explodes in my chest. I grip her tightly and lead my mystery girl right into the dark.

Chapter Twenty-Nine

CADENCE

I can't make sense of him.

Dutch went to all that trouble to contact me.

He chased me into the night.

And now he has me alone.

We're in an elevator. My skin is buzzing from being this close to him, but he's staying a respectful distance away.

If I weren't in this red wig, would he have such self-control? I close my eyes and picture the times he threw me over his shoulder in school. Or when he backed me up against the coffee machines. Dutch never seems to know what personal space is when he's with the other me.

The real me.

Awkwardly, I lick my lips and glance at him. He's dressed in all black, as if he wants to blend into the shadows. But a guy that looks like him could never blend in anywhere. His eyes are two bright, golden suns peering out of a face crafted to perfection. His body is a weapon of mass destruction. Tats climb up and disappear under the sleeve of his shirt. His muscles bulge when he folds his arms over his chest.

Dutch glances at me and holds my eyes. There's no hint of discomfort. He's cocky as always. Annoyingly at ease.

This isn't what I pictured when he told me we were going to a hotel. I expected a key card and a beeping sensor. I expected his hands all over me, finding the soft places, the quiet places. Exploring parts of me that I'd never exposed to anyone before.

Didn't we both know what his invitation meant? Didn't I accept it?

I was ready. Willing, even.

Anything to escape the pounding dread that's gathering like storm clouds in my heart.

The darkness I've run from my whole life is breathing down my neck. It crept out of the shadows when I saw my brother. Rick's eyes when he admitted to not being able to afford our rent *and* his is embedded in my mind.

Yet another soul crushed by mom's selfishness and irresponsibility. Yet another weight I have to bear now that I know the truth. How much more until it buries me? Until I'm a mangled mess?

My skin feels too tight. Like I'm about to pop out of it. My heart is hammering behind my ribs. I know what I'm running from. Mom's ghost. She's haunting me tonight like a bad spirit. Dark shadows in every corner. Secrets threatening to spring out like snakes.

I grab Dutch's hand before we get to the rooftop. "What are we doing up here?"

What I mean to say is... why aren't we in one of those hotel rooms?

I don't want to feel right now.

I need him to get rid of my thoughts.

I need to feel his skin so I forget that mine doesn't fit anymore.

Isn't he the prince of Redwood? He's probably popped more cherries than he can count on his fingers and toes. Are we really walking up here to gaze at stars and talk about our feelings?

I don't want to do that. I want to escape into something that'll take my breath away.

"You'll see," he says, smiling slightly. Taking my hand, he leads me forward.

On the rooftop, lanterns strung from lights flutter in the breeze. Flower bushes lift their faces to the sky. In the center of it all sits a grand piano. Moonlight glints against the shiny black paint.

I stop in my tracks. "How... how did you get this up here?"

Dutch releases my hand and takes a seat behind it. Without a word, he starts to play. His fingers are long and slender, perfect for the piano. They drift over the keys without hesitation.

I recognize the melody. It's a slowed down version of the piece I did at the show case just before I started Redwood Prep.

Uncertainty grips me by the throat when I realize I'm in way over my head. I thought Dutch would touch me physically, but he's gone much darker. Much deeper. Because he couldn't be satisfied with just taking my body tonight. He's trying to touch my heart.

As he continues to play, I approach the piano. The buzzing that I felt between us in the elevator jumps another degree.

With his head bowed and his eyes closed, he looks like a

sculpture come to life. Warm. Magnetic. Alive. He's nothing like the cold, obnoxious Dutch that prowls the halls of Redwood Prep.

Tonight, his guard is lowered. There's darkness, yes. But there's something else. Brokenness. Emptiness. A longing for more. He's letting me see the rawness that lingers just beneath the surface.

Something shifts inside me.

"I didn't know you could play piano," I say.

"There's a lot you don't know about me," he says with a low laugh.

I smirk. "You'd be surprised how wrong you are."

"Tell me then. Who do you think I am?" he challenges.

"Someone who always gets his way." I take the seat beside him and begin a duet. With my fingers drawing out the music, teasing a new layer to the melody, the piece turns full and haunting. "Someone who doesn't take no for an answer," I add. I think of what he did to Mr. Mulliez and to me. "Someone who isn't afraid to be cruel."

"You think I'm evil."

"I think it's easier to choose darkness than light." I play the dark keys to prove my point. "That way, rather than being hurt, you're the one doing the hurting."

He takes one hand off the keyboard and I impulsively fill in the missing notes.

"You're right. I'm not a good person." Dutch's eyes are hot on my face. "But if there's any light left inside me, it's all drawn to you."

A burst of air hits my lungs and I look up at him, suspending the chord.

"You're in my head." He keeps one hand on the keyboard, stands and places his other arm around me, playing with me between his arms. "And what I hate even more," Dutch whispers into my hair, "is that I can't tell if I'm inside yours."

A sick feeling wrenches my stomach. Because... he is.

I have no idea when things started to change, but I'm drawn to him. To the brokenness in him. Maybe there's a dark, twisted part of me that thrives on it. That loves how even someone like Dutch—rich, handsome, and with the world at his fingertips—can be impaled by life.

"Tell me you don't feel this too." His breath hits the shell of my ear, sending skitters of desire racing up my spine.

It's a challenge.

My eyebrows tighten. "You must be very popular with the girls if this is how you repay your debts."

His gaze slides down to the piano. A low chuckle rumbles through his chest and since he's right behind me, I feel every vibration. My heart does a strange flip, but I maintain my cold expression and keep my focus on the music.

I play softly, choosing my own chords rather than the ones that belong to this piece.

"No other girl comes close to you," he says with dark confidence.

Caught off guard by the frank confession, I sweep my gaze in his direction.

"Now that your doubts have been addressed," he continues, his lips skating from my ear to my cheek, "do you have any other questions for me?"

My body feels languid. I press my fingers to the piano, but I've already forgotten what song we're playing. All I can think about is the memory of our last kiss. The heat of his mouth on mine. Rough callouses on my sensitive flesh. A wet tongue sliding below my collar.

He's lying.

There's another girl.

Me.

My heart stutters. "Why me?"

Why not Cadence Without Makeup? Is it because he's into red heads? Or green eyes? Is it because I'm a fantasy?

"Because your music speaks to me." He leaves one hand on the piano and the other presses a chord into my back. "Because," he shifts his hands lower "when I hear you play, it makes me *feel*. It's been a long freaking time since I've felt anything. It's been forever since I've felt *everything*." His hands skate back to the piano and he finishes the note that I've left hanging. "You force me to face the truth, even if the truth is more cruel than I could ever be."

His touch is a drug. I'm melting into him, seeking the warmth of his chest. The hardness of his abs. The promise of his kiss.

Still, I make a half-ditched effort to keep control. "How would I even know if you were telling the truth?" I ask.

His laughter is low and gripping. The music shifts again. My fingers are digging deeper into the keys. It produces a different kind of sound. One full of decadence, as if we're approaching something thrilling but dangerous.

"I guess you'd have to call my bluff," he says.

"And if I did?" I turn my face to the side, breathing heavily.

He lowers himself over my shoulder. Abandoning the piano, his coarse fingers grip my chin.

My heart races until I'm sure it'll burst out of my chest.

Dutch leans down and speaks right against my lips. "Then I would have to show you how much I want you."

I don't realize I'm holding my breath until his gaze drops to my lips and I exhale on impact. The moment he sees my mouth part, his amber eyes go dark. Then his lips crash down on mine.

Every vein in my body comes alive at the feel of his mouth parting, caressing, and teasing.

My hands leave the keyboard completely and band around his waist to drag him closer. He holds still, lingering, as if he wants me to get used to him being there. As if he's giving me time to push him away if this isn't really what I want.

He's dragging out the moments.

Torture.

I need friction so much it's tearing me apart. I want to scream with it.

"Wait," I whisper.

He eases back immediately, looking down at me.

"Don't touch my hair," I demand. Then I surge forward and kiss him.

Even if all he can offer is pain, I want to get lost in Dutch tonight.

* * *

DUTCH

I press my mouth to hers and hold steady.

I just want to feel her for a heartbeat. Two.

Then she kisses me the same as she did in the changing room.

My resolve to be a gentleman shatters.

She gasps when I grab her hips and thrust her on top of the piano. Discordant notes play. Her fingers press into the keys while she wildly tries to find her balance.

I steady her with a hand on the back of her neck, pushing her into me so I can deepen the kiss. Her hand pushes against the keys as she meets my passion with her own.

More disjointed notes burst from the piano.

Pure chaos.

The tension before the crescendo.

"This is so…" she sucks on my bottom lip, "disrespectful… to the piano."

"Don't worry about it." I breathe her in. "Be a bad girl tonight."

My thoughts dissolve as my tongue explores her mouth. She groans low in her throat and I grip her tighter, needing to hear that sound again. Needing to be closer to her.

It's not enough. I need more of her skin.

I try to step between her legs and bump into the lid of the keyboard instead. Frustrated, I grunt and ease back to assess.

She looks up at me, eyes half-closed and mouth wet. Moonlight shines on top of the red hair that's off limits. Her green eyes are dark and sultry, like a cat about to pounce.

She's sexy as hell, but I realize her perch on the keys isn't the best for what I need to do. Determined, I grab her thighs. Her squeal of surprise makes my heart trip.

Lifting her higher, I set her on the desk of the piano.

"Better?" I growl.

She swings around so her legs are dangling off the side. "Maybe."

Heat sweeps over my entire body. Wrapping my fingers around one ankle, I tug decisively until she's at the edge of the piano and step between her legs.

"You're a hard girl to please," I mumble.

Her eyes are dark. "If it makes you feel any better, you're not doing too bad right now."

My pulse hammers in my chest when she curls her leg against my body to pin me in place.

I crash into her again. Then, ripping my lips away from her mouth, I press kisses down her neck while my hands work to free her from her blouse.

Her fingers skate against my scalp and over my back. A burning sensation skitters everywhere she touches.

Throwing aside her shirt, I chase the trail of goosebumps prickling down her shoulder. Her skin is softer than a lily. I need this so much I'm almost going blind.

Mine.

Mine.

She has to understand that after tonight.

Her fingers grip and tug at my hair as I remove her bra. The taste of her is familiar. So are the sounds she makes.

Her little pants make my tongue move faster and I focus on the moment. It's just her in my head. No one else. She can't be compared to Cadence. I won't allow it.

When I feel her slender hands tugging on my T-shirt hem, I release her just long enough to tear my T-shirt off. Her eyes widen, but I don't give her time to admire my tattoos. She'll trace each of them, know them all by heart, by the time I'm done with her.

When we kiss again, breaths damn-near erratic, I guide her hand to feel me. Electricity skitters everywhere her hands touch. I guide her over my pecs. My abs. Lower. Lower.

She rips a groan from me and then she smiles like she just found a new toy.

I growl out a warning, "Careful now."

Her eyes are flashing with lust. One side of her lips curls up in a sexy little smirk. I hiss when she cups my face in one hand and presses her full, red lips against my pulse, as if she's a vampire trying to suck the life out of me. It drives me freaking insane.

My mouth collides with hers and I tip her backward until the upper half of her body is flat on the piano desk. Her eyes fall shut when I unclip the button of her pants.

My desperation makes my hands tremble.

I've never felt like this before. I'd give it all to her.

Everything.

Let her sink into all the places where only music was allowed.

The zipper is loud when I drag it down. The sound makes her bite down on her bottom lip.

"You okay?" I ask, noticing.

"Yeah." Her voice trembles.

I bend over her so my upper body is flattening her on top of the piano and my hip is pinning in her place. The feel of her naked chest pricking into mine makes my head spin.

"Have you done this before?" I ask gravely.

She swallows and her delicate throat bobs.

I slide my fingers into hers and pin her wrists on either side of her head. The surface of the piano is cold and I rub on her for friction and warmth.

"Answer me."

"N-no," she admits, her face flushing an even deeper red.

Damn it. I don't deal with virgins. They place way too much stock on their first times. Build up fantasies in their heads about spending their lives with me.

But there's only a moment of hesitation before I throw those worries away.

"You want to do this with me?" I growl.

She gives me a nervous nod.

I didn't think she could make me break any more of my

rules, but here I am. Eager as a freaking bee to get into a honey trap.

I'm rolling her jeans down when my phone vibrates in my pocket. At first, I ignore it. I'm concentrating.

But the phone doesn't stop ringing.

I squeeze my eyes shut, annoyed as hell.

"Maybe it's important," she says.

I look into her face, unsure if she's trying to push me away so she doesn't have to do this.

Her hand disappears into my jeans like she owns it and I stare at her with a dazed expression when she takes my phone right out of my pocket and shoves it at me.

I want to throw that buzzing thing off the roof, spread her legs and play her like an instrument until she screams louder than my guitar.

But I can't.

Because the name flashing across the screen is my brother's.

Finn wouldn't call me nonstop if it wasn't an emergency.

I put the phone to my ear. "Hello?"

"Dutch."

I stiffen instantly. My brother's never been the cheerful one of the three of us, but he's also never sounded that unhinged.

Redhead must sense something in my expression because she sits up right away and closes her legs. The monster inside me grunts in displeasure. I want her to keep those legs open. I want to be her first. I want to get inside her pretty little body the way she's gotten into my head.

Instead, I grip the phone tighter.

"It's Sol, man." Finn sounds panicked. "He tried to commit suicide."

Everything inside me shuts down.

I can't wrap my head around those words. *Sol? Suicide?*

"Zane's at the hospital," Finn says. "I'm heading there now too."

My heart drops out of my chest. "I'm on my way."

When I turn around, Redhead's already hopped down from the piano. She's bending over to collect her clothes.

I help her out, handing her the bra that somehow landed on the piano bench. Then I locate my shirt and drag it over my head.

"I have to go," I tell her.

"I gathered that. Is something wrong?" She looks concerned rather than shy.

"Yeah. It's..."

Sol... suicide.

I can't even finish the sentence. There's no way Sol would hurt himself. No way.

The world is spinning. Guilt chews me alive. It's my fault. If I hadn't gotten him into this mess over summer break, if I hadn't abandoned him, if I hadn't taken my time to deal with Cadence, none of this would have happened.

As I'm spinning out, something grounds me.

I glance down.

Pale fingers slide over my hand and hold me tight. For a second, I just stare at her hand.

I'm not the guy who does the walk on the beach, holding hands crap. But her hand in mine feels right, so I don't pull away.

We sprint to the elevator and I use my free hand to dial Zane on my phone.

He finally answers. "Dutch."

"How's Sol? What are they saying?"

"He's okay for now, but it's bad, man." His voice cracks

and it sounds like he might be on the verge of a mental breakdown.

I know my brother and when Zane feels helpless, he does one of two things—bang his drums or bang a chick. Since he's stuck at the hospital, there's no possibility of doing either of those things.

"Calm down—"

"Don't freaking tell me to calm down," Zane explodes. "Sol tried to kill himself. And if he'd succeeded, it would have been our fault."

I glance at Redhead. She's staring up at me. I know she's probably hearing Zane's loud screams and wondering what's going on.

I squeeze her hand and then I turn slightly away. "You're right. I've been dragging my feet with Cadence. But I'm done with that."

Redhead's hand slips out of mine.

"What are we going to do?" Zane asks.

"What I should have done from the start." I huff out a breath, my mind alert and churning with all my next steps. "You stay with Sol and his family. I'll be there when I've handled business."

Cadence has been tearing me up inside, but I can't afford to be hesitant any longer.

Sol's life is at stake.

The elevator opens.

I gesture for Redhead to leave first. Her eyes are wide and her face has gone pale. I want to ask her what's wrong, but my phone rings again.

It's Finn.

"Any update?" My brother asks. "I'm stuck in traffic."

I give him the update and then add, "I've decided. It's time we deal with Cadence for good."

I pause. It feels like someone's glaring at me but, when I turn to see if Redhead is watching, she quickly glances away.

"What do you want us to do?" Finn asks.

I step through the glass doors of the hotel and jog down the stairs with Redhead beside me.

"We get her scholarship revoked." I lower my voice. I don't want to scare Redhead, but this needs to happen. Tonight. "Get the IT guy to flub her grades. I'll tell Christa to get her dad involved."

"You think that'll work?"

"There's no way she's getting out of this." I slip the phone back into my pocket and touch Redhead's shoulder. Even in the midst of my panic and fear, there's a hint of affection for her. "I'm sorry about tonight. I'll make it up to you."

Her face turned, she waves me away. "Go."

Something doesn't feel right, but I don't have time to follow up on it. My steps are slow as I back away from her, but she doesn't even look at me as she hurries around the corner.

I'll definitely make it up to her, I promise myself.

And then I turn and sprint straight to my car.

Chapter Thirty

CADENCE

Cold water pours over my head as I stand, shivering in the shower. I scrub and scrub and scrub my skin until it's rubbed raw. Water splashes at my feet, soaring down the drain, but it's not taking the film of disgust with it.

My heart is beating at *allegrissimo*—one of the fastest tempos in music. I keep scrubbing until my skin burns and lean over, a hand against the wall and my hair clumping in front of my face.

Dutch made a plan to ruin me and he did it *right in front of my face.* No mercy. No hesitation. He was every bit as cold and cruel as ever.

I pound the wall again. My forehead eases against the shower. It's cool to the touch.

My mind runs in circles. Before Dutch got that phone call, I was sliding my arms around his neck and kissing him like my life depended on it. I was digging my fingers into his shoulders and moaning while he undid my jeans.

I was preparing to give it all to him.

Something precious. Something that he didn't deserve.

Idiot.

The frustration grows and I hit the faucet to turn it off. Scooping my hair back and away from my face, I breathe in. I can still smell him on me. The fragrance of sandalwood and mint and money. I can still feel his fingers digging into my thighs as he prepared to unwrap me like a present at Christmas.

Then that call came.

And it changed everything.

I hit the wall again. And again.

The most ridiculous part of this is that, before he exposed his plans, I genuinely felt for him. When Dutch got that first call, his entire face went pale.

I stared into his vibrant amber eyes, saw the panic flashing there and my first instinct wasn't to revel in his pain.

It was to protect him.

After all the horrible things he'd done to me, all the ways he'd ruined me, all the times he made my life miserable, I still wanted to hold his hand, hug him and ease the strain.

'I'll deal with Cadence.'

But my care of him was one-sided.

He was eager, desperate even, to take me down. A hit man would probably have more of a heart. It was that coldness, that complete lack of humanity, that reminded me exactly who I was dealing with.

A monster.

"Ah." I hold a hand over my mouth to muffle the cry of frustration and regret. It feels like my heart is on the verge of ramming out of my chest.

I wish I could say Dutch caught me at a weak moment, but the blinding energy between us was unavoidable. It wasn't a moment of temporary insanity.

It was a choice.

My choice.

The full scope of my feelings for him exploded the moment he played the piano. There was not a part of me—not a single inch of me—that wanted him to stop.

In his arms, I felt safe. Like an idiot, I thought I was seeing beyond his cold exterior to the real Dutch, the one who rescued me from drowning and pushed me to overcome my stage fright.

But a beast doesn't know how to do anything but destroy.

I climb out of the shower. My steps are plodding. I'm dripping water everywhere, but I don't care.

It's dark when I slip into the hallway. Viola woke up when I came home, took one look at me and then stalked away. She's still angry that I yelled at her. Just another point where I've failed.

I lock myself in my bedroom and sink against the old mattress. It creaks as it accepts my weight. My keyboard stands out in the shadows. The glistening black and white keys remind me of Dutch.

Desperately, I launch up and throw a blanket over it so it's out of sight.

I pick up my phone, debating if I should call my best friend. I decide against it. Breeze will only tell me 'I told you so'. She warned me that a guy like Dutch wasn't to be trusted. It's my own fault for not avoiding him like the plague.

My chest moves up and down as my breathing thickens. Anxiety spins my head in a freefall.

Is this the end for me at Redwood?

I shift through the regret and brush aside the disgust in favor of something much better—anger. It surges through me like a hurricane, destroying the hopelessness inside.

No, I can't go down like this.

Tonight is my fault. I'll accept that.

I opened my legs for Dutch. I let him get close to me.

Maybe that makes me an idiot. But I don't have to pair that with being a victim. Why should I be the only one to suffer? Why should he walk off into the sunset while I cower in the darkness?

Despite being weak, I have something I didn't before.

Information.

Tonight's revelation is a blessing in disguise.

The shift in my thinking makes my blood pound in a different way. I can't help but jump to my feet and pace my room as I think about what to do next.

Dutch has all the power at Redwood. He's got Christa's dad in his back pocket too. I need someone higher than them. Someone with more influence. Someone who the entire school would believe.

I stop in my tracks when it hits me.

Jinx.

Rolling my shoulders to work out the knots, I send a text.

Cadence: I'm ready to do business.

Anxiety attacks me hard while I wait for a response.

My phone chirps.

I pounce on it.

Jinx: A secret for a secret, New Girl.

Cadence: Dutch plans to flub my grades so I lose my scholarship and get kicked out of Redwood.

Jinx: Evidence?

The inkling of hope that had been growing in my chest dies a violent death.

Evidence?

I tap my phone in my palm and pace in the other direction.

Jinx: Sorry New Girl. No evidence, no deal.

Cadence: I'm telling the truth.

Jinx: You can't believe how many scorned women try to use me for revenge. I need more than that if it'll be worth anything.

Grunting in frustration, I toss my phone back on the bed and keep pacing. My anger's stronger than the disappointment. Just because one door closed doesn't mean another won't open.

I take a few deep breaths and pull myself together. Who else can I turn to?

Back and forth.

Back and forth.

I keep going until I stumble on another path—Mr. Mulliez.

The idea loses steam when his phone goes to voicemail. I send him a text, but there's no response. Miss Jamieson told me he left the country to further his studies.

Damn it.

I start to put my phone down until I remember I have one more option. Miss Jamieson. She believed me and Mr. Mulliez. And she gave me encouragement when Christa tried to blame me for busting her lip.

"Where did I put her number?" I mumble desperately. Books thud to the ground as I upend my school bag. Dropping to my knees, I desperately shove aside lotions, sugar packets and notes until I find the tiny slip of paper with her number on it.

Relief seeps through me and I dial it quickly.

I don't breathe as I listen to it ring.

There's a click.

And then…

"Hello?"

"Miss Jamieson," I call urgently.

"Who's this?"

"I—I'm Cadence Cooper. Sorry to bother you but I really didn't know what else to do."

"Cadence?" The sound of bed sheets rustling tells me I woke her out of bed.

"Who's that?" A male voice says.

"Just a student." She clears her throat. "Give me a second, Cadence."

"Sure."

I hear more rustling then a door creaks open and clicks shut.

"Are you okay?" she asks. From the reverb in her voice, I can tell she's in a bathroom.

"No, not really." My words erupt in a gush. "Look, if I had anyone else to turn to, I wouldn't be bothering you in your private time, but if I don't do something, I'm going to get kicked out of Redwood unfairly and I can't…" My breath stalls. "I can't let Dutch win. I'd die first."

"Sweetheart, calm down, okay. Start from the top. Tell me what happened."

I tell her about Dutch's plan. "It sounded like they were going to change the grades tonight."

"Are you sure?"

I recall the moment in the elevator. "Yes."

She blows out a breath.

I tap a finger against my foot. "Christa already hates me and with her dad being the chairman of the board at Redwood, it doesn't matter what the truth is."

"Why would they do this to you? Seriously, what the hell is wrong with those boys? One of them goes around lying about his age and the other—"

"Did Dutch lie about his age?" I ask. That seems unlike him. He might be a despicable bastard, but he doesn't hide it.

There's a long pause as if Miss Jamieson probably exposed something she didn't mean to.

After a moment, she speaks again in a more composed tone. "If it was a matter of simply changing your grades unfairly, I could intervene. The problem is if they're taking it straight to the board. There's a chain of command at Redwood Prep. Once the situation has escalated, we can't do much to reverse it from our level."

I groan and fall against my bed. "So you're saying I'm screwed."

"I'm saying we have to move faster than they do or we find someone higher than the chairman to support you."

"Who's higher than the chairman?"

There's a moment of silence.

"I might know of someone. Well, not me. Mr. Mulliez has a connection we can explore."

"I tried to call him, but he didn't answer," I tell her.

"He got a new phone number when he moved from the US."

Hope springs to life again. "So you're saying…"

"Let me talk to Mr. Mulliez. Even if this is a dead end, we'll keep fighting. We're not going to let them win, Cadence."

After that conversation, I can't sleep. My mind is too busy cycling through all the things that could go wrong with her plan.

When Miss Jamieson finally calls me back the next morning, I haven't gotten a wink of sleep.

Snatching the phone up, I croak, "What did Mr. Mulliez say?"

"He's cashing in a favor from an old friend."

"You mean..."

"I mean you're not leaving Redwood."

My entire body caves in on a sigh. "Well, do I have to do anything or attend a meeting to explain why my grades are suddenly low?"

"No." She pauses. "But I do have one question."

"What is it?"

"Do you like dramatic entrances?"

Chapter Thirty-One

DUTCH

"Careful, man." I grab Sol's arm as he shuffles out of the car.

He laughs sheepishly and wrenches his arm away. "Damn, I'm not an invalid. I can walk."

That's hard to believe since just a few days ago, he was on death's door.

When I got to the hospital that night, Sol refused to see any of us. His mom was bawling her eyes out and Zane had barely managed to calm her down.

All three of us left the hospital ready to do whatever it took to make things right.

There was no other alternative.

Cadence Cooper had to go.

For all the effort I put in before this, getting Cadence out of Redwood was, surprisingly, easy.

Maybe a little too easy.

Once we snuck into the system and changed Cadence's

grades, Christa made the call to her dad. He sent the order right away and Principal Harris delivered the verdict.

No fuss.

No drama.

Or so I heard.

I haven't been to Redwood in a few days. The first two, I was sick at home, fighting off a flu that came out of nowhere. After that, my brothers and I went to the hospital, banging on Sol's door until he stopped being an idiot and agreed to see us.

He's been cleared to go to school for half day, but he still has to go to the psych hospital for a check in regularly.

"It's been a while, Redwood," Sol says to the main building. He closes his eyes and takes a deep breath.

"Been a while for us too," Finn comments. He arches an eyebrow at me. "Almost felt like some of us were avoiding this place."

I ignore my brother's dig at me.

So what if I didn't want to see Cadence off? I'm pretty sure she would have punched me in the mouth if she ran into me and then I'd be in pain and she'd be in handcuffs.

I'm not going to apologize for what I did to kick her out. Life isn't a walk in the freaking park. Sometimes, hard choices have to be made.

Cadence didn't belong at Redwood Prep in the first place. Plus, she had her chance to accept the money and go somewhere else willingly.

She didn't.

Every choice has consequences.

She made hers.

"Hey, Sol."

"Sol."

"Sol, you're back."

Students stop and take notice as we saunter through the hallway. It feels good to have Sol walking beside me again, where he belongs.

"Man, this place is a lot fancier than I remember," Sol says, stopping in front of his locker.

Zane slings an arm over Sol's shoulder. "We've got assembly today. The text went out on our school app."

"They're going to announce that you're back. You gonna be okay?" Finn asks in a sober voice.

"They're not going to," Sol glances down and pulls at the sleeve of his sweater, "say why I was gone, are they?"

"No one knows except us." I nod at me and my brothers.

"And maybe Jinx," Zane says.

I give him a dark look.

"What?" My brother shrugs. "That creep seems to know everything."

Christa floats by, flanked by two of her dance team members. She's wearing her cheerleading uniform and has her hair up in two ponytails.

"Hey, boys. You excited about the rally?" The greeting is aimed at all of us, but her eyes linger on me.

Zane laughs and punches me on the arm. "I don't think she's talking to us, bro."

My expression doesn't change.

"Dutch," Christa calls my name pointedly.

I do a chin-up nod and look away from her. She helped us out for her own selfish reasons. I'm not going to feed her delusions by making her think we're a thing now.

Her smile drops and she scowls at me.

Finn pulls his lips in to hide his laughter.

Christa doesn't take my rejection well. "So you're just going to ignore me now?"

"Pretty much," I say coldly.

Christa's eyes turn hot as flames. She looks like she wants to say more but, when she notices her friends eyeing her, she huffs at me. "You think you can use me and get away with it, Dutch? Think the hell again."

I watch as she stalks off, her pride hurt and her skirt fluffing around her butt cheeks.

Sol leans in to whisper, "What's up with you and Christa? I heard she was all over you when you came back from tour."

"Our dear brother's tastes have changed." Zane flashes me a smile. "He likes his girls redheaded and mysterious now."

Sol's eyes widen with interest. "You got yourself a girlfriend?"

"She's not my girlfriend," I correct him.

Even if I wanted her to be, Redhead dipped before I could get her name or her number. The manager at the lounge wouldn't give me her information and I knew that tricking her into showing up wouldn't work again.

Kicking myself for not getting her name at least, I went looking for the security guard she'd been talking to, thinking he might have a lead, but I couldn't find him either.

After all my efforts failed, I gave up, tucked my tail between my legs and went to Jinx.

'All will be revealed in time' was her response.

Freaking scam artist.

Now I'm back to square one.

Redhead is in the wind. She might as well have been a dream.

Finn slaps my shoulder when the bells chime. "Time to go."

I'm walking in front when I feel Sol lagging behind.

THE DARKEST NOTE

Finn notices too. He catches my eye and juts his chin at Sol. Zane hones in on our silent communication, sees where Finn is watching and arches an eyebrow at me.

I wave for them to walk ahead and slow my stride so I'm in step with Sol. "You okay, man?"

"Yeah." He scrubs the side of his face. "It's just… a lot of things have happened since I was last here. It kind of feels like culture shock."

"You belong here, Sol," I say intently.

"Hm." He tosses me a thoughtful look. "I heard there was someone who took my place at the start of the school year. How'd you get her to quit?"

Something that feels a lot like guilt slides through my chest. But that can't be right because that would mean I actually felt something other than resentment for Cadence.

I didn't.

I deal with the guilt fast and lift my chin. "Don't worry about that. All that matters is you're here now."

He looks concerned.

I chuckle. "We're the princes of Redwood, Sol. No one's going to get in our way."

That makes him smile a bit.

Seeing that he's in a better mood, I walk a little faster so we can catch up with my brothers. Together, we take a seat at the top of the bleachers.

Kids clamor to sit around us, keeping a healthy distance away—out of fear or nerves, I don't know and I don't care.

I look out over the assembly and feel peace flood my chest.

Sol is back where he belongs.

Balance has been restored.

All I have to do now is find Redhead and I'll have my queen. Everything will be perfect.

Principal Harris walks to the center of the gymnasium. He's in a too-tight suit and his belly's straining against the button. The bald spot in the middle of his head shines like a disco ball in the sunlight.

"Settle down, everyone," he drones in his dry, thin voice. The man couldn't sound weaker if he sucked on a helium balloon first. "In this morning assembly, we have a very special return student..."

Zane elbows Sol in the side.

He knocks my brother's hand away, ducking his head shyly.

"... And I'm sure he needs no introduction," Principal Harris adds.

Finn leans over to me. "When did Harris become such a butt kisser?"

I shrug. Something doesn't feel right to me either.

"... Everyone, let's hear a round of applause for..." Harris tosses a hand at the gym doors.

They break open.

Light blasts from behind a tall figure in a black T-shirt, ripped jeans and sunglasses.

My body coils and I nearly pounce out of my seat.

Dad?

"Jarod Cross!"

The gym erupts with screams and cries of *oh my gosh*.

"What the hell is he doing here?" Zane demands.

Finn is looking on with wide eyes.

Dad lifts his hands like he's at one of his sold out concerts. He strides confidently to the microphone. The voice that stole a million hearts and sold four hundred times that in records booms around the room.

"Hello, Redwood!"

The smile on dad's face makes a scowl grow on mine.

Uneasiness digs under my skin.

Something's up.

"Did dad tell you he was coming to Redwood?" Zane hisses.

"I thought he was still on tour," Finn answers.

I keep quiet. Something tells me this isn't the worst part and I brace myself for the other shoe to drop.

"Redwood Prep has a long, vibrant history of producing excellence in every field but," he gestures to himself, "especially in music."

Finn snorts.

Zane rolls his eyes. "Way to toot your own horn."

Sol laughs softly.

None of us join him.

"That's why I made it my mission to build the music program and fill it with talents. Like my sons." Dad's eyes swerve to us and he raises a hand in our direction.

The entire student body swings around, staring at us too.

I grit my teeth. What the hell is this show about? Why is he really here?

Dad never pulls stunts like this unless he has to cover up something. And since the last horrible secret I had to keep for him, I'm not eager to earn any more.

"And not just my sons," dad chuckles, "but one very special young lady who happened to get on my radar."

The door opens again and all of a sudden, the air gets sucked out of the room.

I hear the *click, click, click* of heels like someone's closing up my coffin while I'm still inside. My heart slows to match the rhythm of the steps. As she comes into view, my eyes slide up her heeled loafers, to the white socks, the too-short skirt, and the blouse that's obviously too small for her.

When my eyes crash into hers, everything inside me goes still.

"Cadence Cooper," dad announces.

The gym falls into shocked silence. Everyone knows we kicked Cadence out of Redwood.

Whispers fire up around us.

Finn gives me a stunned look.

Zane's eyes are about to roll on the floor.

Sol looks uneasy.

I only take a moment to soak in their reactions before I pin my gaze back on Cadence. She's looking right at me, her brown eyes narrowed and her lips up in a smirk.

My phone buzzes.

Jinx: Your search for Cinderella requires no glass slippers. The one you want is already in front of you.

I tap on the video she sent along with the message, unable to breathe when I see it.

Redhead. Outside the back-to-school showcase. Taking off her wig.

My heart is racing and I'm on my feet, pouncing down the bleachers before I even realize where I'm going. People duck to keep from being trampled. Dad stops in the middle of his speech.

It doesn't matter.

I have to get to her.

How is it possible that Cadence is Redhead? Has she been playing me all along?

I can hardly breathe when I get to the middle of the gym. Dad is staring at me. The entire freaking *school* is staring at me. I look like a maniac on a war path. But Cadence doesn't look scared at all.

In fact, her smile turns cruel. "Do you need something, Dutch?"

"Who the hell are you?" I hiss, baring down on her.

She steps close to me. Goes toe to toe. In a dark, warning voice, she whispers, "I'm your worst nightmare."

* * *

Jinx: Hello, citizens of Redwood. I'm sending my royal proclamation through our school app for the last time. Going forward, no one's secrets will be hidden. If you want to know what's happening with the highest of the elite at Redwood, all you have to do is subscribe to my new app.

Here's a juicy little tidbit for free. Redwood's very own Cinderella was seen poofing into the gym on the arm of her fairy god-father. And there was one prince who wasn't very happy with that.

It looks like a war may be brewing between Prince Charming and his working class love, but this Cinderella is not to be underestimated. Today's showdown is proof. How will our blonde prince deliver his first blow? Join my app and you'll be the first to know.

Until the next post, keep your enemies close and your secrets even closer.

- Jinx

TO BE CONTINUED IN *THE RUTHLESS NOTE...*

A Word From The Author

Thank you for reading **The Darkest Note**, Book 1 in the Redwood Kings Series. If you've enjoyed visiting Redwood Prep, show other readers by leaving a review.

The series continues with Book 2 **THE RUTHLESS NOTE**! Visit neliaalarcon.com to learn more.

The Ruthless Note Sneak Peek
CADENCE

THE CRESCENDO IS my favorite part of a musical piece.

It's like gathering electricity, the kind that builds and builds until it buzzes through your entire body. Until everywhere, from your fingers to your toes is on fire. Different from a climax, it *isn't* the peak. It's not the part that will rip the audience's breath from their throats or cause a tear to fall from their eye.

It's the build-up.

And it's special because only the musician knows it's coming. A secret trapped in her hands, in her mind, in her piano. A shifting in the air that makes the audience nervous. Makes their throats bob and their eyes dart from side to side.

A rubber band pulling back, back, back.

No one is sure when it will snap.

No one can do anything about it.

In that moment, in the crescendo, the people who are listening... they're under my control.

I feel that electricity when Dutch storms down the bleachers, his amber eyes hot enough to burn me to a crisp.

His boots hit the metal stands in loud thuds. *Thump. Thump.* Rhythmic percussions. Students jump out of his way, knowing he won't stop. Knowing they'll get crushed like cockroaches if they're stupid enough to remain in place.

I watch the wave that flows and ebbs around Dutch's descent. The air around him is charged. Musical notes pluck through my mind. The shrieking melody of an electric guitar to match the frantic pace of his footsteps. His boots land on the gym floor and he barrels at me like a bull seeing red.

For a moment, my breath clogs in my throat.

The Prince of Redwood Prep.

Dangerous.

Beastly.

Violent.

There's a weight to Dutch that goes far beyond the wide chest and shoulders straining against his preppy vest, an intensity that has nothing to do with the slightly unhinged glint in his eyes or the hardness in the planes of his face.

Can I really do this? Can I go toe-to-toe with a ruthless king like him?

Brushing the thought away quickly, I square my shoulders. There is no other choice. He didn't *give* me another choice.

"Do you need something, Dutch?" I ask coldly.

His eyes drill into mine with the precision of a laser. His voice sounds like it's scraping against shards of broken glass when he hisses, "Who the hell are you?"

My heart wobbles, but I beat it back into submission. Nights ago, after dropping my defenses—and almost dropping my panties—I found out swiftly that Dutch Cross would stop at nothing to destroy me. He made the call to get me kicked out of Redwood. He didn't give a damn about what that would do to me, to my future or to my family.

He cares about only one thing: himself.

Now that I've managed to scramble out of the hole he tried to bury me in, I won't forget who put me there.

I step close to him and tip my chin up to meet his stormy gaze. "I'm your worst nightmare."

His eyes narrow. His nostrils flare.

So much anger. It's a flood running through his lithe, gorgeous body. I can practically see it charging in his veins and sparking from his glowing hazel eyes. Chiseled jaw muscles clench and unclench as he struggles to make sense of who I am and how he should respond to me.

"Dutch?" A voice rings through the school gym. It's deep and husky, the kind of voice that can capture a stadium full of men and women and make them believe in love.

I turn and lock eyes with Jarod Cross.

The respectable black turtleneck and pressed trousers can't snuff out the 'rockstar' ingrained beneath his skin. With his thick chestnut hair, slightly wavy as if he couldn't care less about hair products, the thick sideburns, the heavy silver necklace and the tattoos creeping out of his throat and on the back of his hands, he screams musical chaos.

I've never been an active fan of Jarod Cross, but there's not a person on this *planet* who hasn't heard his music. From triple platinum albums to the soundtracks behind the most iconic action movie scenes to simply featuring on another band's track, he's *everywhere*.

Dutch rips his gaze away from me and focuses on his dad. The two share a long, charged staredown. Beneath their unblinking gazes is a dangerous hint of animosity.

The truth shakes loose before my eyes. Jarod Cross didn't jump to my rescue to help out Mr. Mulliez or to log a point in his book of good deeds. There's more to his appearance at Redwood Prep.

"You want to explain why you're making a scene?" Jarod Cross snarls beneath his breath.

"I have nothing to say to you," Dutch snaps back.

The pressure in the air mounts like a plane taking off on a runway.

What's going on between Dutch and his dad?

The gym doors burst open before I can dig into it. Both Jarod Cross and Dutch glance around. Apprehension flickers through Jarod's eyes when he sees the police. He takes a step back.

But the cops aren't looking at him. Their eyes swerve through the gym, intently searching for their target.

Whispers and gasps rise from the student body. In all their elite, privileged lives, they've never brushed against a moment like this.

I hear the crescendo in my head.

Relentless momentum.

Crashing dominos.

Phones are out now, some already suspecting that, whatever's going down, it's worthy of being recorded.

"What in the heavens?" Principal Harris exclaims from his perch next to the podium. Sweat leaks out of his bald head and pours down the side of his face. "Why are there police officers?"

Everyone in the bleachers leans forward, anticipating a show.

But it's not the kind they're expecting.

The officers march straight to the cheerleaders who are clumped together on a bench. Pretty, toned, and privileged, they wear their careless abandon like they do their sparkly outfits with the pleated skirts and plastic pompoms.

I watch the dancers' shocked reactions when the cops get closer. Each of their faces devolve into masks of discomfort. Their eyes dart to one another. Teeth tugging into bottom lips. Hands tightening around their pompoms.

The buzz in my veins gets worse. Was I always this greedy for revenge? Have I always been a destructive person or did Redwood Prep turn me into this monster?

I feel Dutch's gaze boring into my head. Diverting my attention from the cops to the furious god of Redwood Prep, I arch a brow in challenge.

He steps toward me. His chest brushes my arm and sends an unwanted spark of awareness thrumming through my body.

Voice low and head tucked close to my ear, Dutch growls, "What. Did. You. Do?"

"Me?" I whisper innocently.

He grabs my arm. His fingers are almost painful when they clamp around my wrist. "Cadence."

A shriek ricochets around the gym, temporarily averting Dutch's venomous gaze. We both look to the front where the cops have pointed out Christa.

"Get your hands *off* me!" the blonde screams.

Principal Harris throws helpless eyes at Jarod Cross as if invoking some kind of supernatural creature to do his bidding. The rockstar remains rooted in place. His fingers are relaxed. One corner of his lips arches up in amusement.

The police succeed in getting Christa to her feet. I'm too far away to hear what they're saying, but I know why they're here.

And I know why Christa's face turns pale.

Her blue eyes shoot over the gym and skewer me. Pink lips curl up in an animalistic sneer.

I should be scared, but I'm not.

The crescendo is building.

A D D# E

Pulling. Pulling. Pulling.

No release in sight.

The police escort Christa out of the gym. Gasps ripple through the crowd. Phone lights flash and blink.

Principal Harris produces a handkerchief, sops up the sweat on his face, and motions to the disappearing police. "I should see what's going on."

In the chaos of students shooting to their feet and teachers fighting to keep order, Dutch yanks me right up against him. His breath hits my neck like fingers grasping at my throat and every muscle in my body pulls taut.

"I don't know what the hell you're plotting, but I will end it." Eyes narrowing to slits, he hisses, "I will *end* you."

His threat ricochets through my body.

Before I can say anything, one of the officers returns to the gym.

The students go quiet again.

Jarod Cross stiffens.

Dutch is the only one who doesn't seem to know or care that he's practically manhandling me in front of law enforcement.

"Cadence Cooper?" the cop drawls.

I turn, my hand still held hostage in Dutch's giant paws.

"You need to come with me."

"Sure." I wrench my hand back and spear Dutch with a dark look.

He returns the glower with an even icier one. Pale

fingers clench into fists. His amber eyes convey only one thing—*this isn't over*.

I *feel* the weight of his promise and I fear the damage he'll do to me. Not because Dutch is big and intimidating. Not because he and his brothers rule Redwood Prep with an iron fist. Not even because he has no respect for his father, authority in general or the law.

But because I don't trust the way my body will react to him. Even if I hate him with my every breath, there's a twisted, dark piece of me that beats to life when I'm near him.

Maybe it's a good thing I'm being taken away.

I follow the cop into the empty hallway. "Why did you need to see me? Wasn't the video enough?"

Last week, I made a deal with Jinx to get evidence of Christa shoving me into the pool. Christa was stupid enough to have her friends film her that day.

In exchange for the footage, I had to leak one of my biggest secrets to Jinx. A part of me thinks I might have jumped straight out of the frying pan and into the fire. But if making a deal with the devil keeps me alive long enough to protect myself and my future, I'll do anything.

We turn the bend.

The officer motions me forward.

"We need to get your official statement in order to charge Miss Miller with aggravated assault." He hands me a filled-out report.

"The hell is going on here!" A man in a suit storms into view. "I'm Reginald Miller, Christa's dad and chairman of the board at Redwood Prep. Why is my daughter being questioned? Do you have any idea the hell my lawyers will rain—"

"We have evidence of your daughter instigating a near-fatal drowning. This is a very serious matter, Mr. Miller."

"My daughter would *never*—"

The cop lifts his phone and plays the video.

Giggling pours from the speakers, then someone whispers *sh*. On screen, Christa is tiptoeing toward me. Her hands are out-stretched. Then they're slamming against my back.

I watch my body lurch into the inky blue water and my throat gets tight as if I'm reliving the horror of that moment all over again.

My enemies are ruthless.

Which is why I have to be even more so.

Miller's face turns whiter than my sheet music. His eyes dart to me and back to the video.

"We also have a statement from the nurse detailing Miss Cooper's injuries, as well as a corroborating medical report from the hospital. This is not an unfounded accusation. It is our responsibility to look into this case carefully and methodically. We ask for your cooperation."

Miller's mouth opens and closes. He looks at me again but, this time, there's a hint of desperation. Gone is the man who swaggered into Redwood Prep demanding that heads roll.

Now he's ready to bow.

I rise unsteadily from the desk. "Before I sign, I need to use the bathroom."

The officer steps away to let me pass. When I'm in front of Miller, I stop to whisper, "Meet me in the hallway out front."

His stiffening shoulders are the only indication that he heard me.

I wash my hands in the bathroom, take a few deep breaths and then meet Miller in the shadows.

His blue eyes—so much like Christa's—are pleading. "I'm hoping you didn't ask to meet privately because you have something over my daughter that would make this worse."

"Relax." I straighten my shoulders and hope my voice doesn't tremble the way my knees are. "I want to make things better. Not worse."

His eyes take on a skeptical sheen. "You set this up."

"Oh no. I didn't force your daughter to try and *murder* me, Mr. Miller. That would be foolish of me."

"You're exaggerating."

"This case can easily become an attempted homicidal drowning. Since Christa's eighteen, she'd be tried in a criminal court. At worst, she'll do a few years behind bars. At best, her chances of going to a fancy Ivy League goes *poof*." I gesture with my hands.

His tongue darts out to swipe his bottom lip. His eyebrows wrinkle. "I'm willing to do anything. Just," he waves his arms frantically, "make this go away."

A D D# E

The swell before a lashing tsunami. A wave that's rising and frothing at the mouth.

I feel the electricity in my bones.

"Anything?" I whisper.

"Yes. Just tell me what you want."

"I want Dutch Cross's head on a platter."

His lips curl down. Annoyance skitters through his eyes. "Is that what all the fuss is about?" He scowls. "You're threatening my daughter's future for petty high school revenge?"

I take out my phone, spin it between my fingers and say

casually, "I wonder what fraud charges would look like on top of attempted murder charges?"

His eyes bug.

"Christa, Dutch and his brothers changed my grades to get me kicked out of Redwood Prep and you, dear Chairman of the Board, you were their accomplice." My stare hardens. "Does this still sound like petty high school revenge to you?"

Miller tugs at his collar. His Adam's apple bounces up and down. "I can't touch Dutch."

"Why the hell not?" I hiss. Is that monster really a god? Not even the head of the board at Redwood Prep wants to take him down.

"Why do you think you could just come waltzing back to school after being kicked out?" Miller spits.

My eyelashes flutter. "Jarod Cross."

"Even *I* don't have the kind of power to take Cross on yet."

"Hm." I tap my fingers on the cell phone. "Then I guess I'll have to send this video of Christa to the local news. And who knows how widely it'll spread? People love to see the mighty falling off their pedestals. They'll make this bigger and bigger until your daughter won't be able to lift her head in public again."

"Wait. Wait." He holds out a hand and stares pleadingly. "I can't touch the Cross boys, but I can do something else. Anything else. Name it."

My heart beating fast, I contemplate the offer. "Fine. Put my grades back to where they were before."

"W-what?"

"I'll send you a snapshot of all my test papers. You can consult with my teachers to verify. I want it done in a day—"

"A day?"

"—And if, in the next twenty-four hours, my grades aren't returned to what they were," I step close to him and smile tauntingly, "the police aren't the only ones I'll be visiting. You can look forward to seeing your daughter's mug shot everywhere."

He trembles. "I really don't know if I can make it happen in a day."

"Well," I smooth out his collar, "we'll see how much time your daughter has then."

Miller gulps.

I take a step away and then I stop. Turn around. Stare coolly at him. "Oh, and Miller, from now on, keep your daughter in check. If she comes at me again, I won't let her off easy."

He nods desperately.

I glide past him, my head held high. The moment I turn the bend, I crash against the lockers and struggle to catch my breath.

I feel like I'm on a slippery slope with rabid sharks beneath me. But what other choice do I have? Now that Dutch didn't get his way and Christa's been publicly humiliated, they'll both be on the war path. I'll need to become something new, something stronger, if I'm going to survive in Redwood.

My fingers dig into the locker.

I close my eyes and count backwards from ten.

My throat is closing up.

It hurts to breathe.

In. Out. In. Out.

When I no longer feel like throwing up, I straighten and find an empty classroom to hide out from the police. I have a feeling that Miller won't waste any time holding up his end of the deal.

And when that happens, it'll be my turn to make all this go away.

* * *

Jinx: Hell hath no fury like a mermaid without her legs.

Turns out, New Girl and water aren't the best of friends.

Not surprisingly, New Girl and Pompoms aren't chummy either.

So why did our resident Cinderella tell the cops her little make-out session with Redwood's chlorine-soaked pool water was a 'little misunderstanding between friends'?

And you thought rock legend Jarod Cross's surprise visit to Redwood would be the talk of the decade? Turns out, all it took was a little shakedown from the boys in blue to usurp the strongest star in the Redwood sky.

Speaking of Redwood stars, our resident Prince Charming is yet to make a move now that his father and his rebellious Cinderella are in the spotlight. I wonder… why is he hesitating? Is it true love or is our king losing his golden touch?

Until the next post, keep your enemies close and your secrets even closer.

- Jinx

* * *

Visit neliaalarcon.com to purchase THE RUTHLESS NOTE.

Written By Nelia Alarcon

The Redwood Kings Series

The Darkest Note

The Ruthless Note

The Broken Note

Printed in Great Britain
by Amazon